Mr Darcy's Proposal

A Pride & Prejudice Variation

By

Martine Jane Roberts

<u>Dedication</u>

To Peggy, who I love more than words can say.

Also by

Mr Darcy's Struggle

What if, after initially refusing Mr Darcy's offer of marriage at the parsonage, Elizabeth finds herself in the position where she is forced to accept his proposal? The proud Mr Darcy has only six weeks to prove himself and make Elizabeth fall in love with him. Taking her reproofs to heart, he is determined to woo her *and* become a better man. Then days before the wedding Elizabeth receives another offer. Will she meet Darcy at the altar or run to the arms of another?

Mr Darcy's Struggle is a variation on Jane Austen's Pride & Prejudice and therefore does not follow the original timeline.
UK English, spellings, grammar and terminology are used throughout this book.

Darcy to the Rescue

When Elizabeth's parents joined together and insisted that she accept Mr Collins proposal, she decides to take matters into her own hands.
The consequences of this see her reputation in tatters and a proposal from Mr Darcy. However, will Mr Darcy honour this proposal when he discovers Elizabeth already has an offer of marriage?
Will Caroline Bingley relinquish her plans to marry Darcy herself, or will she fight to become the mistress of Pemberley?
Or will Elizabeth be forced to marry her odious cousin instead?

Darcy to the Rescue is a light-hearted alternative to Jane Austen's version of events after the Netherfield Ball.
UK English, spellings, grammar and terminology are used throughout this book.

To Love Mr Darcy

The day after the Netherfield Ball, Elizabeth Bennet received an unexpected caller at Longbourn.
With Mr Bennet's full blessing, Fitzwilliam Darcy informs Elizabeth they are to be married.
Furious to have her future decided for her, Elizabeth sets out to change Darcy's mind. However, the untimely interference of Lady Catherine de Bourgh and Darcy's subsequent action, makes it impossible for Elizabeth to break their engagement.
The events that follow lead to betrayal, a renewal of affection, and even death.
Yet, in the midst of all this chaos, love blossoms, and in the most unlikely manner...

To Love Mr Darcy is an exciting alternative to the original Pride & Prejudice novel by Jane Austen.
UK English, spellings, grammar and terminology are used throughout this book.

Contact Details

www.martinejaneroberts.com

www.twitter.com/LizzieAndDarcyx

www.facebook.com/lovejaneausten2

Mailing List Link
http://eepurl.com/cgH5IX

Table of Content

Chapter One

The rider dug his heels into the horse's flanks, urging him to increase his pace. Moving as one they flew over the uneven terrain.

Unaccustomed to his master riding him with such fierce determination, Odin sporadically bucked his back legs in protest as they raced over the emerald landscape. Finally, as they approached a tall, but shallow hedge, the stallion, foaming at the bit with the exertion of the pace, decided enough was enough. As his rider leant forward in preparation for the jump, Odin dug his hooves into the ground and promptly stopped.

Darcy, who had resolved to ride until his black mood was exhausted, found himself momentarily airborne, before landing unceremoniously in a heap on the other side of the fence.

Relieved to be rid of his ill-tempered burden, Odin trotted over to a patch of green, winter pasture and lowered his head to sample the long blades, unconcerned with the fate of his rider.

Winded by the fall, Darcy lay on the ground and tried to catch his breath. He could not blame his faithful steed for throwing him. He had ridden Odin hard for almost an hour as he tried to banish a particular image from his mind, and from his memory. The image of George Wickham touching Elizabeth.

As Darcy lay prostrate on the hard ground waited for his breathing to become easier, the events of the last week played out in his mind.

Darcy decided it would be prudent for him to also quit Netherfield, leaving only two days after the ball and one day after Mr Bingley. Miss Elizabeth Bennet and her fine eyes were a pleasant distraction, but he could not think of her as a suitable candidate for his affections. As for Miss Bingley and Mrs Hurst, it had been easy to persuade them of the necessity to return to Town; he had only to mention the words Charles, Jane Bennet and matrimony in one breath and they too had insisted on following their brother.

Having arrived at Mr Bingley's London residence, it took the three of them very little time to persuade Charles that Jane Bennet did not love him. Indeed, they pointed out; Miss Bennet had bestowed her serene smile on all who had engaged with her. It had not been reserved for Charles in particular; Caroline delighted in pointing out.

Crestfallen, Charles had to agree with her, Jane's outward appearance had not quickened when in his presence.

However, that was not the only reason Darcy had wanted to leave the shire. Miss Elizabeth Bennet had begun to have an alarming effect on him, discomposing his emotions, and intruding upon his ability to think rationally. He had even begun to look forward to their encounters, however brief or cutting they might be. Therefore, it made sense for him to extract himself from her influence before he made a fool of himself. She was, after all, too far removed from his level in society to be a serious contender as his wife.

Now home, and away from Elizabeth's charms, Darcy was sure he would soon forget her.

However, he had underestimated the effect the fairer sex could have on a red blooded man in his prime.

Having stayed to dine with Charles and his sisters, Darcy returned home late that evening. Convinced he could put Elizabeth from his mind, and return to his usual pursuits, he settled down in his favourite armchair with a book and a small brandy.

Thirty minutes later, he was frustrated to find that he had not read a single page, a single paragraph or even a single sentence. Miss Elizabeth Bennet was the only subject on his mind.

He tried to reason with himself. Elizabeth had nothing to recommend her to a man such as he. No connections, no fortune, her inferior birth and her ridiculous family..., and yet..., she seemed to have found a way under his skin and into his heart.

Darcy closed the book and slammed it down on the side table. He rose and paced the floor as he tried to convince himself of her unsuitability. He knew an alliance with her was unthinkable! His family would never accept her, society would never accept her... but... as he thought of never seeing her again, a physical pain made its presence felt in the centre of his chest.

Finally, Darcy realised it was time he stopped deluding himself. He could no longer deny the depth of his feeling for Elizabeth Bennet.

He loved her, ardently.

Angry at his own lack of willpower, Darcy pulled open the library door and bellowed for his butler.

Startled to be summoned in such a manner, Miller hurried to see what was amiss with his master.

"Miller," Darcy barked, "inform Fletcher to repack my trunks, we are returning to Hertfordshire."

"And the duration of your stay, sir," Miller asked in his most professional voice.

"Indefinitely," Darcy replied, only to hastily change it to "Undetermined."

A true professional, Miller merely said, "Yes sir." And then hurried off to do his bidding, while Darcy sat at his desk, dashed off two brief notes.

The first was to his sister, and the other to Mr Bingley, asking his permission to stay at Netherfield Park again, although he gave no explanation as to why he was returning to Hertfordshire so soon after leaving.

Then Darcy rang for a footman and instructed him to deliver them without delay.

Only then, and with his emotions still in turmoil, did Darcy retire to his bed. Self-loathing at his lack of determination and suppressed excitement fought to win the upper hand, but as he slipped into unconsciousness, the latter prevailed.

A gentle grin played on Darcy's lips as he dreamt of Miss Elizabeth Bennet, smiling…laughing…teasing.

On the journey back to Netherfield, the carriage had passed through the town of Meryton. With skill, the driver navigated through the busy streets, and Darcy looked out of the window, scanning the inhabitant's faces for the one he hoped to see.

Then, as if in answer to his silent prayer, there was Elizabeth. She was standing outside the bookstore talking to an officer in a red coat. With their faces in profile, Darcy did not recognise him at first.

Then Elizabeth must have disclosed something amusing, for the officer threw back his head and laughed raucously.

Next, as if in slow motion, Darcy watched as the man reached out and stroked Elizabeth's arm in a familiar way. At that moment, his identity became clear. It was none other than George Wickham!

⁓

Elizabeth, who was enjoying an extended morning walk, watched in disbelief as a man appeared from nowhere and landed at her feet.

Startled, she retreated a few steps, then instinct took over, and she rushed to his aid.

"Are you injured, sir?" Elizabeth asked as she knelt by his side.

Only when the man turned towards her, with a familiar scowl on his face, did Elizabeth recognised him.

"Why, Mr Darcy?" Elizabeth exclaimed with surprise, "We understood you had left Hertfordshire and returned to the Town?"

His mood, already black from suffering an undignified parting from his horse, darkened as he realised his demise had been witnessed.

The fact that it was Miss Elizabeth Bennet who had been party to the shambolic event, only deepened his anger and embarrassment.

Brushing off Elizabeth's attempt to assist him, Darcy replied gruffly,

"Thank you, but I am in no need of assistance."

Although Elizabeth had no brothers, she understood the concept of male pride and would have forgiven Mr Darcy for his rudeness, had he not been bleeding from a graze on his brow.

Ignoring his black scowl, Elizabeth withdrew a handkerchief from her reticule and as she reached out to dab at the wound said,

"May I?"

"No," he barked, "I have already stated that I am in no need of assistance, madam. I must ask you to desist."

Humiliated, Darcy rolled over onto his stomach and tried to stand, however, he could only manage to struggle to his knees. Silently cursing, Darcy wished Elizabeth would leave him to his humiliation and allow him to recover in private.

Managing to regain his breath, he quickly realised the exertion of moving had rewarded him with a thumping in his head and a spell of dizziness. Momentarily defeated, he knew he needed to rest for a while longer before attempting to stand again.

His harsh words did not deter Elizabeth.

On several occasions when visiting her father's tenant, she had tended to the scraped knees of their children. Neither the child's verbal protests nor the sight of their bloodied knees or nose had swayed her from her task.

So, sitting back on her heels, Elizabeth watched as Mr Darcy tried again to scramble to his feet, only to fall back onto his hands and knees.

Now, with only one foot resting on the ground, it quickly became apparent that the gentleman was unable to stand under his own volition.

As Darcy paused in this half sitting, half kneeling position, Elizabeth said,

"Sir, while I hate to contradict you, it is obvious to me that you most definitely are in need of assistance. Now, if you could stop being so stubborn for one minute, and take my arm, I am sure we could have you back in the saddle...." Elizabeth's sentence was left unfinished.

"So far, I have been tolerant of your interference, Madam, but no more. You will kindly desist in your attempts to nurse me and remove yourself from this property."

When Elizabeth made no move to leave, Darcy added,

"Trespassing is an offence, you know?"

If Elizabeth was shocked or stung by the severity of his address, she did not show it. Instead, she carefully folded the handkerchief and returned it to her purse.

Standing, she brushed the dried leaves from her dress and then paused to look at the dishevelled man kneeling before her. Had she not already experienced several encounters with the proud and unpleasant, Mr Darcy, Elizabeth might have taken offence at his curt words, his brisk tone or even his dark scowl, but she now deemed them to be part of his character long ago, even when one was trying to be helpful towards him.

"Very well, sir, I will leave you to your fate, but not because you order me from this property, but because I choose to leave. Besides, Netherfield Park ended with this boundary fence. You are now on Longbourn property."

Elizabeth waited until she had her back to Darcy before letting a broad smile graced her lips.

Chapter Two

"Oh, Mr Bennet, have you heard what happened this morning?" Mrs Bennet asked her husband as she entered the parlour behind Elizabeth.

"Lizzy had a most unfortunate encounter with Mr Darcy, of all people. Apparently, he was thrown from that beast of a horse of his, and when Lizzy offered him her assistance, he dismissed her as one might dismiss an ordinary servant. In fact, he threatened her. Now, what do you make of that, sir?"

Mr Bennet rested his book on his knees and turned to his wife of more than twenty years. She was still a handsome woman even though she was in her fifth decade, and the bearing of five daughters had done little to sabotage her figure. Some might say she was prone to exaggerations or indulged a bit too much in self-promotion, but these character foibles had made their life together both happy and amusing, leastways for him. Willingly, he admitted, without her constant daily interruptions to share some snippet of gossip she had just gleaned from one neighbour or another, his days might have been a little less diverting.

"Well, my dear." Mr Bennet said, "I think any man foolish enough to slight our Lizzy, does not deserve to know her true worth."

Turned to Elizabeth, he asked,

"And pray, Lizzy, what assistance did Mr Darcy need that he could reject your offer so out of hand?"

"It was quite amusing really, Papa. Apparently, he was thrown from his horse, but imagine my surprise when the gentleman landed squarely at my feet, and..."

"He could have killed her, Mr Bennet." interrupted Mrs Bennet, exaggerating the actions of Mr Darcy travelling through the air with her arms. "Flying through the air in such a cavalier manner, and with no regards for where, or whom he landed on. Such a proud and disagreeable man, I cannot afford him any charity in the matter. Now, if it had been that nice Mr Bingley..." her words trailed off.

Mr Bennet rolled his eyes and then indicated for Elizabeth to continue.

"I had not meant to walk as far as Netherfield, Papa, but the morning was mild and the solitude welcome. Once I had recovered my wits, I offered to help him home, or at least back to his mount. But he not only declined my assistance, he then ordered me from his property." Then Elizabeth laughed, saying, "But I was not offended Papa, for the jest was on him."

"How so, Lizzy?"

Still laughing, Elizabeth replied.

"When Mr Darcy took me to task for trespassing, he did not realise that his horse had deposited him on the Longbourn side of the boundary."

Mr Bennet and Elizabeth's sisters joined in her mirth, while Mrs Bennet failed to see what was so amusing. Only when Jane pointed out that it was Mr Darcy who was trespassing, did Mrs Bennet understand.

Choosing not to see the humour in the situation, Mrs Bennet said,

"Well, I think Lizzy was very fortunate not to be injured, which I quite expect one of these days with all her walking about the countryside. She wanders here, and she wanders there, with no servant for company or protection." Turning back to face her daughter, Mrs Bennet reprimanded her for the umpteenth time. "You could at least ask one of your sisters to walk with you Lizzy; goodness knows what our neighbours must think of you."

"I can assure, mamma, there is none that would wish me harm in the local area, and as for our neighbours, they have better things to do than gossip about me taking a little exercise. Besides, Papa is the only one up when I leave."

Deciding Elizabeth had been scolded enough, Mr Bennet broke into the conversation.

"And I am too busy with estate business to chaperone Lizzy. Let the girl enjoy her freedom for a while longer, Mother." Said Mr Bennet, referring to his wife by his pet name. "Now, I suppose I am obliged to pay Mr Darcy a call, knowing that he was injured on my property."

Mr Bennet paused to sigh.

"It is a chore to be sure, but I can see no way of avoiding it. Still, once I am confident he will survive his injuries, I see no reason to extend the acquaintance."

Mr Bennet was gone a relatively short time the next morning when paying his call on Mr Darcy. On his return, he went directly to the parlour and stood before the hearth. Raising his coat tails to aid the circulation of air, Mr Bennet warmed himself before the glowing embers.

"The cold seems to have worked its way through to my bones this morning. I hope you were sufficiently layered for your constitutional this morning, Lizzy? We wouldn't want another one of you girls confined to bed with a chill," he said jovially and winked in the direction of his favourite child.

Elizabeth returned his smile and then went back to reading her book.

It was clear her papa was referring to Jane's forced stay at Netherfield Park earlier in the year. Mrs Bennet had insisted that Jane rides on horseback rather than in the carriage, to take lunch with Miss Bingley. Sadly for Jane, the skies opened up, and a deluge of rain washed down on her, resulting in her catching a chill.

Mr Bennet, as the only male member of the family, was quite used to being left to his own devices. Indeed, a great deal of his time was spent in his study, which boasted an excellent selection of books for such a small estate. He liked nothing more than after dealing with the day's estate business, to retreat into his study and lose himself in the pages of a good novel, away from female talk of fashion and fancies. And if Lizzy decided to join him for a spell of companionable reading, so much the better. Her sharp mind and whimsical sense of the ridiculous saw them often laugh at the world in general.

Gazing down at his ladies, Mr Bennet was surprised by their total lack of interest on his visit to Netherfield Park.

After some minutes of disinterest from his family, he said,

"I am pleased to say the gentleman will survive his injuries. You need not reproach yourself for Mr Darcy stubborn refusal of help, Lizzy. Indeed, the gentleman assured me he recovered almost the instant you had left."

Fanny Bennet glanced up at her husband.

"Mr Darcy, Mr Darcy, I am sick of hearing his name. Did you ask why he had returned to Netherfield and is Mr Bingley to join him?"

Mr Bennet took a moment to savoured the knowledge that he alone held, before saying,

"Mrs Bennet, he confided only that his business was of a personal nature. But he did intimate that his sister, one Miss Georgiana Darcy, might be joining him in the near future."

Everyone lifted their eyes and looked at the now chuckling, Mr Bennet. No longer ignored, he was the focal point for six pairs of questioning eyes.

Taking a deep breath, Mr Bennet prepared himself for the barrage of questions that would now inevitably fly his way.

Mrs Bennet, Kitty, and Lydia bombarded him with a dozen questions all at once. Their voices battling with each other to have their query heard, and answered first.

Holding up his hand to silence them all, Mr Bennet turned to his wife and said,

"I gleaned as much information as I could, without being impertinent. If you remain quiet for but a moment, dearest, I will endeavour to relay all that I know to both you and our offspring."

The room fell silent.

"Mr Darcy is aware that his sister has led a somewhat sheltered existence. He confided that, at present, she is too shy to be presented at court. However, Mr Darcy hopes that if he is successful in the business he intends to conduct while in Meryton, she might be coaxed to visit him at Netherfield within the next few weeks."

"I cannot see Mr Bingley returning to Netherfield if Mr Darcy is merely attending to business. How very annoying, I must say," interrupted Mrs Bennet. "Did he say how long he intends to stay?"

"He hopes to winter in Hertfordshire before returning to his estate in Derbyshire early in the New Year."

Mr Bennet paused briefly, and in those few seconds, the cacophony of noise again began to rise.

Then, very softly and with no fanfare at all, Mr Bennet added,

"I have invited him to dine with us this evening."

After a moment of stunned silence, Fanny Bennet erupted into action.

"This evening, Mr Bennet? *This* evening? Oh, my Lord, I must speak to cook without delay. I cannot serve Mr Darcy mutton stew! And we must have at least three sauces. Hill... Hill?" Mrs Bennet called for her housekeeper then rushed from the room in search of her.

Close behind their mother was Lydia and Kitty, who raced upstairs, squealing at the prospect of a male guest. It did not matter that it was the annoying Mr Darcy, the boring Mr Darcy. Though he was not as handsome as the militia officers in their fine red coats, they still saw it as an opportunity to put on their favourite ball gowns.

Mr Bennet looked at his remaining daughters, his eyes coming to rest on his middle child, Mary.

Seeing her father's expectant expression, Mary said,

"*I* take no pleasure in welcoming a single gentleman to our table, but I understand that Jane or Lizzy may benefit from such a guest in our midst in the form of a suitor," Mary stated flatly and without malice.

"Wise words, Mary. You stick to your sermons and music. Much better company than single gentlemen." Mr Bennet replied.

Satisfied that she had made her views known, Mary gave a nod, picked up her pile of sheet music and went off to practise on the pianoforte.

Now, with only Jane and Elizabeth to keep him company, Mr Bennet spoke freely.

"Poor Mary. Too plain and sober-minded to snare a husband for herself, while Kitty and Lydia are too silly to attract a sensible minded man."

His gaze shifted between Elizabeth and Jane until he finally confided in them.

"If Mr Bingley does not return and make an offer for you, Jane, then I fear your mother will expect one of you to encourage the affections of Mr Darcy. I also fear she will not be happy until she has deprived me of the only two sensible people in my household."

Then, in an unusual show of affection, Mr Bennet, kissed Jane and Elizabeth on the cheek before withdrawing to his study until their guest arrived.

Chapter Three

"Damn and blast," cursed Fitzwilliam Darcy as the footman closed the door on the retreating figure of Mr Bennet.

He stood for a long moment in the atrium of Netherfield House, brushing a hand through his dark wavy hair, a habit he unconsciously executed for a variety of emotions.

Then, bounding up the stairs two at a time, he bellowed, "Fletcher!"

Mr Fletcher, or Fletcher as he was known, was Mr Darcy's valet. He had been engaged by Mr Darcy Sr. to look after the young master when he went to university in Cambridge.

Old Mr Darcy had deemed Fletcher, being a single man in his late thirties, suitably mature to serve his son while he concluded his education, and then to accompany him on his grand tour. Unfortunately, circumstances had seen the latter postponed indefinitely when Mr Darcy Sr. passed away unexpectedly.

Fletcher preferred the young Mr Darcy to any other employer he had previously served. He treated him well and paid him handsomely. And unlike several of his contemporaries who bemoaned their lot in life, Fletcher liked his work *and* his employer.

Since old Mr Darcy's death, Fletcher, who had no family of his own but an older sister, viewed himself as a surrogate father to the young master. Others might say he overstepped the boundaries of a servant, but Fletcher, rightly or wrongly, saw it not only as his duty to take care of his master, but as a privilege. Indeed, Mr Darcy was the most honourable man Mr Fletcher had ever known.

Even before Darcy reached the door to his chambers, Fletcher turned the handle and smoothly pulled the door open from the inside, allowing Darcy to enter without pause.

Darcy stood before the mirror and waited for Fletcher to remove his jacket and waistcoat.

"I see you have survived your first caller, sir," Fletcher ventured.

"I did not journey out of town to be harangued by a deluge of rustic callers, Fletcher," Darcy replied with ill humour.

Fletcher knew this mood well. Darcy disliked engaging in meaningless chit chat, especially with strangers, and although the Bennet's were known to him, he had not spent any time alone with them.

Usually, Mr Bingley or his sisters were by Darcy's side when making calls or receiving visitors, thus easing the path of conversation. Then, once Darcy felt comfortable, he would begin to contribute to the discussion.

Sensing Fletcher was still waiting for a reply, Darcy said,

"Mr Bennet has invited me to dine with his family tonight."

"A quaint custom sir, not uncommon in the Shires. Did you accept?" Fletcher asked.

"I felt as compelled to accept his invitation as he did in offering it."

Fletcher said nothing, but his raised eyebrow spoke volumes.

"Odin threw me yesterday morning, and I had the misfortune to land on Longbourn property. Hence the invitation."

Fletcher, who knew all about his master's unfortunate accident, suppressed a wry smile, and said,

"I am sure the horse did not do it intentionally, sir."

Darcy gave Fletcher a sideways glance. He should berate him for being over familiar, but in truth, Fletcher had a point. It was not the animals fault; it was his. Odin was a noble and magnificent beast, not unlike his master. Having been ridden like a common plough horse, he had every right to dislodge his abuser.

Having done his best to refuse the squire's offer, even assuring Mr Bennet that his injuries were more to his pride than to his flesh, the man would not be dissuaded.

"Nonsense, Sir, you must let me offer you restitution in the way of a hearty meal with my family."

In truth, he had finally accepted because it was the perfect way to rekindle his acquaintance with the Bennet's without slighting any of Bingley's other neighbours. To say his reintroduction to Meryton society had not gone as he planned was an understatement.

Initially, he had intended to make an appointment with Mr Bennet and seek his permission to formally court Elizabeth without anyone else aware of his intentions. That way, if the squire refused his consent, only the two of them would know of his failed suit. But his unfortunate meeting with Elizabeth had meant that idea had been scrapped. At least this way, he did not have to concoct another plan, another meeting. The foundations to speak to Mr Bennet were already laid and by the gentleman himself.

Fletcher opened the wardrobe door and retrieved his master's dressing gown, and then eased the garment over Darcy's broad shoulders.

Sinking into the comfortable chair by the fire, Darcy waited for his bath to be filled.

As a stream of servants filed in with buckets of steaming, hot water, Fletcher cast him a sideways glance.

Seeing his master was deep in thought, Fletcher uncharacteristically misread the reason why.

When the last footman had closed the door behind him, Fletcher ventured to say,

"I understand that a meal of two courses may last only a few hours. You could be home by ten, sir."

"Yes," Darcy concurred absently, not really hearing him.

Having spent several minutes contemplating the forthcoming evening, Darcy's thoughts then turned to wondering if there had been any changes during his week-long absence.

"So, what news have you managed to glean from the local populace?" he asked.

If Fletcher considered he knew his master well, then by default, he must also concede the same of Mr Darcy.

Mr Darcy had been conscious of Fletcher's worth for years, as were many of his acquaintances. He was charming, intelligent, had impeccable manners, was loyal, honest and above all, trustworthy. Indeed, several of Darcy's lesser friends had tried to poach Fletcher away from him with offers of financial reward.

He was grateful for Fletcher's loyalty.

"I understand a proposal of marriage has been made to one of the Bennet girls, sir," Fletcher imparted.

Shocked to hear these words, Darcy jumped to his feet and began to fire a string of questions at him.

"A proposal? Was it accepted? Who made it and to whom?"

Before Fletcher had time to answer, Darcy grabbed him by the shoulders and asked with urgency,

"Which sister, man?"

"The second eldest, sir, Miss Elizabeth Bennet."

Darcy's hands dropped to his sides, and he turned his face away. He was too late. Knowing how desperate Mrs Bennet was to secure husbands for her offspring, there could be no doubt that Elizabeth would now be engaged.

Fletcher stared at his master. Mr Darcy had never laid a hand on him in the ten years he had been his valet. Undeniably it was a shock, but as Fletcher focused on Darcy downturned features, the reason for his actions became clear.

His pained expression announced he was a man in love.

Fletcher quickly added,

"Miss Bennet refused the Parson's offer, sir, there is no engagement."

Darcy turned to face Fletcher with such speed he almost felt dizzy.

"Elizabeth refused him, are you sure?"

"Oh, yes, sir. Although I gather the girl's mother was exceedingly displeased with her," Fletcher replied, pleased to note the look of relief that had swept over his gentleman's face.

Inhaling deeply, Darcy allowed a wide grin to curl his lips. He wished he had been a fly on the wall when Elizabeth had turned the obnoxious Parson down. Elizabeth was far too spirited to be leg-shackled to a man like William Collins.

Easing himself into the steaming tub, Darcy suddenly thought dinner with the Bennet's didn't seem quite such a daunting prospect after all.

A few minutes before seven, Darcy was shown into the drawing-room at Longbourn. Assembled before him was the entire Bennet family.

Mr Bennet, who was standing before the fireplace, moved forward to greet him.

"Ah, Mr Darcy, welcome to, Longbourn." Mr Bennet said as he shook Darcy's hand. "I believe no introductions are necessary."

Darcy scanned the faces of the six women, and coming to rest on Elizabeth's, he said,

"No, sir. I am acquainted with all your ladies. Good evening." The ladies stood and curtsied, to which Darcy replied with a single bow.

"Now, we dine unfashionably late at Longbourn as I expect you recall. I take it you have no objections, sir?"

"None, sir. I am content to fit in with your usual practice."

Turning his gaze to the rest of the gathering, Darcy waited until the women were seated once more before selecting the empty chair next to Mrs Bennet. A choice he would later regret.

Mrs Bennet gave him a strained smile and then asked,

"Mr Darcy, how nice to see you sustained no serious injury after your mishap the other day. I trust your horse also came to no harm?"

"Odin is quite well, thank you."

Elizabeth turned to her father and discreetly raised her eyebrows. It was evident that Mr Darcy had not changed in the essentials, he appeared to possess a taciturn nature still.

"If Mary will play the pianoforte for us after dinner, would you join us in a dance, Mr Darcy?" Lydia blurted out randomly.

Darcy knew he was being baited, but if he wanted to spend more time with Elizabeth, it meant he also had to spend *some* time with her relations.

"I seldom dance, Miss Lydia," Darcy replied politely, hoping that his curt reply would curtail any further ideas in that direction.

"Why not, you danced with Lizzy at Mr Bingley's ball?" Lydia persisted, a childish pout forming on her lips.

Formatting a reply that would not cause offence, Darcy said,

"Finding a partner that matches my exacting standards is not always easy, Miss Lydia. If one is to partake in an activity, it is preferable to do so to the best of one's ability, is it not?" While Darcy maintained a calm countenance, inside, he was horrified at the girl's rudeness. Although approximately the same age Lydia, and Georgiana were nothing alike.

Had she just been insulted, or complimented? She wasn't sure. As she was the only local he had deigned to dance with since he arrived in Meryton, it could be a compliment. On the other hand, he did not say she met those high standards he sought in a partner. Maybe an insult after all?

Again, Elizabeth raised her brows in the direction of her father.

Lydia opened her mouth to challenge Darcy again, but the sudden pressure from her father's hand on her shoulder told her she should not. Instead, she folded her arms across her chest and released an exaggerated sigh. It was evident to all present that she was sulking

Thankfully, Hobbs, the butler entered as the clock struck seven and announced that dinner was served.

The soup course was eaten in relative silence, with only the odd, *pass the bread please*, being uttered.

As they waited for the next course to be served, Mr Darcy turned to Elizabeth.

"Do you continue with your early morning walks, Miss Elizabeth?"

"Yes, I do, unless the weather is very inclement," She replied.

"Would you be open to sharing some of the routes with me? I would be most obliged if you said yes."

"You do not strike me as the type of man who would enjoy long walks in the countryside, sir."

"Oh, but I do, Miss Elizabeth. Walking is beneficial for both the body and mind. Do you not agree?"

"Yes, very beneficial."

"So, will you share some of your routes, or better still, may I accompany you in person?"

Elizabeth was on the verge of saying she preferred to walk alone when Mrs Bennet shot her a warning glare.

Ignoring her mother's steely gaze and the scolding she had received earlier, Elizabeth still tried to politely refuse.

"The paths I walk are quite simple to find, sir. They are well worn and free from obstruction. I do not think a guide is necessary. You, as a man, would have little trouble in finding and negotiating them, Mr Darcy.?"

"Then you object to me accompanying you, Miss Elizabeth?" Darcy asked, crestfallen at being so soundly rebuffed.

A throaty cough from the direction of her mother told Elizabeth she had pushed her luck far enough.

"Not at all, sir, though I hope you will not find my conversation... or lack of it, too tiresome," Elizabeth replied with a faint smile.

"I assure you, Miss Elizabeth, with a sister of sixteen, I am well able to converse on the latest fashions." Darcy finished with a smile.

"You surprise me, Mr Darcy. I did not think a man of your status would concern himself with such frivolous items as lace and ribbons."

"Yes, I am a man, Miss Elizabeth, but that does not exclude me from taking an interest in what young ladies of fashion are wearing. On several occasions, I have even purchased such trimmings for my sister as gifts."

Mrs Bennet's eyes went back and forth as she watched Darcy and Elizabeth's dance of verbal sparring. Although he seemed quite capable of matching Lizzy, as the hostess, she was aghast that Elizabeth appeared to be actually arguing with him.

"I understand your sister is to join you in a few weeks, Mr Darcy. I believe she is of a similar age to Kitty and Lydia? Well, Miss Darcy is welcome to join my girls when they walk into Meryton any time she likes. Sometimes they go as often as two or three times a week," she offered.

Mr Darcy acknowledged her offer was meant with kindness, but having witnessed Lydia and Kitty's behaviour over the past few weeks, he could not recommend it for Georgiana.

Seeing the expectant look on his hostesses' face, Darcy replied,

"Thank you, madam, but Georgiana is a shy natured girl, unaccustomed to socialising with others."

"Oh, Mr Darcy, my girls will soon bring her out of her shell. There are officers aplenty for her to practise her skills on," Mrs Bennet gushed.

Darcy had no intention of letting his sister, already emotionally scarred from her encounter with George Wickham, parade herself before the militia as Kitty and Lydia Bennet did.

Replying a little harshly, he said,

"That will not be possible, madam." Suddenly, every face was turned towards him.

Trying to cover his outburst, Darcy hastened to say,

"I am afraid Georgiana has a delicate constitution, ma'am. When…if Georgiana decides to visit, walking in the grounds of Netherfield House with be sufficient exercise for her."

Deflated by Darcy's sharp tone and negative words, Mrs Bennet could only say,

"Oh, I see."

With the lull in the conversation stretching on, Elizabeth asked,

"Mr Darcy, do you expect Mr Bingley and his sisters to join you?"

Moistening his potatoes in a puddle of gravy, Mr Darcy paused before answering.

After having advised Charles that there was little hope of him finding happiness with Miss Jane Bennet, while he, his best friend, now actively pursued Miss Elizabeth Bennet, well it seemed somewhat hypocritical. However, in all honesty, Darcy did not know what his young friend's plans were. Indeed, had he not left the Shires himself with no intention of returning? Yet here he was, breaking bread with the very family he vowed to avoid?

"I am not aware that Mr Bingley or his sisters have any immediate plans to return to Hertfordshire, Miss Elizabeth…, but he may do. Charles' lease on Netherfield Park does not expire until next Michaelmas."

Mrs Bennet turned her eyes towards Jane and gave an exaggerated sigh.

"Such a shame." She said in a wistful tone, "I was sure he was going to propose to our Jane."

Darcy felt a flush rising over his collar. Even though Mrs Bennet could not possibly know how instrumental Darcy had been in separating the young lovers, he felt his guilt acutely at that moment

Not liking the direction this conversation was going in, Mr Bennet stepped in before his wife could further embarrass their guest or humiliate her daughters.

"Well, well, my dear, this is an excellent spread and no mistake, and with the choice of three sauces. Cook certainly has excelled herself tonight."

It was now Mrs Bennet's turn to be mortified. She had intended for Mr Darcy to assume this was their usual standard of fare. Suitably embarrassed, Mrs Bennet shot her husband an angry look, but his single raised brow and tight lips signalled her that a reply would not be welcome.

The rest of the meal was eaten with relatively little conversation. Lydia was still sulking, Kitty and Mary were uninterested in their elders and talked only to each other, while Jane and Elizabeth were deep in thought at Mr Darcy's last comment. Only the occasional request for one of the three sauces broke the silence.

Pleased to be leaving the gentlemen to their brandy and cigars, Mrs Bennet ushered her daughter out of the dining room.

Mr Bennet waited until the door was firmly closed behind his retreating womenfolk, before turning to Mr Darcy and saying,

"So, Mr Darcy, what brings you back to the country so quickly? Are you eager to indulge in more shooting and fishing, is that it?"

Darcy accepted a snifter of brandy and took a small sip. Never one to shy away from confrontation, and known for speaking his mind in the directest of manners, Darcy replied,

"My return was prompted by something of a more personal nature, sir, an affair of the heart, you might say."

"A lover, Mr Darcy? I did not think you the type to indulge in meaningless trysts."

"And nor am I, sir." Darcy retorted, annoyed by Mr Bennet's insinuation. "What I seek is a wife, not a whore."

"Ah, well that is quite a different matter then," replied Mr Bennet soberly while swirling the amber liquid around his glass, mystified as to where this conversation could now go.

Trying to lighten the now heavy atmosphere that hung between them, Mr Bennet asked,

"And tell me, do you intend to examine the entire female population of Meryton to find this woman, or perhaps you have someone special in mind already?"

It was an off the cuff remark, meant to inject a touch of levity into their conversation. However, Mr Bennet was dumbfounded by his drinking companion's next revelation.

"It's your daughter, sir, Miss Elizabeth, who has caught my eye."

Mr Bennet, who was mid swallow when Darcy revealed the name of his intended bride, coughed and spluttered as the fiery liquid went down the wrong way.

Wiping his chin with the back of his hand, he asked,

"Elizabeth? *My* Elizabeth?"

"Yes sir, your daughter, Miss Elizabeth Bennet."

"There is not much in this world that surprises me, Mr Darcy, but I must confess that you have managed it tonight." Mr Bennet drained his glass, and then refilled it with a more generous portion.

So, Mr Darcy, the man who never looked at a woman but to see a blemish, wanted to marry his Lizzy. He wondered, was Elizabeth aware of Darcy's regard, or would she be as shocked as he had just been. If she was aware of his intention, or indeed returned his regard, then she had managed to conceal her attachment admirably.

Darcy knew he had shocked Elizabeth's father with his confession. The truth was, he had not intended to blurt it out like that, but he had been affronted by the older man's insinuation that he was merely interested in a dalliance.

At his age, Darcy could not deny there had been a number of women in his life. But his time for flirtations and visits to bordellos had passed. He was weary of having no-one to share his life with, his accomplishments and achievements, his hopes and dreams, and yes, even his fears. He was ready to settle down, more than ready. The sowing of his proverbial wild oats was all done and behind him.

With the silence between them stretching on into the minutes rather than seconds, Darcy realised he must state his case less abruptly, defining the advantages of their match. After all, without Mr Bennet's permission, he had no doubt Elizabeth would reject him.

"I realise a declaration towards one of your daughters was not what you were expecting when you invited me into your home tonight, but I have for some time now, harboured feelings towards your daughter Elizabeth of a most ardent nature. Elizabeth…Miss Elizabeth that is, has all the qualities I would look for in a wife. She is kind and generous, and beautiful and witty. Honest and brave and constant and disciplined. She is also intelligent with a keen and inquiring mind, perfect company for those long winter evening in the country. Elizabeth is all of these things and more… so much more."

Mr Bennet sat wide-eyed. This was the most number of words he had heard Mr Darcy string together since he had made his acquaintance. Love, it appeared had turned him into a veritable chatterbox. But, they were only words. As Elizabeth's father, he wanted to know if Elizabeth was aware of Mr Darcy's regard for her. Did she return his sentiment? And if so, then how long had she loved him? He could not imagine she had already consented to be his wife without first discussing it with her papa.

These were only a few of the questions he intended to ask Mr Darcy, but he started with,

"Well, well, Miss Elizabeth, is it? And does Elizabeth return your sentiment, sir, have you already made her an offer?"

"I…that is…err, no sir. I have not broached the subject of my affection with Miss Elizabeth yet."

"You know she has no fortune, no dowry?"

"I do, sir, but it is of no consequence to me. I have more than enough money for both of us."

"And when I die, which might be quite soon if I receive many such shocks like this, will you take on the responsibility and burden of care for my widow and any unmarried children of mine?"

This was one of the main reasons Darcy had tried to fight his attraction to Elizabeth. It would not be an understatement to say that apart from Elizabeth and her sister Jane, the entire Bennet family fell far short of what he would consider acceptable acquaintances, let alone describing them as a family. And there was no doubt, most of his family would consider them beneath their notice.

However, Elizabeth was worth the degradation of her relations.

"I do," Darcy stated confidently. "Let me reassure you, sir, in such circumstances, I would honour my obligations regarding the comfort and welfare of *all* my extended family."

Darcy wanted to move forward with the discussion, to gain Mr Bennet's approval for the match. With so much to offer, Darcy could not imagine anyone, least of all a country squire, refusing him anything. Besides, if possible, he would like to broach the subject with Elizabeth, tonight.

"I take it you do not object to me as a son-in-law, sir?"

"Me? No, I have no objections to you, sir."

"You would look on my suit with favour then? Give us your blessing?"

Mr Bennet had to admire the nerve of this young man. He had not even declared himself to Lizzie, yet he wanted his consent and blessing to marry her.

Chuckling aloud, he said,

"I do not think it is my consent you should be concerned with Mr Darcy, but Elizabeth's. Lizzy possesses a strong and independent nature, as I am sure you remember. If I understand you correctly, sir, at present, Elizabeth has no idea that you are in love with her?"

"That is so, sir, but I am sure I can convince her of the advantages an alliance with me would bring to both her and her family, should she accept my proposal."

Mr Bennet paused for a moment, taking the opportunity to swallow a little more of his drink while he mulled over his options. He could, of course, forbid the match outright, and Elizabeth would never know about his conversation with Mr Darcy, but did he have the right to deprive his favourite child such an opportunity? Undoubtedly, the possible future Mr Darcy offered was far removed from the one mapped out for her at present? Legally he could forestall any wedding until Elizabeth was of age at one and twenty, but morally? The realisation was quick. Not even as her father, did he have the right to deny her this opportunity?

Knowing he must make some reply to the proud young man who stood expectantly before him, Mr Bennet cleared his throat, and said,

"Mr Darcy, I cannot, nor would I force Elizabeth into accepting any man that made an offer for her. Only last week I rejected an offer for Lizzy's hand from my own cousin, much to the consternation of Mrs Bennet. So, my advice to you is this. Tomorrow, you must speak to Elizabeth as you have me. Propose to her if you must, but keep this condition in mind. I will allow you to embark on a month-long courtship, but if by Christmastide Elizabeth still has not declared her love for you, you must give her up. However, if she grows to love you and admits as much, then I will give your union my blessing."

It was not an unreasonable offer, but one month's courtship was uncommonly short. Also, the emphasis Mr Bennet had put on tomorrow, clearly meant he did not have his permission to speak to Elizabeth tonight.

Though he did not show it, Darcy was apprehensive. Could he successfully woo and win Elizabeth's heart in one month? Only time would tell.

Extending his hand towards Elizabeth's father, Darcy said, "Agreed."

Chapter Four

Slipping his arms into the great coat that Fletcher was holding up for him, Darcy felt as if his stomach was tied up in knots. Never before had he been this anxious about anything in his life. Meeting Miss Elizabeth for a morning walk was turning out to be very stressful.

On his departure last evening, Mrs Bennet had visibly pushed Elizabeth forward, saying,

"Elizabeth has something to say to you, Mr Darcy. Don't you Lizzy?"

Elizabeth inhaled a deep and calming breath before saying,

"Would you care to join me on my walk tomorrow morning, Mr Darcy?"

"That is most kind of you, Miss Elizabeth. Shall we say nine thirty?" he offered.

Having been forced into asking Mr Darcy to join her, Elizabeth was not about to be dictated to when she should go.

Wearing her best, false smile, she said,

"Goodness, no. Half of the day has gone by then. I think eight o'clock is quite late enough. Can you be ready and here at such an early hour, Mr Darcy?"

It was clear to Darcy that Elizabeth had been forced to invite him. In return, she was trying to dictate what she thought was an unreasonably early hour to set off, but, as he usually rose around six thirty, an eight o'clock meeting time was no hardship to him.

"I think I can manage that, Miss Elizabeth. Until tomorrow," he said.

Then turning to Mrs Bennet, Darcy thanked her for an excellent meal, bowed and said goodnight.

Elizabeth was waiting in the hallway of Longbourn when Mr Darcy pulled on the doorbell. If she must act as a guide, she wanted it

over as quickly as possible. Besides, she felt guilty about having to drag Daisy away from her duties to act as their chaperone.

With the civilities out of the way, Elizabeth set off at a brisk pace.

The speed at which Miss Elizabeth was walking was a reasonable pace for Darcy, but he knew it must be excessive for Elizabeth.

After almost a mile of striding out, Darcy felt it was up to him to break the silence.

"The weather is mild for this time of year, is it not, Miss Elizabeth?"

Without stopping or even slowing her pace, Elizabeth replied,

"Yes, it is mild, but do not be deceived, Mr Darcy, winter will surprise us yet."

Seizing on her reply, Darcy continued along the same vein.

"So, you predict we will have snow Miss Elizabeth? Can you also predict when?" he joked.

"Unfortunately, not, Mr Darcy, my education did not run to meteorology."

All too soon, the peak of Oakham Mount rose before them, and Darcy realised that Elizabeth intended for their time together to be of a short duration.

If he was to broach the topic of courtship, Darcy knew he must turn the conversation to the one that interested him.

"I have heard it mentioned that you recently received a marriage proposal, Miss Elizabeth. Have I been remiss in wishing you joy?"

Not for the first time, Elizabeth mentally cursed the gossip mongers, who seemed to know everyone's business the moment it occurred.

"It is true that I received a proposal of marriage. However, I turned the gentleman down."

"May I ask why?"

"We would not have suited each other," she replied honestly.

"That is a broad spectrum for me to speculate on, Miss Elizabeth."

Elizabeth could not explain why, but it grieved her that a man such as Mr Darcy, should know that she had received a proposal from a man such as her cousin Collins. Suppose he thought Mr Collins was the best kind of man she could attract? What if Mr Darcy agreed with Mr Collins, concurred with his observation that she might never receive another proposal? After all, Elizabeth reasoned, Meryton was not a big town, and there were many single young ladies of marriageable age residing there. The local marriage market certainly favoured the local bachelor's and widowers.

Elizabeth stopped and turned to face him.

"I did not love him, Mr Darcy. Is that singular enough for you?"

Clearly, his chosen topic had irritated Elizabeth, yet it had given him more information than he could ever have hoped for. Elizabeth wanted to marry for love. It gave him hope. Although hard to achieve in one month, it was not impossible.

Elizabeth, who enjoyed walking on most days, was extraordinarily pleased to reach the scattering of seat size boulders and logs on the ridge at Oakham Mount. Although it was she who had set the fast pace, the last few uphill yards had been a struggle.

A little breathless, Elizabeth sat on one of the lower stones and untied her bonnet. The fresh air felt cold on her exposed head, but it was a welcome chill after the heat of the pace. She hoped that Mr Darcy would not question her about Mr Collins anymore. Somehow, she always seemed to reveal things about herself to this man that she had no intention of doing.

Darcy joined Elizabeth, taking a seat on the boulder at right angles to her, from where he could better admire her.

Having caught her breath, Elizabeth turned to Darcy.

"What about you, Mr Darcy? You are what...seven and twenty, eight and twenty, and also unmarried. Have you ever been engaged?"

"I have yet to ask a woman to be my wife, but it is something I hope to remedy in the very near future, Miss Elizabeth."

This was not the reply Elizabeth had expected. For some reason, she felt both intrigued and wary.

Deciding to delve further, she asked,

"You sound as if you have someone in mind, Mr Darcy? Is that the reason you returned to Meryton, to conduct your courtship?"

Unwittingly, Elizabeth had started a conversation on the very subject he wanted to pursue, but first, he must dispel her belief that he had somehow wronged George Wickham. If he proposed to her while she still thought ill of him, he would have no hope.

Aware of the falsehoods Wickham was spreading amongst the residents of Meryton, Darcy suspected he had embellished his tale of woe for Elizabeth's, consumption purely because Darcy had shown an interest in her.

Therefore, Darcy decided to seize on the last time they had spoken about Wickham to start his defence.

"Miss Elizabeth, do you remember the night of Mr Bingley's ball, when we spoke of Mr Wickham and my relationship with him?"

Elizabeth screwed up her nose. It had not escaped her notice that Mr Darcy had changed the topic of conversation. He had done so once before, at the ball. *Reports may vary greatly with respect to me; and I could wish, Miss Bennet, that you were not to sketch my character at the present moment, as there is reason to fear that the performance would reflect no credit on either of us."*

Then, he had politely been telling her it was none of her business, but now he appeared to be willing to talk about it. And, as Mr Darcy's relationship with Mr Wickham was a subject all of Meryton was eagerly awaiting clarification on, she decided to indulge him.

"I do, but as I recall you were more than a little evasive, sir."

"I am still not at liberty to divulge all the particulars at present, but, if I tell you that he once tried, and almost succeeded, in dishonouring a gentlewoman of my acquaintance, merely to obtain her considerable fortune, would it change your opinion of him?"

Seeing Elizabeth's startled expression, Darcy tried to reassure her.

"Thankfully, Providence stepped in, and saved the young woman from ruin, but not without consequences to her health, her confidence and her trust in her fellow man. As for Mr Wickham, he has shown not the slightest hint of remorse or regret for his actions, and I cannot forgive him." Darcy could not hide his bitterness, nor did he try.

"I do not tell you this out of malice, Miss Elizabeth, but as a warning. Mr Wickham is not the gentleman he professes to be, and you should not trust him, or his words. Providence may not be so generous next time."

Elizabeth was shocked. If this accusation were true, then it would drastically change her opinion of Mr Wickham. Though there was no way she could substantiate Darcy's accusations? The despoiling of virgins was hardly a subject a gentlewoman could raise in polite conversation.

"I...I think you know it is an allegation I cannot substantiate with Mr Wickham. Without further details... or proof of some kind, I feel I must still give Mr Wickham the benefit of the doubt.

Darcy was disappointed.

"It is not my secret to reveal, Miss Elizabeth. But be assured, if it were, I would not hesitate to tell you the particulars."

Elizabeth could see that it had been hard for Darcy to broach this subject, which gave her pause for thought. If a man as proud as Mr Darcy was willing to reveal such a painful happening, and to a close acquaintance, then there must be some truth in it.

"I can see that it was not easy for you to divulge, Mr Darcy. So, I will promise you this; from now on, I will be more circumspect in my dealings with Mr Wickham."

"Then I am satisfied... for now," Darcy said.

From the corner of his eye, Darcy saw the serving girl fidget as the cold from the stone penetrated her thin cloak. This, he suspected, would prompt Elizabeth to begin their descent back to Longbourn.

Pushing on with his final question, Darcy asked,

"And your opinion of me, Miss Bennet?"

Again, his question had taken her by surprise. It was unthinkable to offend a man such as Mr Darcy to his face, although she had been quite vocal in doing so behind his back. She had the good grace to blush a little when she thought of all she had said. And now, how was it possible to answer this question without giving offence?

Pausing to reflect on their acquaintance, Elizabeth examined their dealings together.

Her dislike of him had only been minor until fuelled by Mr Wickham's account of his ill-treatment at Darcy's hands, yet that was now a questionable source of information. The only negative fact she personally could hold against him, was his unkind words at the assembly. Yet, was he not entitled to his opinion? Had she not done and said the same about Miss Caroline Bingley? The only difference was, she had taken care that her conversation was not overheard. His words had not injured her, only wounded her pride.

She had to admit, Mr Darcy had never served her ill.

She replied quietly,

"My opinion of you...it is a question that should not be asked."

"But you don't like me, do you, Miss Bennet?"

"Those are your words, sir, not mine."

Darcy had given Elizabeth the chance to confirm her dislike for him, in which case he would have returned to London and licked his wounds. But she had not.

Elated, and seeing an opportunity to wipe the slate clean, Darcy said,

"Miss Elizabeth, I think neither of us would like to be measured by our first impression of one another, would you agree?"

Elizabeth neither confirmed nor denied his statement verbally, only inclining her head a little and then waited for him to continue.

"Might I propose that we start anew?"

The opportunity of delving into the mind of such a man as Mr Darcy fascinated Elizabeth. Since his arrival in Meryton, the village had been divided in their opinion of him. They either admired or detested him. Courted or avoided him. Loved or loathed him. Her curiosity won the day.

Elizabeth slowly inclined her head, and then said,

"Very well, Mr Darcy, I accept your offer."

Springing to his feet, Darcy could not hide his joy and a smile spread over his face.

"Fitzwilliam Darcy, at your service, ma'am," and he bowed low.

Elizabeth couldn't help but be swept up in his cheerful mood.

"Elizabeth Bennet, sir," and she executed a deep curtsy.

Standing facing each other, they smiled at the silliness of it all, until Darcy suddenly stopped smiling and took a step closer to her.

"Elizabeth..." he said.

The very persistent cough from behind them brought Darcy back to his senses, although he inwardly cursed at the untimely interruption from Elizabeth's serving girl.

Instead of revealing his emotions, he said,

"May I walk with you again, eight o'clock tomorrow?"

"You may," Elizabeth replied, with a smile.

Chapter Five

The next morning, Darcy again arrived promptly on the stroke of eight at Longbourn. Mrs Hill opened the door, and Elizabeth stepped out. Today she was accompanied not by Daisy, but by her sister Mary.

Elizabeth explained.

"Mary has agreed to keep us company today, Mr Darcy. I hope you do not mind, only Mrs Hill cannot spare Daisy for a second day."

He did not want an audience when he made his offer to Elizabeth, but each day that he did not make her aware of his feelings was a day wasted. Darcy gave a half smile and dipped his head in acknowledgement.

Mary, he thought, was a strange girl.

Having heard the news from Fletcher that Charlotte Lucas was to marry Mr Collins instead of Elizabeth, he had thought that the pious and plain Mary Bennet would have suited him better. Not only that, but he suspected his Aunt Catherine would have also considered it a better match. Lady Catherine saw no reason for an estate to be entailed away from the female line, as with her own daughter. Lady Catherine's only child, Anne, would inherit a vast estate and fortune on her mother's demise, rather than it passing to Darcy or her other cousin, Colonel Fitzwilliam. In Darcy's opinion, if Mr Collins had married his cousin Mary, he would have gained even greater favour with his stern and opinionated patroness.

Darcy took heart when he saw the book in Mary's hand. Hopefully, she would engross herself in the pages of that, rather than join in with their conversation.

Today, they set off a slower pace than the previous day, and Darcy took this as a sign that Elizabeth was happier to be in his company.

"I am pleased we travel at a more sedate pace today, Miss Elizabeth. It will allow us more time to talk." Darcy said.

"Oh, it is not my design to tarry, Mr Darcy. Mary has a blister on her heel."

A deflated Darcy could only say, "I see."

Winding their way along a different path, through a less dense part of the woods, Elizabeth guided them to a small clearing, where several trees had been felled and were awaiting collection from the local sawmill.

Mary followed Elizabeth, and Darcy followed Mary.

"I will sit over here, Lizzy," Mary said in her monotone voice.

Elizabeth smiled at her sister and sat on one of the other tree trunks.

"Longbourn is situated in a charming part of Hertfordshire," Darcy said, trying to initiate a conversation on a neutral subject. Complimenting their home seemed a safe topic.

"We did not choose our ancestral home's location, Mr Darcy; it was here when we were born. It will remain here when we die," chimed in Mary.

"Yes, quite so, thank you, Mary," Elizabeth said, although she could not stop the rosy tint of embarrassment from staining her cheeks.

Mary's comment had given the air a feeling of awkwardness, and even Elizabeth was in a quandary as to how to move on.

It was Darcy who broke the stalemate of silence.

"I was thinking of calling on a few of Mr Bingley's neighbours. I understand my previous impression did not show me in a favourable light. Who would you recommend I send my card to first, Miss Elizabeth, Sir Lucas?"

Seizing the chance to stifle the awkwardness created by her own sister, Elizabeth replied,

"Yes, Sir Lucas is a good choice. Although he is new to the nobility, he is the only titled gentleman in the area, and very well respected."

"Then it is settled, I will leave my card on the way home."

Elizabeth knew her mamma had invited the Lucas' and Colonel Forster to dine with them the next evening. Unfortunately, at the last minute, Colonel Forster had to drop out, which vexed Mrs Bennet greatly, and she had voiced her displeasure several times. *Now, not only will we be an odd number, but there are too many ladies.* Elizabeth had suggested that she reschedule the meal for when Colonel Forster could attend, but her mother would not hear of it. She was determined to show Lady Lucas that they supported Elizabeth wholeheartedly in her refusal of Mr Collins proposal. With five daughters to support and husbands to find for each of them, nothing could be farther from the truth, especially as they only had one thousand pounds' dowry each. Indeed, she had been so annoyed by her daughter's disobedience and refusal, that she had vowed never to speak to Elizabeth again.

Elizabeth had smiled to herself. If only that were a vow her mother had kept, but her daily outbursts to remind everyone that Mr Collins and that sly Charlotte Lucas could turn them out with only a day's notice after Mr Bennet's death, belied her oath.

However, if she were to invite Mr Darcy to join them, not only would it even out the numbers, but it would add another gentleman to their party, which she hoped would go some way to restoring her in her mamma's good grace. After all, he was quite the richest man they had ever met, or were likely to meet, with ten thousand pounds a year!

"Mr Darcy," she began nervously, "...do you have plans tomorrow evening? I ask because Sir William and Lady Lucas are to dine with us, and I am sure our mother would like us to extend the invitation to you also." She finished, casting Mary a glance.

Mary made a face and shrugged her shoulders. Only one man had been of interest to her, and now he was spoken for. She returned to her book.

Darcy wanted to spend time with Elizabeth, not her family. Conducting a courtship in plain view of her family was one thing, sharing it with them was quite another. However, if it meant additional time in Elizabeth's company, he was sure he could tolerate them for one more evening

"That is very generous of you, Miss Elizabeth. If you are confident it will not be an imposition, then I accept."

Elizabeth was surprised by Mr Darcy's exuberant response. It was the most animated she had ever seen him.

Their mood of mutual civility was broken when Mary said,

"I'm cold and want to go home, Lizzy, now."

On the ride back to Netherfield, Darcy thought he had made some progress with his cause. Although they had shared only a relatively short conversation, it has been both congenial and productive. A dinner invitation and a chance to repair both the Bennets' and the Lucas' opinion of him.

"Well it is too late to retract the offer now, Elizabeth, so I suppose we will just have to make the best of it," moaned Mrs Bennet.

"But Mamma, having a man of Mr Darcy's consequence sitting at our table must be of some advantage to us?" Elizabeth said, hating to use Mr Darcy's status as leverage. "Where is our charity, mamma? Mr Darcy is alone at Netherfield and knows very few people in the area."

"And whose fault is that? If Mr Darcy had not acted so above his company, I dare say there would be many families willing to invite him to dine," retorted Mrs Bennet.

"Singling us out as his principal acquaintances will significantly add to our standing, Mamma, and not just in our community, but in all of Hertfordshire."

"Very well, my dear, it is done now. As you say, we cannot retract the invitation now. Myself, I will enjoy the additional presence of another male in the fray. Too often I am outnumbered by the female of the species," Mr Bennet winked in Elizabeth's direction.

But Mrs Bennet would not be silenced on the matter.

"That is all very easy for you to say, Mr Bennet, but Cook and I have planned the meal and courses to fit the number of guests precisely. How am I to conjure up another brace of quail that have been hung to my specifications?"

"Mr Darcy can have one of mine, Mamma," offered Elizabeth.

"And one of mine, Mrs Bennet. It is settled then."

"It most certainly is not," exclaimed Mrs Bennet. "And have Mr Darcy think us too poor to serve a proper meal. No, I will have to go into Meryton myself and speak to the butcher. As if I don't have enough to do."

Closing the door firmly behind her, Mr Bennet and Elizabeth were left in no doubt as to Mrs Bennet's displeasure in the matter.

Elizabeth had been relieved to discover her mamma in the library with her father. He had, as anticipated, lent her his moral support when informing her mother about their extra guest.

Deciding it would be prudent for her to avoid her mother, for the time being at least, Elizabeth elected to remain in the library with her papa. Choosing a book of verse by Lord Byron, she then made herself comfortable on the tuffet by the fire.

Elizabeth loved this room, and it wasn't just because her mother and sisters rarely ventured into it, or even that it was somewhere she and her father could spend time together. It was because of the books. Elizabeth's thirst for knowledge had set her apart from her sisters. In some circles, she would be labelled a bluestocking, but she did not care. Having a sharp and inquisitive mind had moulded her into the woman she was today, and though she sometimes envied Jane her looks, she was quite content with her lot in life.

Ten minutes before seven, Darcy arrived at Longbourn. He anticipated being the first guest to arrive but was disappointed to see that he was, in fact, the last.

Darcy detested being the last to arrive, and it was as he expected. Moving into the room, he immediately felt uncomfortable as the gathered company focused their attention solely on him, expectantly waiting for him to say something witty or charming.

He gave a curt bow, then said,

"Good evening."

Elizabeth waited for one of her parents to excuse themselves, to remember their manners and welcome Mr Darcy as they should, but both appeared absorbed in conversation. Her father was exchanging views with Sir William on the variety of local pig breeding stock, while her mother was extolling the virtues of their new scullery maid to Lady Lucas.

Whether they had genuinely not seen Mr Darcy enter or not, Elizabeth did not know, but it was unthinkable for no-one to greet him officially. Having extended the invitation herself, she could not just leave the poor man standing there, floundering on the perimeter of the gathered company.

Moving forward, Elizabeth said,

"Mr Darcy, I hope my greeting will suffice. As you see, my parents are engaged at present, but you are very welcome." She motioned for him to sit in the free seat between Jane and herself.

Relieved to have someone to talk to, Darcy accepted Elizabeth's offer and took the chair placed between the sisters.

Looking around, he realised that during his previous three-month stay in Hertfordshire, he had only been to Longbourn a handful of times. It must have been a handsome property in its time, and still was, only it needed some time and money spent on it to restore it to its former glory. Most people would not notice these insignificant faults that Darcy did, but then he was pedantic about such things.

In one corner, there was a small piece of paper peeling away where it met the ceiling cornice, and the flooring, although expensive oak planks, needed a new coat of varnish. And while the windows were large and impressive, the frames had a few flakes of paint missing here and there.

Turning his attention to the occupants of the room, he noticed that Mr Bennet's clothes were probably two seasons out of date, as were Sir William's. However, this was not the case with the ladies. All of them were dressed in fashionable attire, and, he noticed, following the latest trend for simple accessories. Jane wore a single strand of coral beads about her neck, while Mary and Elizabeth had chosen a small gold cross and chain. Apart from these few things and the married women's wedding bands, there was no ostentatious show of wealth or superior position.

With typical county promptness, as the clock struck seven, so the butler announced dinner.

In the dining room, Mrs Bennet made herself busy, directing her guests to their allocated seats, before taking her own seat at the opposite end of the table to her husband.

Elizabeth, as usual, was sitting next to her father, with Mr Darcy on her right, followed by Kitty and Mary. Next to Mrs Bennet on her right was Lady Lucas, Jane, Lydia, and finally Sir William on Mr Bennet's left.

Darcy, as usual, spoke little to start with, but he was not bored. He was listening.

"Of course, Charlotte had no choice but to accept Mr Collins' proposal. At her age, there could be little chance she would receive another. As it is, there might still be time for her to be blessed with children," Mrs Bennet cooed to Lady Lucas.

"My dear Mrs Bennet, Mr Collins was, I believe, merely following his patroness's instruction in proposing to Elizabeth first. Lady Catherine felt he should make some attempt to counteract the entail on Longbourn. Though, in reality, Charlotte was always Mr Collins' preferred choice for a bride," responded Lady Lucas.

"How old is Charlotte, seven and twenty? Can you still have babies when you're that old?" chimed in Lydia.

"Of course, you can. Mamma was about that age when she had you, silly," said Kitty.

"Why would any woman want to be married with babies? Flirting with the officers is much more fun," Lydia announced with a giggle.

"The Bible instructs us to procreate, to populate the world and spread the word of God. To do that a man and woman must marry," added Mary in her usual flat tone.

"Well, Zelda Murphy has a baby, and she has no husband!" exclaimed Lydia.

"Lydia!" berated Elizabeth in a firm but hushed tone. "Miss Murphy is not a suitable subject to discuss at the dinner table. If you want to know more, I will explain her circumstances when our guests have gone."

Making an inordinate amount of fuss as she put her cutlery down, Lydia folded her arms across her chest and then proceeded to turn her mouth upside down in a severe pout.

"Such a high-spirited girl," Mrs Bennet said, as she tried to cover Lydia's rudeness with humour.

Finally, Mr Bennet found his voice.

"Well, well, never a dull moment,"

Once the ladies had excused themselves and moved through to the withdrawing room, the remaining three men enjoyed a snifter of brandy.

Darcy was pleasantly surprised by the contents of his glass, which appeared to be the finest Napoleon Brandy.

"You approve?" asked Mr Bennet.

More comfortable now he was in the company of only men, Darcy nodded and said,

"I do, sir. It is French, if I am not mistaken?"

"Quite so, sir. It is my only weakness, but what would life be without at least one vice, aye?"

Sir William Lucas, who had received his knighthood for giving a speech praising the king when the king had passed through Meryton, was, by nature, a gentle man. Newly titled, he moved his family to a bigger and better property, naming it Lucas Lodge. Next, Sir William sold his business and became a man of leisure, which suited him greatly. Being of a friendly disposition meant he seldom saw the darker side of people's personalities, only their good and kind traits permeated into his field of vision.

"Dinner was a lively affair, was it not gentlemen? The young people of today are so passionate about everything," Sir William said.

"I fear my two youngest girls have yet to learn the meaning of the word restraint," Mr Bennet said opening a box of cigars and offering them to Darcy and Sir William.

"A taste I have yet to acquire, but I know some like to indulge."

Both declined.

"So, a daughter to be married, Sir William? When is the happy event?" asked Mr Bennet.

"Early in the New Year, I believe. Mr Collins has gone to ask for Lady Catherine's blessing. I think they are well suited. My Charlotte is a sensible girl and will make Mr Collins an excellent wife."

"Quite so, Sir William, quite so." Replied Mr Bennet. Turning to Darcy, he asked,

"So, have you acted on the matter we discussed, sir?"

Darcy was sure Mr Bennet knew he had not, but as he had raised the subject, it was an opportunity to act on it now.

"I have not, sir, but if you could provide me with some privacy, I would like to resolve that situation this evening."

Nodding, Mr Bennet said,

"Very well, Sir Lucas and I will rejoin the ladies, and I will send Elizabeth to you."

Darcy paced the room as he waited for Elizabeth to arrive. How he wished he had prepared his proposal in advance. But he had not.

Lost in thought, he was alerted to Elizabeth's presence when her questioning voice behind him asked,

"Mr Darcy, Papa said you wished to speak to me?"

Elizabeth was puzzled. What could Mr Darcy possibly want to talk to her about, and so urgently that it could not wait until their next morning walk?

Gesturing for her to take a seat, Darcy waited until she was settled before he spoke.

"Miss Bennet, we have been acquaintances for some weeks now, and although we have not always agreed on many subjects, I have enjoyed our encounters and conversations immensely. You have shown to me that you have a keen mind and possess a sharp wit, while still being able to boast of a generous nature. These are all attributes that I admire...in moderation. Putting aside your lack of fortune, vague connections, and station in life, I have, for some time now, felt that you would make an excellent wife and mother. Therefore, I would like to make you an offer of marriage."

Elizabeth remained silent, and Darcy, who was inexperienced in matters of the heart, repeated his offer.

"I said, would you to consider being my wife, Miss Elizabeth?"

Elizabeth had not expected a proposal of marriage from Mr Darcy and was completely taken aback when he delivered his offer. He had complimented her in several ways, yet insulted her too. And though she was not insensible to the honour his offer bestowed on her, there had been no mention of love. He *enjoyed* their conversations, he *admired* her attributes, he *felt* as if she would make an excellent wife, but no love. On the other hand, should she dismiss his proposal so quickly, without giving it the due consideration any proposal deserved? No, the least she could do was consider it.

"I thank you for the offer, Mr Darcy, although I am a little surprised by it. May I have some time to consider it? Perhaps I could give you my answer tomorrow?" Elizabeth replied.

Darcy did not wish his agony to be prolonged for another twenty-four hours. In a half pleading, half annoyed tone, he said,

"You cannot tell me now?"

How typical of a man to assume that selecting a lifetime mate was as simple as saying yay or nay.

Explaining the delay, she replied,

"I understand your impatience, sir, but marriage, for a woman at least, is agreeing to put their future life and freedom into the hands of their husband until the day they die. To serve and please them, to be controlled and subjected to their wishes, to rely first on their father and then on their husband for their every comfort and consideration. It is not something a woman should enter into lightly."

Feeling foolish for his impatience, Darcy shuffled his weight from one foot to the other.

"My apologies, Miss Bennet, clearly my proposal was unexpected. However, if you deem to accept my offer, I would like to begin a formal courtship as soon as possible."

"I understand. You will have my answer in the morning, Mr Darcy. Now, shall we rejoin the others?" Elizabeth said more calmly than she felt.

Sometime later, after their guests had returned to their homes, and everyone had retired for the night, Elizabeth sat in her bed, her knees drawn up, and her chin resting on them. She was replaying the words of Mr Darcy's proposal in her head, comparing it to the one she had received from Mr Collins. The latter had at least said he loved her, however untrue it was, while Mr Darcy had not mentioned love at all. Though, Mr Collins had proposed only because his patroness wanted him to marry, not because the idea of matrimony had appealed to him or that he sincerely loved her. Whereas Mr Darcy wanted to be married, and what's more, he wanted to be married to her. Had he not told her himself that he had never proposed to a woman before? And she could not believe he would have proposed at all, if he was solely attracted to her for her company and their lively exchanges.

Elizabeth absently wrapped a glossy tendril of hair around her index finger, and then admired the spiral it had formed as she released it from her grasp.

Of course, she could not ignore the financial stability a marriage to Mr Darcy would bring to all her family. The entail on Longbourn would no longer be a consideration when her father died. Undoubtedly, being able to secure the financial future of all her sisters was an appealing incentive, but it must not be the only reason she accepted him. Then, as her mamma had so often pointed out before Mr Bingley's sudden departure, having a rich a son-in-law would ensure the younger girls were introduced to other wealthy men. Though being related to Mr Darcy should be consideration enough, if he added a few thousand pounds to each of their dowries…but she was getting ahead of herself.

With these points firmly turning her mind towards accepting his offer, Elizabeth knew it was not her family that would have to deal with Mr Darcy, live with Mr Darcy, or be loved by Mr Darcy. That burden would fall on her shoulders alone.

Falling back onto her pillows, Elizabeth tried to imagine herself being embraced and kissed by both men that had proposed to her. A shudder of revulsion rippled through her entire body when she thought of Mr Collins placing his lips against her mouth. Thankfully though, that would now never happen. Then she turned her thoughts to Mr Darcy. He was intelligent, articulate and well read. But could she bear to be to be kissed by him, embraced by him, loved by him? Admittedly he was a handsome man, with the appearance of a firm and well-formed body. It would not be so abhorrent, Elizabeth decided, to allow Mr Darcy such liberties.

Then, quite involuntary, as her mind imagined Mr Darcy's lips pressed against her own, a few hairs at the nape of her neck responded, producing a pleasant, yet strangely unsettling sensation.

Giving herself a mental reprimand, she thought of what her mother might think. As Mrs Fitzwilliam Darcy, she would want for nothing. Fashionable clothes and jewels, and servants aplenty. Properties, foreign travel, and influential acquaintances. Yes, there was a lot he could offer her, but would these be enough without love?

And what if she did accept him? Having made no secret of her dislike of Mr Darcy, to her family and close friends, should she now confess her prior dislike to him? Surely one of them would reveal her past opinion of him if she did not. How she wished she had been more guarded in her opinions.

Eventually, she decided if the right moment arose, then she would confess her previous opinion of him, aware that by then she might be his wife.

Finally, there was one point that she would not compromise on. She would not enter into a marriage with a lie between them. She did not love Mr Darcy, not at present, but she imagined…hoped she could learn to love him. If this was acceptable to him, and he could answer all her questions satisfactorily, then there was, she decided, a strong possibility she would soon be Mrs Elizabeth Darcy.

Elizabeth slept very little that night, and when she did sleep, her dreams were a jumble of Mr Darcy and Mr Collins fighting a duel over who should take her, as the prize.

Chapter Six

Darcy was up long before the cockerel crowed. Pacing back and forth in his bed chamber, berating himself for his woefully inadequate proposal to Elizabeth yesterday. He concluded that if he were she, he would refuse him. What had possessed him to mention her inferior birth and lack of fortune, and why had he not declared that he loved her and had done so for some time instead of wittering on about how he enjoyed their arguing.

Frustration saw him slam his fist into the wall. Not for the first time, he wished that he possessed an easy way with words like his friend Charles Bingley.

Sitting astride Odin at the bottom of the lane, Darcy had to cool his heels for a full twenty minutes before it was time for him to call on Elizabeth.

During this period of inaction, his loyal steed pawed at the hard ground, preferring to race across open fields to hovering on a dirt road.

With a few minutes to spare, Darcy handed Odin's reins to the stable boy and ordered him to give him a good rub down.

When the butler opened the door, he informed Darcy that, Miss Elizabeth was expecting him, and if quite convenient, would he mind joining her in the back parlour.

Standing before the closed door, Darcy took a deep breath, then, sure of rejection, he strode in.

Elizabeth was accustomed to seeing only two expressions on Mr Darcy's face. One of languid indifference, which he usually wore when in company, and the other was a dark scowl.

Which, she wondered, would he honour her with today?

Having wrestled most of the night, trying to weigh up the pros and cons of his proposal, she had decided there were several things that must be asked, and answered before she could make her final decision.

With the weather chillier than it had been of late, she hoped he would not mind if they stayed inside today.

Leaving the door ajar for propriety sake, Darcy went to greet Elizabeth formally.

He bowed, she curtsied.

Elizabeth sat down, while Darcy preferred to stand.

"You are too generous to trifle with me, Miss Bennet, have you reached a decision?"

Elizabeth raised her brows.

"As usual, Mr Darcy, your subject is singular, but before I give you my answer, there are some questions I would ask of you."

"Of course, ask whatever you will, Miss Bennet."

Where to start, she wondered. There was much she wanted to say, but there was also no profit in aggravating him with irrelevant questions.

"Do you remember our conversation the first day you walked with me?"

"I do."

"Then you also recall why I said I could not marry Mr Collins?"

"Yes, because you did not love him," Darcy replied stoically, anticipating the direction of her reply.

"Sir, while your proposal honours me, I must tell you that neither do I love you."

"Then you reject my offer!" Darcy said, his tone harder than he intended.

Her declaration had hurt him more than he thought. Although entirely expected, to hear the words spoken aloud, was nevertheless a painful experience.

"No... not yet. In truth, I am still undecided, sir."

Puzzled, Darcy frowned.

"Why do you want to marry me, Mr Darcy? Is it merely because I amuse you, will bear your children, and keep your house?"

Seizing the opportunity to expunge his disastrous proposal of last evening, Darcy took a step closer to Elizabeth's chair, and said,

"No...yes, it is all those things, Miss Bennet, but if that were all I wanted in a wife, there are dozens of debutantes I might choose from."

Darcy pulled up a chair and sat opposite her.

"At first, I felt only a deep admiration towards you. Your conduct in difficult situations set you apart from others around you. The time you spent at Netherfield caring for your sister, demonstrated to me that you possessed a kind and companionate nature. When Miss Bingley, and Mrs Hurst, were cruel and unkind to you, you could have retaliated, yet you did not. You answered them with wit and humour. You have been generous to your friend Charlotte, defending her decision to accept Mr Collins proposal, even when others were malicious and uncharitable. My admiration for you has grown with our every encounter, until I can now say, with complete honesty, that I love you, most ardently, Miss Bennet. And while I am willing to accept that you do not love me now, I would hope that you could come to love me, in time."

Elizabeth had never seen Mr Darcy so animated, heard him so vocal, or so passionate about anything. The thought that he had become so when talking about his affection for her felt oddly satisfying.

"You... love me, Mr Darcy?"

"Passionately, Miss Bennet. Believe me, Elizabeth, I view my feeling for you with perfect clarity."

Darcy noticed the rose colour of her cheeks had turned a darker shade of scarlet.

The warm feeling Elizabeth experienced while listening to Mr Darcy declare himself faded a little as his declaration threw up another question in her mind.

"But in time, Mr Darcy, would your passion wane and give way to regret?"

"Never," he replied firmly.

Elizabeth rose and took a few paces away from him, before turning to say,

"Sir, did you not say only yesterday, that you had overcome your objections to my family, to my lack of fortune and the deficiency of me having any worthy connections, to make me this offer? How then, do I know that these feelings will not resurface in the future in the form of resentment?"

She looked down for a moment, then, nervously she wet her lips, lifted her chin and in a faltering voice, said,

"I could not bear to be married to a man, who... after the first flush of passion had faded...regretted me."

"Knowing I love you, is still new to you, Elizabeth, but I have lived with these feelings for many weeks and months now. It does not diminish, Elizabeth, but grows stronger each day. I do not anticipate a downturn in my affection."

"And my family, sir, could you overcome your feelings of degradation at being associated with such relations? To withstand the censure of society for such a connection?"

The Bennet's, it was true, would not normally be in his circle of acquaintances, not by choice anyway, but they were Elizabeth's family, and she could not be separated from them.

"I am ashamed for expressing such sentiments, Miss Bennet. However, I considered all my objections thoroughly before I returned to Hertfordshire. There is no eventuality that I am not prepared for, either from your family, from my family or from society in general. The opportunity to spend my lifetime loving you, Elizabeth, is worth it."

Elizabeth coloured at his frankness, but his words were reassuring.

"And my family, sir, you would allow me to visit them?"

"I would have no objections to you visiting your family from time to time, within reason, of course. Also, I want to assure you, Miss Bennet, that I would take my responsibility of caring for my extended family very seriously."

Elizabeth took comfort in this. Darcy had declared his intention to look after her mother and sisters when her father died. It had been another concern she had wanted to raise, but it appeared that also had been considered, and resolved by Mr Darcy.

"Thank you, sir," Elizabeth said, sounding a little breathless as her emotions rose.

Taking a moment to regain her composure, Elizabeth asked,

"And where would we live, Mr Darcy?"

"Mainly at my estate in Derbyshire. I consider Pemberley my home, Miss Bennet. I would, of course, take you to London as often, or as seldom as you wished, but my hope would be that you too, would grow to love Pemberley as I do."

"And the duration of our engagement?"

"Does that mean you accept my offer, Elizabeth?" Darcy asked, unable to conceal the eagerness in his voice.

"Perhaps..." Elizabeth said hesitantly.

Hardly hearing the hesitation in her voice, Darcy went on to say,

"I would like for us to be married before the New Year, Miss Bennet. I have been away from Pemberley for some time now, and although my estate manager can oversee most of the business, there are some things that I must tend to in person."

"So soon," Elizabeth said aloud as she thought of all that must be done.

Darcy waited, his breath caught in his throat as she paused to think. His entire future happiness rested in the palm of Elizabeth's hand. She had the power to make him the happiest man alive, of to crush him in an instant. To cause him ecstasy or despair, euphoria or desolation, joy or sorry. It was alien to him, to feel powerless with the direction of his own fate.

"Are you quite sure you want to marry me, Mr Darcy? Knowing that at present I do not return your sentiment, that I may never return your sentiment in an equal measure?" she asked finally.

Darcy stood, and closed the short space between them. Then, taking hold of her upper arms, his voice ladened with a myriad of emotions, he said,

"I do. But Elizabeth, if you accept me, it is to be a full marriage, not one of convenience. I will love you and protect you, honour you and cherish you. I will respect you and defend you, provide all you need, and give you all you want. All this I will do gladly, but in return, you must give me your loyalty, your attention, your respect and your time, and although you do not love me now, you must be willing to try to love me. We will be man and wife in the full, biblical sense, Elizabeth, and your favours are to be given only to me. Is that clear?"

Mesmerised by the passion of his speech, Elizabeth look up at him with wide eyes, and could only nod, and say,

"Yes, I understand."

She had never been witness to such ardour before. His words left her in no doubt as to the strength and passion of his love, his desire for her, and she felt breathless and overwhelmed by this knowledge.

"Is there anything else you wish to ask me? Any concern you might have that I have not attended to?"

Elizabeth could think of no other objection to his proposal. He had addressed all her concerns and soothed all her fears. There was nothing left to do now but give him her answer.

In a soft voice, Elizabeth said,

"Would you ask me the question again, Mr Darcy?"

Daring to feel optimistic, Darcy felt his pulse quicken, but he would not let his guard down, or his hopes rise until he had a firm yes or no.

Deciding to repeat his proposal in the established mode, Darcy fell onto one knee, and taking her childlike hands into his own, he asked,

"Miss Bennet, Elizabeth, it would be my greatest honour, if you would accept my hand in marriage and consent to be my wife."

Elizabeth looked down. His strong hands were surprisingly tender as he absently stroked the back of her hands with his thumbs.

Could she ask for anything more from a husband than what Mr Darcy had offered? She did not think so. He had promised her everything. His heart, his protection, his wealth, his respect, his devotion and his love. Yes…his love

Having made her decision, Elizabeth felt calm as she lowered her eyes to meet his, and replied,

"I will."

<u>Chapter Seven</u>

Darcy stood, and he raised Elizabeth up with him. He lifted his hand and brushed her cheek with the back of his fingers, silently admiring the softness of her skin. Letting his hand wander down, Darcy traced the outline of her mouth with his thumb. She was so beautiful; how could he ever have thought her plain. He cringed as he recalled the unwarranted slight he had delivered when first he made her acquaintance, and now... there was no other that could be compared to the exquisite face before him. He wanted to kiss her, to possess her lips, to let her know that there would be no denying him, not now, not ever.

Slowly, he lowered his head

The entirety of the time Darcy had been caressing her face Elizabeth looked up into his eyes, compelled to return his gaze. She knew he was about to kiss her, to lay claim to her. He would kiss her because now he had that right to kiss her.

It was a soft kiss, a brief kiss, but nevertheless a kiss of ownership. She had accepted him, and now he had the right to become familiar with her, intimate with her. First her mouth, and soon her body.

Elizabeth did not return the kiss. Having never been kissed before it was a new and strange experience for her, though not an unpleasant one. Soon, she would become accustomed to such liberties, and maybe in time, she would learn to enjoy and return such expressions of affection.

As Darcy broke away and raised his head, Elizabeth saw a smile break over his face as she had never seen before. He was happy. She had made him happy. Now, she hoped, and yes, prayed that he would make her happy too.

Having agreed to marry him, Elizabeth expected Mr Darcy to go to her father to seek his blessing. However, to find that he had already spoken to him was a shock. Elizabeth felt as if she had somehow been...manoeuvred into accepting his offer. Who else had prior knowledge of his impending proposal, she wondered.

"If you will excuse me, sir, I must go and speak to my father. I am sure he will be eager to share our news with the rest of my family," She said, leaving Darcy to cool his heels alone, in the back parlour.

"So, you have accepted Mr Darcy. Well, Lizzy, I can't say I am surprised."

"You suspected that I would, Papa?"

"Opposites attract, although you do share some interests, you are quite unlike in the essentials, Lizzy. Still, I do believe if anyone can soften Mr Darcy's character, it's you."

"We have your blessing then, Papa?"

Mr Bennet knew Elizabeth would not have accepted Mr Darcy's proposal if she was not content to do so, but he could not stop himself from asking,

"But you do not love him, Lizzy?"

Having ridiculed Mr Darcy on several occasions with her papa, Elizabeth suspected that he would ask this question. However, she predicted that he already knew the answer.

Choosing her words with care, she said,

"I will, in time. We have spoken at length this morning, and Mr Darcy has acquitted himself very well. We discussed several issues that I voiced my concern over, and he addressed them all to my satisfaction." Seeing her father's concern, worried that his favourite child would be unhappy, Elizabeth leant forward in her chair and touched his hand.

"Mr Darcy loves me, Papa, and I must be sensible. Am I likely to meet another man of such consequence? For him to fall in love with me, and brave societies censure to make me his wife? I do not think so. It is a good offer, Papa...I will be happy,"

Mr Bennet placed one of his hands over Elizabeth's and gave a weak smile. So, he was to lose his muse, his companion, his daughter. He would miss her terribly.

Elizabeth closed the door of her father's study and made her way back to where she had left Mr Darcy. As she neared the door, which was still ajar, she could hear her mother's voice, filling the hallway with excited chatter.

"Oh, Mr Darcy, how sly you are. I did not know that you thought of Lizzy in that way, as a marriage candidate. And to think, Lizzy...our Lizzy is to be mistress of Pemberley. You have several carriages I expect, and a house in town as well as your estate in Derbyshire? Yes of course you do, what am I saying..."

"Mamma, there will be ample time to speak to Mr Darcy of such things later. I suspect he is eager to be on his way," turning red-faced to Mr Darcy, Elizabeth continued, "If we go out the back door, I can walk you to the stable yard."

Having endured several minutes of Mrs Bennet effervescing over his wealth and his assets, Darcy seized on Elizabeth's suggested opportunity to escape.

He gave Mrs Bennet a faltering smile, bowed and then hurried after his betrothed.

Passing through the kitchen, Elizabeth picked up a carrot and an apple and then popped the carrot into her pocket.

Seeing Mr Darcy frown, she explained,

"One for Odin and the other is for me." And she bit into the apple.

For part of the way, they walked in silence, neither sure of what to say now everything seemed settled between them.

Until Mr Darcy said,

"Your father was kind to you?"

"Papa is never unkind, sir, though he seemed to have anticipated my reply. Why is that, I wonder?"

Elizabeth cast him a questioning glance before turning her eyes forward again to continue along the path.

It was a reasonable question, and there was no logic to him hiding the fact that he had taken her father into his confidence.

Unabashed, he said,

"I made you father privy to my intentions several days before seeking you out. I knew...I assumed that without his blessing you would not accept me. Was I wrong?"

No longer in the mood to eat, Elizabeth looked down at her half-eaten apple sullenly. It irked her to think of Mr Darcy and her father being friends and sharing confidences, especially when she was the confidence. His assumption had been correct. While she had found him a difficult man to read, and considered she knew him very little, it appeared that Mr Darcy knew her quite well.

"No."

They walked on for several minutes more, again with no words being exchanged. Though Darcy was comfortable with the silence between them, he sensed that his revelation had upset his companion. He wished he possessed the ability to talk freely and confidently as others did, but as a child, he was taught that men of his consequence did not have to seek out acquaintances or make an effort to please or appease others. His lofty position in society meant that he could cherry pick who he wanted to be friends with, and in general, ignore the remaining populace. It was widely known that the Master of Pemberley was not to be trifled with. But now, with his reputation firmly in place as a proud and somewhat difficult man, Darcy envied anyone who did not suffer the restraints that he suffered, namely a well-hidden shyness and fear of rejection.

Seeing Elizabeth's displeasure with the apple, Darcy asked,

"Is the fruit not to your liking, Elizabeth?"

Unaccustomed to hearing him use her given name, Elizabeth bit back the set down that almost spilt from her lips. They were engaged, and he now had the right to call her Elizabeth, or even Lizzy if he so preferred. Although somehow, she just could not imagine Mr Darcy calling her Lizzy. No, for him she would always be Elizabeth.

Sighing, she wondered if she should now call him Fitzwilliam?

Pulling in a breath to give her reply, she went to say his name, Fitzwilliam, but at the last moment, an attack of nerves got the better of her.

"Fi…forgive me. I was wool-gathering. The apple is sweet, but I find that my appetite is gone."

There was no need for Elizabeth to explain, Darcy knew she felt betrayed by her father and probably him too. After all, Elizabeth's relationship with her father was a close one, uncommon in today's society of wet nurses and nannies. Most parents chose to spend only a few hours a week with their offspring, but in Elizabeth's case, and thankfully his own too, this was not true. But whereas Elizabeth's bond was with her father, his own had been with his mother, Anne.

It was a poor start to their courtship.

"Elizabeth, as you know, I am almost eight and twenty, but you are the only woman I have asked to be my wife. Protocol dictated that I ask your fathers for his permission to court you. It grieves me to have caused you pain so soon into our engagement, but as a gentleman, it is important to me to adhere to the proprieties," Darcy said.

There was truth in his words, but Elizabeth felt compelled to say,

"This is 1811, sir, not the dark ages."

"The gossip mongers will have more than enough to talk about when they learn of our betrothal. I will not give them further cause to slander my good name, or by association Elizabeth, yours."

Stung by his words, Elizabeth stopped walking and turned to face him.

"You sought me out, sir. If you feel being associated with my family and me such a degradation, you may withdraw your offer at any time."

"You know that is not what I meant, Elizabeth," Darcy said firmly. "I have, for a number of years, been considered a... desirable catch." A vivid flush crept over his collar. "Every season there has been speculation about whom I would marry. Consequently, any woman I have shown more than a passing interest in has been drawn into this speculation. Theories about why I might choose her, interest in her circumstances, her background, her family. I would not want your family exposed or involved in such a media circus."

Elizabeth felt thoroughly ashamed of herself, jumping to the conclusion that she had. Would Darcy berate her? He had every right to. While Darcy was thinking only of her family, and how best to protect them, she had assumed he was thinking of himself, his reputation, his pride.

"I...I am sorry. It was naïve of me to think that no-one beyond our families would be interested in our marriage. I forget who I am engaged to."

Darcy reached out, taking one of her hands and clasping it between his own.

"The Darcy's have been one of the country's leading families for generations, Elizabeth. People look to us to uphold the law and to lead by example. Unfortunately, this also means that people feel they have a right to know about every aspect of our lives. Thankfully, city reporters rarely venture as far north as Pemberley." Seeing her downturned expression, Darcy chucked her under the chin and said,

"Once we are married, and back at Pemberley, I am sure the Prince Regent and Beau Brummel will draw the attention away from us."

This did nothing to reassure Elizabeth. Now, she was even more concerned about marrying him.

"You think our marriage will draw media attention?"

"Possibly. But I know the editors of most of the reputable papers. They will be sympathetic in their coverage. The others are merely for gossip mongers. No-one of consequence reads them anyway."

Elizabeth was pleased to know that Darcy was not overly concerned about the newspapers, but she did not dare reveal that her mother and younger sisters enjoyed pawing over such publication, relishing every bit of gossip concealed within their pages, whether it was true or not.

As they reached the stable yard, Elizabeth realised Mr Darcy still had hold of her hand, and she instantly felt awkward and self-conscious.

"The carrot is for Odin," she said shyly.

Darcy brought her hand to his lips and placed a feather kiss on her fingers before releasing it.

Having retrieved the carrot from her pocket, Elizabeth waited for Odin to be drawn out and saddled.

Darcy stood by and watched his horse crunch greedily on the orange vegetable until Elizabeth fed him the last morsel. The grateful horse nuzzled her hand, searching for more, but when it became evident there was none, he happily let her pet him instead.

"Do you ride, Elizabeth?" Darcy asked.

"No. I have tried, but sitting at such an angle, well, I found it to be most uncomfortable. Now, if I could ride astride like a man…"

Darcy was about to relay his shock at such a suggestion when he saw the glint of mirth in her eye.

"I do not think society is ready for the sight of a woman riding astride, Miss Bennet," he said in a playful scold.

Darcy likes to see Elizabeth smile. It relayed her genuine pleasure in something, or he hoped…someone.

Suddenly remembering he had a gift for her, Darcy reached into his pocket and pulled out a handkerchief.

Fascinated, Elizabeth watched as Darcy carefully unfurled the cloth and then proffered its contents to her.

"I picked this from Bingley's hothouse."

Elizabeth looked down at Darcy's gift. A single, red rose bud, its petals on the brink of bursting open. The universal symbol of love.

"It…it is a truly beautiful specimen, sir, I thank you."

"There may be many flowers in a man's life, Elizabeth, but there is only ever one rose."

Elizabeth knew if she looked up into Darcy's eyes at that moment, he would kiss her.

Darcy waited, hoping she would offer him a gesture of affection. But when Elizabeth looked up, it was clear her smile and thanks were all she was prepared to give him, today at least.

Darcy returned her smile and accepted defeat with good grace.

Happy they were parting on good term, Darcy bent over her hand once more.

"Until tomorrow, Elizabeth."
"Until tomorrow, Mr Darcy."

Chapter Eight

With Mr Darcy on his way back to Netherfield, Elizabeth found herself unexpectedly free for the rest of the day. Walking towards her father's study, she heard voices coming from the front parlour.

Pushing the door open, she saw Lydia, Kitty and their mother talking to Mr Wickham and his friend, Mr Denny.

This was the first time she had seen Mr Wickham since Mr Darcy had spoken to her about him.

Committed to greeting them, Elizabeth entered fully, saying,

"Mr Wickham, Mr Denny, this is a surprise. What brings you to Longbourn?"

Wickham and his friend stood as she entered, saluting her with a half bow. Then, Wickham let his chocolate brown eyes linger on Elizabeth's mouth briefly, before raising his gaze to meet her eyes.

"A pleasant one I hope," Wickham said smiling warmly. "The cold weather has driven both men and officers into their lodgings. We were in desperate need of some good company. Where else would we find a welcome as warm as the one afforded to us by, Mrs Bennet and her charming daughters? Take pity on us, Miss Elizabeth, as country boys, we cannot abide large crowds, is that not so, Denny?

For the first time. Elizabeth felt uncomfortable in Wickham's presence. He appeared the same, as did Denny, but something had changed. She had changed. Darcy's words, whether true or not, now made her look at Wickham from a different perspective. Admittedly, if you ignored his flattery, his smiles, his boyish good looks…there was something not quite…decent, about his overt friendliness, particularly towards women.

"Will you join us, Miss Elizabeth?" Wickham asked with an outstretched hand.

"Oh, yes, Lizzy, do come and sit down." Then leaning in closer to the officers, Mrs Bennet said, "Lizzy spends far too much time with her nose in a book, much better for her to come and share her time with some officers, and such handsome officers too," and she blushed like a teenager.

"Mamma," Lydia pouted, "Wickham and Denny have come to see Kitty and me. Should you not be speaking to Mrs Hill or cook about menus or something? Besides, Lizzy is here now, may she not chaperone us?"

As no-one raised any objections or rallied to Mrs Bennet's defence, she left the young people alone, albeit reluctantly.

Mr Wickham remained standing, waiting until Elizabeth had chosen her seat before moving to sit next to her.

Lydia was annoyed to see Wickham mooning over her sister, especially as she considered herself twice as pretty as Lizzy.

Only later, would Elizabeth and Lydia realise the havoc the young woman's next words would set in motion?

"Lizzy, do not think to keep Wickham all to yourself. You have Mr Darcy now, so Wickham is mine."

The way Wickham next looked at her, with disbelief and suspicion, sent a shiver down Elizabeth's spine.

As there had been no announcement about her engagement, this was clearly news to Mr Wickham.

A full ten seconds elapsed before he asked,

"Can this be true, Miss Elizabeth, you are to marry Darcy?"

A flush of colour rose to cover her cheeks, and Elizabeth silently berated Lydia for sharing her news.

"Yes, Mr Wickham. Mr Darcy and I are engaged to be married. Although it is not a secret, we had not intended to announce it until Mr Darcy had informed his closest relations. Lydia was a little premature in revealing it, sir."

Wickham's mind was racing. When Mr Bingley had deserted Jane Bennet to return to the city, and Darcy had followed only one day later, he had thought to woo and wed one of the more refined Bennet sisters himself. But having checked with a less desirable lawyer friend in London, he had been dismayed to discover that there was an entail on the Longbourn estate. Undefeated, with a little more digging, his lawyer uncovered a well-hidden clause stating that the entail on the Longbourn *could* be passed on to a male grandson. Though even this loophole had a drawback. The child must be born while Mr Bennet still lived.

Though it was no Pemberley, Wickham coveted the prospect of being the master of an estate with two thousand a year. It was almost as appealing as the delightful Miss Elizabeth. But now, this news had changed everything. So, Darcy wanted Elizabeth Bennet as his wife?

Somehow, there must be room for him to extort a sum of money from the situation. Probably nowhere near the thirty thousand pounds, he could have claimed as Georgiana husband, but Darcy should be good for ten thousand if he thought Miss Elizabeth was in danger of being compromised.

Elizabeth could not deny that she still thought Mr Wickham, a handsome man, but as he stared at her, with a broad smile on his lips that did not reach those dark eyes of his, she almost wanted to shudder. For the first time, Elizabeth believed Mr Wickham quite capable of trying to despoil a young woman for monetary gain. Thank goodness, she and her sisters had no fortune.

"I cannot deny that I am shocked to hear such news, Miss Elizabeth. Having confided to you how poorly Darcy treated me, I am surprised that you would even consider binding yourself to such a man. May I be impertinent and ask *when* he gained you affections?"

Elizabeth did not like to lie, but somehow, she could not bring herself to tell him the truth.

Trying to evade the question, she smiled and said,

"Upon my word, Mr Wickham, that is an impertinent question."

Wickham would not be sidelined and persisted with his questioning.

"I felt sure your regard for Darcy reflected my own sentiments. Tell me, am I wrong, Miss Elizabeth?"

This was a statement too far for Elizabeth. She stood up and wrung her hands in an agitated manner.

"My regard for Mr Darcy is a personal matter, of no concern to anyone but Mr Darcy and me. Now, if you will all excuse me."

Forgetting himself, as Elizabeth turned to leave, Wickham reached out and grabbed her hand.

"I had hoped…" before he could finish his sentence, Lydia jumped up and in a raised voice, asked,

"Wickham, why do you hold Elizabeth's hand so? I thought you had come to see me? We are meant to be making arrangements to…"

Dropping Elizabeth's hand, Wickham took a step towards Lydia, and said hastily,

"…arrangements for a winter picnic, yes, I did, but now it will not be a surprise, my impatient girl,"

Elizabeth looked from Lydia to Wickham and then to Kitty and Denny. None of them spoke, but they looked to one another before they all focused on Wickham.

Not convinced by Mr Wickham's brash attempt to silence Lydia, Elizabeth turned to Kitty, the weakest of them all, and asked,

"Tell me, Kitty, is that the purpose of Mr Wickham and Mr Denny's visit this morning, to arrange a winter picnic?"

Sensing Kitty's indecision, whether to be truthful or tell a lie, Elizabeth pressed her.

"Come now Kitty; I am your sister, I will not be angry."

Kitty felt three pairs of eyes burning into her as Wickham, Denny, and Lydia willed her to lie for them.

"I...I..." unable to please everyone, Kitty burst into tears, "I don't know what I am supposed to say, Lydia?" Her sister turned her face from her with a scornful look.

Kitty turned back to Elizabeth, and said,

"I don't think so, Lizzy, but Lydia said I must say that it was so or..."

"Kitty!" Shouted Lydia, as the final word fell from Kitty's mouth,

At this point, Kitty could take it no more and run out of the room sobbing into her sleeve.

Elizabeth turned to look at Lydia, silent, yet accusing.

"What?" Lydia asked defensively, "I don't know what she was talking about, Lizzy. We *were* arranging a winter picnic, and now, thanks to you, the surprise is spoilt. You spoil all my fun, Lizzy. You are just as boring as old Mr Darcy." Then Lydia's followed Kitty's example and storm out of the room too.

The two redcoats stood awkwardly in the room, looking from one another and then to Elizabeth.

With pursed lips, Elizabeth turned on Wickham and Denny, saying,

"I believe you gentlemen were just leaving?" Elizabeth said, making sure to emphasise the last word.

"Miss Elizabeth, I...that is we..."

"Good day to you both," Elizabeth said dismissively, cutting Wickham off midsentence, then she moved aside, leaving their exit path clear.

The instant she heard the front door close behind them, Elizabeth rushed into her father's study, desperate to explain the scene she had just been party too.

With his usual desire, not to be involved in household squabbles, Mr Bennet asked,

"What are you accusing them of Lizzy, plotting to entertain us all in a novel way. I don't see your point, my dear. Are you angry because they did not involve you, is that it?"

"No, Papa, don't you see, I am sure that the picnic plan was a ruse, and Kitty seemed to know nothing about it either. You know Lydia, Papa, she never does anything unless it is of benefit to her. Besides, if it were truly a picnic they were planning, why did Mr Wickham react so?"

Seeing her papa raise his brows and purse his lips, Elizabeth implored him again.

"Could you at least speak to her, father?"

When Elizabeth called him father instead of Papa, he knew it was something she felt passionately about. Although he was still certain it was an innocent misunderstanding.

"And say what, child?"

"Ask her for details about this supposed picnic. It is December after all, and soon the snow will come. So, when was this picnic to be held, and where? Ask whom they were going to invite, have they spoken to cook about preparing the food?" Elizabeth said in exasperation.

Closing his book, Mr Bennet said,

"Very well, Lizzy, send her to me, but if I am satisfied she is telling the truth, there's an end to it."

The slamming of the music room door heralded Lydia's arrival, and Elizabeth ceased playing and waited expectantly.

No doubt Lydia had come to berate her for speaking to their father, but Elizabeth was not repentant. Lydia often acted and spoke without thinking first. She remembered how Lydia had embarrassed poor Mary at their Aunt Phillips supper by insisting she played a different tune so she could dance with the officers. Most people were content to mingle and talk.

"I hate you, Elizabeth Bennet," Lydia stormed, "Papa said I can only walk into Meryton if you or Jane chaperone me. Well, Jane has not ventured further than the garden since Mr Bingley left, and all your time is spent being wooed by Mr Darcy. So, when am I ever to go out of this house again? I want to see the officers?" and Lydia stamped her foot in childish frustration.

Elizabeth remained calm through the entirety of Lydia's tirade. Her words were spoken in anger and said to provoke an argument. Elizabeth would not oblige.

"Lydia, I have recently been made aware of a defect in Mr Wickham's character. If it is proved to be true, it is most alarming. I was…I am, merely seeking to protect a much-loved sister from befalling a terrible fate."

Seeing Lydia's folded arms and her deep frown, Elizabeth knew the girl was not willing to be appeased.

"Lydia, I know the story of a winter picnic was a falsehood. Your words and actions were not of someone being truthful. You knew that the real event you were planning would not meet with father's approval, and so you tried to drag you sister into the lie as well."

Elizabeth paused to see if there was any change in her sister's appearance, but she still wore the same stubborn scowl, with no hint of remorse or contrition.

"I expected you to continue with your deceit when Papa questioned you, but the fact that you are here and obviously angry, tells me that with him at least, you were honest."

Lydia could contain herself no more.

"Defect of his character?" scoffed Lydia, "can you hear yourself, Lizzy? Mr Wickham is a gentleman and has never behaved inappropriately towards me, towards any of us. You are just jealous because you are stuck with dull, old, Mr Darcy. Wickham is ten time the man Mr Darcy is." Having flung these final words at her sister, Lydia turned on her heels and stormed out.

The thud of the slamming door was still ringing in Elizabeth's ears when Jane entered the room.

Lydia's raised voice had reverberated throughout the entire house, and there could be no-one present that did not hear her diatribe.

Seeking to console her sister, Jane put a comforting arm around Elizabeth's shoulder, and said,

"She is still young, Lizzy, her harsh words were spoken on impulse and out of anger and disappointment. She does not mean it."

Elizabeth looked at Jane and gave a rueful smile,

"Oh, yes, she does, for the moment anyway."

"Are you at liberty to share what you heard about Mr Wickham?"

Elizabeth recalled Mr Darcy's words. He had mentioned no names, and so she did not feel as if she were betraying his confidence.

"If this is true, Lizzy, we must distance ourselves from Mr Wickham at once. Did you explain this to papa?"

"I had hoped it would not be necessary, but after today's events, I think I must. Is father still in his study?"

"Yes, tell him now, Lizzy," Jane agreed.

However, Elizabeth was waylaid by her mamma before she could make it even half way to Mr Bennet's study.

"I am not interested in hearing your excuses, Lizzy, but your interference will not curtail Lydia's enjoyment. Now, Lydia wants to go into Meryton, and you must accompany her," Mrs Bennet said with her arms folded across her heaving bosom.

Elizabeth knew that arguing with her mamma over Lydia was futile. She would do as she was bid, and walk into Meryton with Lydia, albeit reluctantly.

Chapter Nine

Even with her warmest coat and bonnet on, Elizabeth was cold. Lydia, who was still in a strop with her, had made a point of striding off in front of Elizabeth, ignoring all her attempts to engage her in conversation. Elizabeth could do no more than try to keep up with her and hope they did not run into Mr Wickham.

With the town centre in sight, Lydia quickened her step and then began to wave frantically.

"Harriet, Harriet,"

Harriet Forster, the new wife of Colonel Forster, waved back. Leaving her husband standing in the street, Harriet hurried forward to greet her new friend.

Elizabeth hastened after them, but as she approached, the two young women linked arms, began to giggle and scuttled off towards the haberdashery shop.

Determined not make an exhibition of *herself*, Elizabeth decided to walk over and greeted Colonel Forster.

"Good day Colonel Forster, I think the weather may be turning,"

They exchanged salutes, and then Colonel Forster replied, in a genial tone,

"I believe you are right Miss Bennet. It would not surprise me if we had a dusting of snow before the week was out. Are you parents well, Miss Bennet, and all your sisters?"

"Yes, sir, I thank you, we are all quite well."

"Mrs Forster is quite taken with Miss Lydia. They appear to have formed a firm friendship in these past weeks. They always seem to have their heads together, laughing and plotting some outrageous ruse to play on my officers," he said good-humouredly.

Since Mr Darcy had divulged the near fate of his female acquaintance, Elizabeth could not help but eye all the officers with suspicion. Though she thought Colonel Forster above reproach, the officers under his command, such as Wickham and Denny, she now viewed differently.

"Well," said the Colonel, "I had better go and pay for my wife's purchases, though goodness knows why she needs more ribbons and bows."

Having asked the Colonel Forster to tell Lydia she would wait for her in the bookshop, Elizabeth turned in the direction of the town square and made her way towards the small, almost hidden door, of the bookstore. It was one of the quirkiest shops in the town, with its entrance partially concealed behind the trunk of a large old beech tree, but Elizabeth loved it.

Unaware she was being observed, Elizabeth's mood lifted at the prospect of buying herself a new novel or book of verse.

With her head bent to shield her face from the cold wind, and only ten feet from the warmth of the shop, Elizabeth did not see Mr Wickham when he first stepped out from behind the tree and blocked her path.

"Miss Bennet, may I speak to you?"

Raising her eyes, Elizabeth looked directly at the red coat blocking her way. Pursed her lips together, Elizabeth made no effort to conceal her displeasure at being approached by the officer.

In anticipation of her negative reply, Mr Wickham spoke before being denied.

"Miss Bennet, have I offended you in some way? If so, please tell me how I might rectify the situation. I must have you as my friend, Miss Elizabeth, it is vital to my being, that I may count you as my friend."

To someone less acquainted with the gentleman, they would have noticed no change in his tone or his manner. To a bystander, he seemed as he had always been, softly spoken and clear in his address. But Elizabeth had detected a hint of desperation in his voice, panic even. Then there was the way he had presented himself, jumping out on her from behind the tree, as if making sure she could not alter her direction to avoid him.

Also, his question made her wonder, why, with so many admirers eager for his company, including Mary King, Lydia, Kitty and Harriet Forster, was her friendship so important to him.

In a barely civil but hushed voice, Elizabeth said,

"You will forgive me if I speak plainly, sir? My sister is not yet sixteen, an age of many transitions. She is neither a child nor a woman, still growing and learning how to act in a world full of expectations and pitfalls. Lydia is easily influenced by others, often by people who are older than she and who should know better. Too often, she does not foresee the consequences her action might bring about."

The look of mortification on Wickham's face did not fool Elizabeth. It seemed...rehearsed.

"My intentions toward Miss Lydia, and indeed any gentlewomen I have met since I joined the militia, is only one of friendship. I am mortified you would think otherwise, Miss Bennet," Wickham said, in a tone of outraged indignation.

Wishing to bring their encounter to a close, Elizabeth tried to excuse herself.

"I am not prepared to discuss my sisters' probity in the open street, sir. If you will excuse me..."

Wickham was unwilling to let Elizabeth go until he had her firm undertaking that they could remain friends.

Sidestepping to block her path again, he said,

"But you do, believe me, Miss Elizabeth, when I say that my intention is for us to just remain friends?" he paused, before adding, "with you and all your sisters?"

But Mr Wickham had miscalculated the strength of Elizabeth's mettle. She would not be drawn into any further discussion on the matter

"If you are a gentleman, Mr Wickham, and your intentions are indeed what you say they are, you will step aside and let me pass." Elizabeth moved to walk past him.

Wickham persisted,

"We are friends then?" and now Wickham made his biggest mistake. Overestimating the strength of his appeal, as Elizabeth drew level with him, Wickham shot out his hand and grabbed her by the elbow.

"I ask again, Miss Elizabeth, we are friends then...?"

He did not see the hand that struck his face, or the hand that rose him up from the ground and threw him several feet away from Elizabeth, but he heard the voice. The unmistakable voice, filled with contempt, loathing, and rage, of Fitzwilliam Darcy.

"If you ever, touch Elizabeth again, it will not be only your pride I will wound, Wickham. I have warned you in the past to stay away from what is mine."

Darcy stood over the cowering form of his nemesis, quaking with rage. It took all his willpower not to give Wickham the thrashing he so richly deserved, here in the open street with dozens of onlookers.

Wickham, he was sure, had followed him and Bingley to Hertfordshire, with the sole intention of executing a plan to further embarrass and extort money from him, or even his friend Charles. Elizabeth, it appeared, had been Wickham's next victim.

Darcy returned to Elizabeth's side and putting a protective hand on her waist, asked,

"Did he hurt you, Elizabeth?"

Elizabeth felt a myriad of emotions. Relief at having been saved from the distasteful encounter. Shock at the violent reaction of her betrothed. Awe at the prowess Mr Darcy had exhibited. Horror and embarrassment at being caught up in such a spectacle. Yet it was the feeling of excitement, as Mr Darcy came to her rescue, which remained with her the longest.

Quietly, but a little breathlessly, she said,

"I am not injured, sir,"

Darcy looked at her upturned face and felt the urge to kiss her. His brave and defiant, Elizabeth. Would she ever cease to amaze and delight him?

With no plans to visit Elizabeth until tomorrow, Darcy had decided to ride into Meryton and purchase a small gift for her. Knowing of her love of reading, he decided on a book.

The bookshop in Meryton was deceptively large. With a small front entrance, half-hidden by a tree, it gave the appearance of a small, one room establishment from the outside. But once through the portal, the interior stretched back to fill the entire ground floor of the property.

The proprietor, a bachelor in his late sixties, lived only on the upper floor.

Having selected the book, Lyrical Ballads, by Wordsworth, Darcy then walked to the window to inspect the condition of his choice. It was then he saw Elizabeth talking to Wickham. Not a fortnight previously had he been witnessed to another encounter such as this, only then Elizabeth had been laughing with Wickham. Two things had changed. Elizabeth appeared distressed by the encounter, and secondly, now she was his.

Mesmerised by the intensity of Darcy stare, Elizabeth could not pull her gaze away. Only the calling of her name broke the spell.

"Elizabeth, are you well? Are you injured at all?" asked Charlotte. "I cannot believe Mr Wickham accosted you in such a fashion, and in the street."

A violent flush stained Elizabeth's cheeks as she turned to her dear friend and replied,

"I am a little shaken Charlotte. I think I must sit down."

Pushing through the large crowd that had gathered, came Mrs Phillips, Elizabeth's aunt, who immediately took charge of the situation. Prising Mr Darcy's hand from Elizabeth's waist, she placed a guiding arm around her shoulder and steered her towards her home.

Once inside, Mrs Philips said,

"Come, Lizzy, and sit by the warm fire will see you right as rain in no time, and Cilla will bring us a nice cup of sweet tea."

Scanning the throng of faces, Mrs Philips called to Charlotte.

"Charlotte, has someone sent for the constable? Mr Wickham cannot be allowed to assault a gentlewoman in broad daylight and go unpunished."

Elizabeth just had time to cast a glance over her shoulder. Her eyes locking onto the receding figure of Mr Darcy, now standing alone, as she was bustled off by her family, friends, and well-wishers.

Darcy gave an almost imperceptible nod, and then turned on his heels and went back into the shop to pay for the book. Though, if he had his way, he would have swept Elizabeth into his arms, holding her tight, while promising to never let Wickham, or any man, harm her again. However, he was sure Elizabeth would have been just as mortified had he done that, as Wickham accosting her.

Fearing the severity of the situation was becoming exaggerated, Elizabeth repeatedly tried to explain that Mr Wickham had only held onto her elbow for the briefest of moments, and only to gain her attention, but no-one would listen. Charlotte and Mrs Phillips were adamant he had made a grab for her with intentions of who knew what, and the constable was sent for.

In all the chaos, Lydia had been totally forgotten. As she emerged from the modiste shop, with a length of ribbon in her reticule that her friend Harriet had purchased for her, she headed for the bookstore to meet Elizabeth.

Using the heel of his boot, Wickham loosened some of the earth from the hard ground, then, scooping up a handful of the black soil, he proceeded to rub it over his face and uniform.

Skulking from view in the shadows of the alley next to Mr Jeremiah's bookstore, he watched and waited for Lydia Bennet.

Chapter Ten

After what seemed like the tenth time of explaining, the constable agreed, if Miss Bennet were quite sure that no assault had taken place, he would issue Mr Wickham with nothing more than a stern warning, this time. Though in truth, having received a number of complaints from the local population about that very gentleman, he would have relished a chance to clap him in irons, if only for one night. The constable had discovered just what a wily character Mr Wickham was, always staying just within the boundaries of the law.

Having done all that he could at Mrs Phillips', the constable then went in search of Mr Wickham.

It was about this time that Lydia was remembered. Charlotte, speaking in a hushed tone so as not to alarm Elizabeth, asked Mrs Phillips,

"Has someone been despatched to bring Lydia here from Miss Pearls? She should accompany Elizabeth home, in case Lizzy has a delayed fit of the vapours. I am surprised she is not here already?"

Elizabeth was mortified to think she had completely forgotten all about her young sister, and a wave of guilt washed over her.

It was only a few minutes after Charlotte's enquiry that Lydia arrived at her Aunt Phillips house.

Watching as everyone fussed over her sister, Lydia stood on the periphery of the room, with a sour pout curling her lips downwards.

However, when her aunt deemed Elizabeth recovered enough to travel home, Lydia refused point blank to ride in the carriage with her. Only when her Aunt Phillips threatened to exclude her from her next supper party, where all her favourite officers would be in attendance, did she capitulate and climb in next to Elizabeth.

As the borrowed conveyance rumbled along the half frozen, half mud track back towards Longbourn, Lydia finally found her tongue.

"I know what you did, Elizabeth," Lydia said, her voice loaded with venom.

"I did nothing, Lydia. It was Mr Wickham who stopped me. If he had let me pass instead of trying to press his point with me, none of this would have happened. Besides, I thought you were in the shop with Mrs Forster. How can you know what occurred?" Elizabeth asked.

"Wickham told me. And what that brute did to him."

Exasperated by Lydia's theatrics, Elizabeth said,

"And whom might that be, Lydia?"

"Mr Darcy, of course. His brutish behaviour has ruined poor Wickham's uniform, and his eye is already swelling where Mr Darcy struck him. But I am glad, for now, everyone will see him for what he truly is, Lizzy, a bully and a liar. You might be blinded by his wealth and position now, Lizzy, but you just wait. Wickham said he wanted you to know you had a friend in him, for when Mr Darcy shows his true colours, you will need all the friends you can get. No wonder he had reached eight and twenty with no wife. No woman will have him!"

"Lydia! That is quite enough. Remember, one day, when Papa is no longer here, it will be Mr Darcy who will provide for us and protect us, including you, Lydia Bennet, who is the most undeserving of sisters. Unless of course, you marry before papa's demise."

Elizabeth waited, expecting Lydia to refute her claim, but she did not. Instead, a sly smile spread across her face as she turned to look out the carriage window. This action concerned Elizabeth more so than if Lydia had continued to shout at her and malign Mr Darcy.

"Lydia?" Elizabeth said, in a questioning tone.

But they had completed the short journey back to Longbourn, and before Elizabeth could question her further, Lydia jumped down the moment the vehicle stopped and ran into the house.

Elizabeth watched as her sibling disappeared inside the house, calling for Kitty as she went.

Elizabeth was torn. Should she tell her parents now what had occurred in town today, or wait until Mr Darcy arrived tomorrow and let him explain?

In the end, Elizabeth decided she would consult with Jane before taking any action.

Sitting on her bed, with Jane at her side, Elizabeth recalled the incident in its entirety, even her conversation with Lydia on their journey home.

Jane pondered for a moment, then said,

"Speak with, Mr Darcy first, Lizzy."

"Why do you say that, Jane?"

"Well," Jane paused, "There is a possibility that it will show Mr Darcy in an unfavourable light. You mentioned he struck Mr Wickham first, did you not?"

Elizabeth mulled over Jane's words for a moment.

"Yes... though he only sought to rescue me from Mr Wickham's unwelcome attention. And Jane, Mr Darcy only hit Mr Wickham once, regardless of what Mr Wickham told Lydia. It is just one more reason for Mamma to voice her dislike of Mr Darcy. Oh, Jane, what if I relay my fears to Papa and then nothing happens, or worse, I say nothing and something awful happens."

"Come, do not fret about mamma, Lizzy. Her dislike of Mr Darcy disappeared the moment you two became engaged."

Confused and perplexed, Elizabeth decided on the former line of action and duly went down to speak to her papa.

Tapping twice on the door, Elizabeth then waited for her father to bid her enter.

"Come in, Lizzy,"

Pushing the door open, Elizabeth was surprised to see Mr Darcy already standing next to her father.

"Mr Darcy!" she exclaimed. "Forgive me; I was not aware you had returned to Longbourn."

Darcy looked at Mr Bennet.

"Yes, well, you two get along now. Fear not, Darcy, I will send a note now and get thing moving on that other matter," said Mr Bennet in an unusually determined tone.

Once the door was closed behind them, Darcy said,

"Is there somewhere we may speak privately, Elizabeth."

Elizabeth led the way to the music room. After checking that Mary was not occupying it, she said,

"We will not be disturbed in here."

Elizabeth sat on the piano stall, and turning to find another seat, Darcy retrieved a particularly stylish chair that was hiding behind the door.

Sitting to face her, he said,

"I know you were not expecting me until tomorrow, Elizabeth, but my conscience would not let me stay away. I felt your father had the right to know what happened in Meryton this afternoon. As a gentleman, I could do no other than give him the opportunity to rescind his consent."

Elizabeth gasped. Without breathing a word of his intention, Mr Darcy had gone to her papa and offered to break their engagement. Elizabeth was appalled and surprisingly...hurt by his actions.

"Oh, fear not, my love. He is still prepared to give us his blessing, but it was my duty, to be honest with him."

Elizabeth's spine stiffened, and her eyes flashed.

Before she thought it through, she had said,

"And Mr Darcy, do you afford me the same courtesy?"

Darcy looked at Elizabeth, first with raised brows, then with drawn brows. He had given no thought to Elizabeth changing her mind. Why should she even consider breaking their engagement when he had merely been protecting what was his?

"I don't understand, Elizabeth? Why would offer you the same courtesy as your father?" he said with incredulity.

Elizabeth resisted the urge to tap her foot in frustration, but nevertheless, her proverbial hackles were up.

"Is it my father you intend to spend the rest of your life with, Mr Darcy, or me? Because listening to the statement you just made, I am no longer sure."

Darcy was confused. If he had done or said something amiss, he was unaware of it, but Elizabeth was clearly upset about something.

"I fail to see why you are grieved, Elizabeth. Would you care to explain?"

Feeling the need to let off some steam, Elizabeth stood up and paced back and forth a few steps.

"Unless I am mistaken, Mr Darcy, it was I, Mr Wickham accosted this afternoon, and it was you who assaulted, Mr Wickham. My father was not involved in either incident, yet you ask him, rather than I, if he still gives his content to see us married?"

By now, Elizabeth's bosom was heaving with disgruntled assertion.

Darcy stood in Elizabeth's path, forcing her to stop her pacing. Taking hold of her hands, he gently pulled her closer to him.

"I was merely protecting what is mine, Elizabeth, you cannot reproach me for that? Would you rather I had not intervened?" then his mood and expression visibly darkened. His grip on Elizabeth's hands became more pronounced, as he said in a guttural tone, "Or perhaps is it because you preferred the company...the touch, of Mr Wickham, to that of your future husband?"

Elizabeth realised that as a mere woman, Mr Darcy did not see her as his equal, and so she was not, but he had hurt her feelings. Had he hurried over to Longbourn, expressing concern for her well-being, she might have been flattered, but he had not. So, in an unusual display of temper, she had insulted him, questioned his morals and yes, acted like a child. At this moment, Mr Darcy must think her more akin to Lydia that the Elizabeth he admired and loved. And to add insult to injury, Darcy had interpreted her speech as a declaration of her partiality for Wickham. But nothing could be further from the truth. If he hadn't done so in the past, Mr Wickham had certainly revealed his true character today. Sighing, Elizabeth realised it was her duty to make amends and smooth Darcy's ruffled feathers. She had no intention of breaking their engagement. She had accepted Mr Darcy Proposal, and there was no going back. Though, if Darcy could learn to consult with her, to trust her to be his ally, to give her a voice and ask her advice and opinion as her father did, then their future might run more smoothly than it was at present.

Full of remorse, Elizabeth was about to offer him an apology, when Darcy suddenly seized her by the shoulders and pulled her into a tight embrace.

"We are to be married, Elizabeth, you are to be my wife. I will not tolerate flirtations of any kind. If it's a man's lips you crave, then they are to be mine, and mine alone." Darcy lowered his head and claimed her lips in a harsh and demanding kiss, covering her mouth with his own until she was gasping for air.

As quickly as he had seized her, so he thrust her away, leaving Elizabeth momentarily disorientated. His kiss had been so harsh, that Elizabeth raised a shaking hand to her bruised and swollen lips.

"There is no damage, Elizabeth. You are not the first woman I have kissed," Darcy spat with contempt.

For a few moments, they stood silently together in the room, yet there was a chasm of misunderstanding between them.

Elizabeth turned to glare back at Darcy, expecting to find a triumphant sneer on his face, but instead, he looked...defeated?

At that moment, there was no forgiveness in Elizabeth's heart. If Darcy expected her to shy away from expressing her views when they were alone together, he was mistaken. She would not cower before him.

Straightening her back, and lifting her chin, Elizabeth replied,

"And are those the actions of a gentleman, sir? You came to my aid today to protect me from the unwanted attention of Mr Wickham, but your behaviour far outstrips his."

Darcy returned to stand before her, and as he stood towering over her, Elizabeth feared he was about to violate her mouth again.

Instead, he said,

"You dare to compare me with that blaggard? You could not have insulted more if you had slapped me, Elizabeth." Darcy said, with hostility, "I am *nothing* like George Wickham. If I were, do you think I would have been satisfied with a single kiss?" Slamming the door behind him, Darcy quit the room.

Standing alone, Elizabeth felt engulfed by a feeling of misery. The minor irritation she had felt due to Mr Darcy consulting with her father rather than her, had seen their verbal exchange escalate to an unprecedented level, leaving her emotionally drained and tearful.

To admit she had deliberately goaded the man who was to be husband into a quarrel, to sooth her ego and garner an apology from him, was easy now he was no longer standing before her.

Brushing her fingertips over her bruised mouth, Elizabeth realised that her ego, and lips were in a sorry state.

Stumbling back onto the pianoforte stool, she felt the first sting of tears as her eyes welled up with the salty fluid. Reflecting on what had just happened, Elizabeth regretted her actions, her quick temper, and her accusations. Her penance was that she must be the one to repair their rift.

Determined to act swiftly and resolved to be humble, Elizabeth decided that as soon as Mr Darcy arrived the next morning, she would go to him and apologise. Then, she would accept his rebuke with quiet humility

Chapter Eleven

The next day, if Mrs Bennet was surprised to see Elizabeth in the morning room before her, she did not show it. But to see Elizabeth looking out of the front window, craning her neck to peer along the driveway, *was* something of a novelty. Smiling to herself, it gladdened Mrs Bennet's heart to see Lizzy anxiously anticipating the arrival of Mr Darcy.

Having listened to Mr Bennet and Elizabeth mock Mr Darcy for the last few months, Mrs Bennet was under no illusion that this was a love match between her daughter and that gentleman. However, as the mother of five daughters, all needing husbands willing to accept a wife with a small dowry, she finally felt proud of her second eldest child. With such an advantageous match in the family, she was sure Mr Darcy could not refuse her request to introduce the other children to his wealthy friends. Especially as Mr Bingley had returned to town with no offer of marriage made to dear Jane. All these things had taken their toll on Mrs Bennet's nerves, and now, the ugly terms of the Longbourn entail had become prominent in her mind again. She was convinced that with Mr Bennet barely cold in his grave, Mr Collins would waste no time in turning them out onto the streets. Having no husband to protect or provide for them, and no money to purchase a home or survive on, they would have to rely on the charity of family and friends to take them in.

Still, that had all changed now that Lizzy had managed to catch herself a rich and well-connected husband, even richer than Mr Bingley. Now, when the sad event of Mr Bennet's death occurred, they would all enjoy a safe and secure future.

"If I am not mistaken, Lizzy, Mr Darcy is a little late this morning. Nine thirty already and no sign of him. Perhaps he has overslept. Do you think a man like Mr Darcy would oversleep, Lizzy?" Mrs Bennet asked.

"No, Mamma, Mr Darcy has a man servant to ensure he does not oversleep," Elizabeth said absently, still craning her neck, hoping to catch a glimpse of Odin carrying Mr Darcy back to her side.

Mrs Bennet sniffed and plumped up the cushion next to her.

"Well, I am sure I don't know what could be keeping him then?"

Then, a thought entered her mind.

"Did you argue with him, Lizzy, tell me you did not you argue with, Mr Darcy?"

Elizabeth looked away from the window and directly at her Mamma, but there were no words needed, Elizabeth's expression confirmed Mrs Bennet's worse fears.

"Oh, no, oh, my goodness. You quarrelled with Mr Darcy," Mrs Bennet wailed as she rocked to and fro. "He has broken the engagement, and now we are all ruined."

Going to the sideboard, Mrs Bennet pulled a sheet of paper and a quill from the drawer and called to Elizabeth.

"Lizzy, you must write Mr Darcy a note this instance, expressing how very sorry you are for being such a shrew."

Elizabeth finally gave her Mamma her full attention. As she listened to her mother prattling on, giving her instructions on what to write, Elizabeth found her voice.

"I am not going to write Mr Darcy a letter, Mamma. We had a minor disagreement that will be resolved the minute he arrives. Besides, even though we were both at fault, I will make my apologies to him in person, when he arrives."

"You mean if he arrives. Oh, no, it's going to be another Mr Collins, I know it. A man willing to secure the families future and you have driven him away with that sharp tongue of yours!" Exclaimed Mrs Bennet sharply.

"I have not driven Mr Darcy away, Mamma. There could be several reasons why he has not called this morning. He may be ill, or injured or even called away on business."

"Even more reason for you to write to him."

"No, Mamma, I am not going to write to Mr Darcy," Elizabeth said, exasperated with the constant badgering.

"You are a heartless girl, Lizzy." Mrs Bennet declared.

Seeing Elizabeth was unmoved to do her bidding, Mrs Bennet tried another approach.

"Very well, we'll see what Mr Bennet has to say about all this." Mrs Bennet stomping out of the room, slamming the door behind her.

Elizabeth sighed, and *that* was the example Lydia followed.

Deciding Mr Darcy must still be annoyed or disappointed with her, Elizabeth knew there was nothing she could do until he either returned to Longbourn, or he invited her to Netherfield.

So, intent on not wasting her day, she went looking for Jane.

In the hallway leading to the small back parlour, one of Jane's favourite rooms, Elizabeth bumped into Mrs Hill, literally.

"Oh, I do beg your pardon, Miss Elizabeth," said Hill.

Elizabeth bent down and helped the older woman pick up the pile of clothes she had dropped.

Laying them on her outstretched arms, Elizabeth asked,

"Where is Becky, Mrs Hill? Doing the laundry is her job, not yours."

"It's Becky's half day, Miss Elizabeth."

"Then leave them until tomorrow, Mrs Hill. No-one will mind."

"I would, Miss, but Miss Lydia said these must be washed and dried as soon as possible."

"Really? Lydia could not possibly have worn all these since the last laundry day." Elizabeth said as she examined a few of the gowns.

"Don't wash them yet, Hill, hang them in the drying room, and I will speak to Lydia."

Picking up the final item, a thick, double lined linen dress of dark blue. Elizabeth failed to notice that it was Lydia's travelling dress.

Jane was pleased to see Elizabeth. She needed someone to bring her out of her reverie. It had been almost two weeks since Mr Bingley had quit Netherfield and returned to the city. Two weeks since she had spoken to him, laughed with him, danced with him.

"Jane," Elizabeth said, then seeing her sister's melancholy expression, asked,

"Are you thinking of Mr Bingley?"

Jane nodded.

"I was so sure Mr Bingley preferred me to any other lady, Lizzy. Do you think I did something to displease him, to drive him away?"

Elizabeth hoped that in due course, that she might be able to convince Mr Darcy to ask Charles Bingley to re-join him at Netherfield. The abundance and variety of fowl this season were a perfect excuse to entice him back to the Shire. Hopefully, once Mr Bingley had seen Jane, he might renew his courtship of her.

In a positive tone, Elizabeth said,

"I have not given up on Mr Bingley yet, Jane, and neither must you. Remember, I am engaged to his most particular friend in all the world."

Jane smiled. It was true. If anyone could convince Mr Bingley to return to Netherfield, it was Mr Darcy.

Before another word was spoken, Lydia stormed in, legs astride and arms firmly resting on her plump, adolescent hips.

"Lizzy, did you tell Hill not to wash my dresses?" before Elizabeth could reply, Lydia continued, "I know you did, I just spoke to her."

Lydia's outbursts were becoming quite a regular occurrence, and Elizabeth reminded herself that hopefully, it was because her sister was between being a child and an adult. A difficult period for every young woman.

Remaining calm, Elizabeth took a deep breath, and said,

"Mrs Hill does not do the laundry, Lydia, Becky does, and…"

"Then let Becky do it," Lydia shouted.

"It is Becky's half day, and she has gone to visit her family. You may ask Becky to wash them tomorrow. But Lydia, there were several dresses there that I am sure you have not worn. Perhaps you could go through them again and select just the ones that are actually soiled?"

"I need them *all* washed."

"Lydia, Mrs Hill is our housekeeper, not our laundry maid. You will not belittle her by asking her to wash your clothes, especially when they don't need washing. You must wait until Becky resumes her duties tomorrow.

"But Hill said she would do them!" Lydia exclaimed persistently.

Fed up with Lydia's tantrum, Elizabeth would broach no further argument from her, merely saying,

"No, Lydia."

"So, I have to wait another day."

"It would appear so. Unless you are prepared to wash your clothes yourself?" Elizabeth added.

Lydia gave a derisory stomp of her foot, before turning and flouncing out of the room.

Elizabeth looked at Jane and rolled her eyes.

"Don't ask," she said.

Having push Odin to go ever fast, Darcy arrived back at Netherfield Park splattered with mud. Leaving instructions with the stable boy to give him a good rub down, he made his way inside and called for Fletcher to have a bath made ready. While he waited, Darcy paced to and fro in his room, oblivious of the dried mud falling from his clothes and Hussar boots and onto Mr Bingley's expensive carpet.

He had long since learnt to control his anger, disgust and resentment towards Wickham, but thinking back on his own behaviour this afternoon, Darcy was angry and disappointed with himself. Not only because he had made an exhibition of himself, but he had involved Elizabeth in it too.

A man comfortable in his own skin, Darcy considered himself an educated man, a likeable man, a superior man. He saw no defects in his character, his behaviour, or his manners.

Yet since knowing Elizabeth Bennet, he had experienced a multitude of emotions he thought he had under good regulation. In the space of a few short months, he had lost his heart, lost his temper, and now, possibly his reputation too.

When young Bingley had invited him to look over a property he was thinking of leasing; Darcy was oblivious to the fact that it would change his life irrevocably. Though he had not been actively looking for a wife, Darcy had for some months realised that he was tired of being a bachelor. The endless rounds of soirees, ball, and theatre outings had become boring and repetitive. He wanted to be settled, to be at ease in his own home, his beloved Pemberley. Every time he ventured out into society the inevitable questions arose; was the master of Pemberley out looking for a wife? Every eligible woman was thrown into his path, either by their mamma's or, god forbid, by their father's.

They came in all shapes and sizes. Many were young, but others were not so young. Some were pretty but had no brains, while others were intelligent but plain to look at. Darcy wanted to marry a woman that was both handsome and smart. The kind of woman that was generous with both her time and her energy. A witty and vivacious woman, who would bear him healthy sons and daughters. But most of all, he wanted a woman to be his wife, his friend, his lover. Yet the continued trend in polite society of encouraging extra-marital affairs and flirtations, also meant Darcy knew he would not choose a woman from the Ton. Fidelity was as important to Darcy as honesty.

Remembering his first encounter with Elizabeth brought a sudden smile to his face. Badgered into accompanying Bingley, his two sisters and brother-in-law Hurst to the Meryton Assembly Rooms,

Darcy had been surprised to see most the revellers were genteel folk. For some unfathomable reason, he had thought they would all be farmers, with their dairy milking wives, buxom daughters and muscle-bound sons in tow.

As their party were paraded around the room and introduced to a few of the more prominent families, Darcy admired the bright eyes and radiant smile of one lady in particular. Miss Elizabeth Bennet. But when she caught him staring at her, he cursed and turned his gaze away.

Bingley was soon dancing with, Jane, the eldest Bennet girl, who was indeed, the prettiest girl in the room, but Darcy only had eyes for Elizabeth Bennet.

His eyes followed her as she danced with a tall, gangly armed youth. Next, she danced with a handsome young man who was in truth a little too tall to partner anyone. Then the next dance she had no partner, and so sat on the sidelines with a rather plain looking girl.

With only one more set before the refreshments were served, Bingley, who had apparently seen Darcy watching Miss Elizabeth, took a break from the frivolities and tried to coax him onto the dance floor. But Darcy could not be persuaded. With all his pride and prestige, he suddenly felt something he had not experienced since he was a lad when chasing the daughter of Pemberley's gamekeeper... a fear of rejection.

Saying the first thing that came into his head, Darcy recalled with perfect clarity what he had said to Bingley. *She is tolerable; but not handsome enough to tempt me.* And then, as if that was not harsh enough, he had continued, *I am in no humour at present to give consequence to young ladies who are slighted by other men.*

Even now, standing alone in his chamber, he blushed at the harshness of his cruel and unkind words.

Nevertheless, he had today, once more unleashed his disdain and anger, only this time it was aimed directly at the woman he loved.

Yes, he had been justified in protecting her from the advances of Wickham, but to then behave in such a disgraceful manner was, in his eyes, utterly reprehensible. Could Elizabeth forgive him, would she forgive him? There was only one way to find out.

As soon as the lark rose, he would ride to Longbourn and beseech Elizabeth to forgive him.

Mrs Bennet stood before her husband, wringing her handkerchief between her hands and intermittently dabbing at invisible tears.

"But husband," she wailed, "if Elizabeth does not apologise, and encourage Mr Darcy to continue with his affections, we may lose him as a son-in-law, and then where will we be if you expire? Will you not speak to Lizzy and instruct her to do my bidding?"

Mr Bennet wanted nothing more than a quiet life, to read his books, to savour an excellent port and to enjoy the odd joke, usually at the expense of his wife. However, on this occasion, he felt comfortable in his languidity, and said,

"I have no plans to expire at present, Mrs Bennet. Darcy is the kind of man that will always be constant in his regard for our daughter. And believe me when I say, I will welcome his return to Longbourn if only to restore my peace and quiet. Now, hurry along, Mother."

"We have no funds reserved to serve us after your demise, husband. How will I manage when you are gone, tell me that?"

Mr Bennet doubted there was little, Mr Darcy would not forgive, Elizabeth; a testament to the strength of his affection for her.

"Mr Darcy has made his intentions quite clear, Mrs Bennet. He has signed the marriage contract, and I for one, do not think him a dishonourable man. This is just some silly lovers spat. He will soon be back at Lizzy's side, mark my words."

Finding no solace in Mr Bennet's words, and Elizabeth as defiant as ever, Mrs Bennet took to her bed, where her nerves were soothed by a visit from her sister, Mrs Phillips, with all the gossip from Meryton.

Chapter Twelve

After the absence of Mr Darcy yesterday, Elizabeth wasn't sure he would come today. But, in the hope that he would, she took special care over her appearance. Having chosen a dress with small yellow roses on it, one which he had once admired, Elizabeth waited impatiently while Cissy weaved a matching ribbon through her hair.

Giving her reflection a final nod of approval, she made her way downstairs.

Entering the breakfast room, Elizabeth expected to meet only her father, who was also an early riser. Instead, she was greeted by the sullen face of Lydia.

Ignoring her scowl, Elizabeth said,

"Good morning, Lydia. We don't usually see you up this early, did you not sleep well?"

"Not particularly, and my head is all fuzzy because I am tired" Lydia replied.

"I am sorry to hear that. Perhaps a brisk walk will make you feel better."

Lydia, due to her youth, did not try to hide the look of loathing she shot her sister. Instead, with eyes burning with resentment, she said,

"That's not funny Lizzy. You know Papa said I am not to leave the house unless you or Jane accompany me."

Remaining calm, Elizabeth said,

"Yes, I remember. That is why I am offering for you to accompany Mr Darcy and me this morning."

"Me...and Mr Darcy," she scoffed, "I wouldn't..." then she paused and thought for a moment.

Elizabeth watched Lydia process her offer, her eyes flicking from side to side as she appeared to mull it over.

"Very well, but only if I can go and visit with Maria Lucas, I promised to loan her some of my dresses for when she visits Charlotte. Then you can collect me on your return."

Seeing Elizabeth waiver, Lydia added,

"I am sure Mr Darcy doesn't want me listening while he talks all lovey-dovey to you."

Deciding it was the start of an olive branch, Elizabeth agreed.

Now all she needed was for Mr Darcy to first turn up, and then for him to agree to Lydia joining them.

Darcy was completely reconciled to making his peace with Elizabeth. Having endured a restless night with a mind that would not be still, and a day full of self-recriminations, he had finally seen reason and admitted the futility of their argument. He *should* have consulted with his betrothed before speaking to her father, and Elizabeth had over reacted at his omission to do so. Darcy sincerely hoped Elizabeth had arrived at the same conclusion too.

Not usually a vain man, Darcy took particular care over his appearance this morning. First, he wanted Elizabeth to see she was not only marrying a wealthy and powerful man but a man that was pleasing to the eye and abreast of the fashions. Secondly, a good suit of clothes was like a shield of armour. Being a man unaccustomed to making apologies, Darcy felt in need of his shield today. Not that he wasn't sure everything could be reconciled with Elizabeth, but...all the same, he was dress for either eventuality.

Though eager to arrive at Longbourn, and riding Odin would have seen him at his destination much quicker, Darcy elected to take the carriage.

Fletcher had tutted and sighed a great deal while removing his muddy clothes two days before. If he wanted to avoid a repeat performance, he must endure a slightly longer journey.

On his arrival at Longbourn, Hill showed Darcy into the breakfast room, where he found Elizabeth alone, and just finishing a cup of tea.

They were very civilised. Darcy executed his salute to Elizabeth, and she acknowledged it with a nod of her head.

Elizabeth spoke first.

"Mr Darcy, I hope you will accept my apology for speaking out of turn last time we met. I see now that you were right to talk to my father," she paused, and before she could help herself, she added, "first."

Darcy, who was up until that point was smiling congenially, raised one eyebrow.

Swallowing the apology that was on his lips, he said,

"It seems I bring out the worse in you, Miss Bennet?"

He was not wrong. Had Elizabeth rehearsed her apology several times, and every time she had stopped at the word father. Why she had added the 'first'; she did not know? To goad him perhaps, into yet another argument. And after two days of her mamma's lamentations about her driving Mr Darcy away, that was the last thing she wanted to do.

Smiling prettily at him, she said,

"I think you must, sir."

"I like your spirit, Elizabeth; it is one of the reasons I fell in love with you. However, do you not think it would be conducive to our future happiness if you tried to refrain from practising it on me with such frequency?"

The upturn corners of his lips had not escaped Elizabeth's notice, and she realised *he* was teasing *her*.

Liking this new side to Darcy, Elizabeth smiled back at him and said,

"I will try, sir."

At that moment, Lydia bound in expecting to find Elizabeth alone.

Looking between Mr Darcy and her sister, who were smiling at each other, her mood changed.

"Oh, you have returned then? We all thought you had jilted Lizzy. Mamma said that she had driven you away with her sharp tongue, is that not so, Lizzy?" Lydia asked with fake innocence.

Elizabeth was about to rebuke her for her rudeness, but Mr Darcy stepping in first.

"Miss Lydia, you could better employ your time by trying to emulate your sister, Elizabeth, rather than trying to humiliate her."

Turning to face Lydia, Darcy took up his usual stance, with his hands clasped behind his back and one knee slightly bent.

Then, in a stern, no-nonsense voice, he addressed Lydia.

"There comes a time in everyone's life when they must leave the school room behind them and begin to act like an adult. That time for you, Miss Lydia, is now. I will ignore your rudeness to me on this occasion, but in future, I will expect you to conduct yourself with the decorum and manners as befits a young woman of breeding. Is that clear?"

Elizabeth suppressed a smile, and the urge to say, bravo.

She loved her father dearly, but this was the dressing down *he* should have administered to Lydia months ago. Instead, it had been left to a virtual stranger to say what needed to be said.

Since Lydia had first been allowed to join her sisters out in society, her behaviour had not matured as expected. She still acted as though she was in the school room. Darcy was quite right. To reap the benefits of being 'out', one had to conduct themselves as an adult and not a spoilt child.

"Well!" Lydia exclaimed.

Darcy raised a single brow in Lydia's direction before turning away, and Elizabeth took the opportunity to walk over to her sister.

Taking her hand, Elizabeth said,

"Run along and put your coat on. And don't forget the parcel for Maria."

Lydia hoped Mr Darcy could feel her angry eyes burning into the back of his head as she flounced out of the room to get ready.

Darcy had not meant to chastise the girl quite so severely, but clearly, Mr Bennet's methods had been ineffective when it came to disciplining his children. From what he had witnessed in the past, Mrs Bennet also indulged her youngest child in every whim and fancy, regardless of whether it was practical or correct.

Darcy felt Elizabeth's hand on his arm. It startled him. It was the first time she had voluntarily touched him.

Reaching out, he covered her hand with his own; Darcy felt his pulse quicken. He wished they had not arranged to go out. He was quite content standing here holding her hand.

Her touch had somehow soothed his ire, and the frown on his brow eased as he waited for her to speak.

"Sir, I hope you will not mind, but I had already made arrangements to walk to Maria Lucas's with Lydia. I have said she may still accompany us as far as the lane leading to Miss Lucas's house."

"You do not mind walking with me alone, Elizabeth, with no chaperone?" he asked warmly and squeezed her hand.

"I think I can control myself, Mr Darcy," and she laughed.

Darcy chuckled too. How like Elizabeth to turn the table on him.

Happier than she had been for two days, Elizabeth excused herself to go and get ready for their outing.

Once Elizabeth had left the room, Mrs Bennet seized the opportunity to speak to Mr Darcy privately. She rushed in and began to mumble about the effect having five daughters had on her nerves.

"It is a strain, you know, trying to find husbands for five daughters. You have only to look at the state of my poor nerves. But, Mr Darcy, we are so thrilled you decided not to break your engagement with Lizzy." Leaning closer still, she whispered, "Elizabeth can be a foolish and headstrong girl at times. I should have listened to my mother. Spare the rod and spoil the child she said, but would I listen…still, if Lizzy becomes troublesome, I'm sure it will be nothing a good beating will not cure. If you feel the need to take a stick to her, you have my blessing."

Darcy looked at his future mother-in-law with abhorrence.

The practice of wife beating was widespread, especially amongst the lower classes, but the very notion of raising his hand to strike Elizabeth made him sick to his stomach.

"And does Mr Bennet beat you, madam?" he asked icily.

Flustered, Mrs Bennet admitted that he did not.

"Then what on God's good earth, makes you think I am the kind of man that would beat *my* wife?" he asked, with incredulity.

Instantly, Mrs Bennet knew she had made a mistake. On reflection, she did not know what had made her say such a thing. Mr Bennet had never raised a hand to her in over twenty-two years of marriage, and neither of them had ever physically chastised any of their five children. And now she realised, Mr Darcy, who made no secret of his disdain for her, would think her even more reprehensible than ever.

Darcy marvelled that such a woman could have produced Elizabeth. Thinking before speaking, was definitely not one of her strong points. However, she *was* Elizabeth's mother, and as such, he felt duty bound to ease the tension between them.

"Let me assure you, Mrs Bennet, there is no animosity between Elizabeth and me. We both spoke rashly before, but everything is forgotten now. Getting to know one another is bound to raise some points we disagree on. Is that not what a courtship is for?"

"Yes, of course. I don't know whatever came over me saying such things."

Seeing her mortification, Darcy offered her a face-saving exit.

"I wonder, Mrs Bennet, would you see how far along Miss Elizabeth and Miss Lydia are? I am eager to enjoy this brief spell of winter sun."

Grasping at his offer with alacrity, she began to back out of the room, saying,

"Yes, though I hear we are soon to expect snow…I will remind the girls to wrap up warm," and she was gone.

The walk out of Longbourn, and along the edge of the field, was made in relative silence.

Lydia was still angry with Darcy for his set down, Elizabeth decided she could not really talk to either of them, less the other resented her for it, and Darcy, well Darcy just wanted to enjoy the prospect of being alone with Elizabeth.

Halfway along the second field track, Lydia turned and addressed Elizabeth, cutting Darcy completely.

"Lizzy, I am going to run on ahead. I will meet you at the crossroads in an hour. Is that sufficient time for you to take the air?"

Darcy gave a cough as he tried to suppress a wry smile. Lydia had spoken in clipped tones, apparently wanting to impress him. Her effort to persuade him that she was indeed, a grown-up fell far short of the mark, as her next action confirmed. Tucking her carpet bag under her arm, Lydia lifted the hem of her dress and began to run down the lane.

Averting his gaze from the sight of stockings and petticoats, Darcy turned towards Elizabeth.

Elizabeth felt his eyes on her. Watching her, searching her face. Unsure of how Darcy would react to Lydia's hoyden like behaviour.

She need not have worried. Meeting his gaze, Elizabeth was surprised and relieved, to see a smile spreading over his face.

"Fifteen, such an awkward age, is it not Mr Darcy?"

"Indeed, it is Elizabeth," Darcy said, momentarily reminded of his sister.

He remembered when Georgiana would beg him to play hide-and-seek as he tried to wrestle with his new role as the owner of a large estate. Yet if her mother were alive, she would be in training for her presentation at court. For a time, he would lay down his quill and indulge her, joining in all the games she asked him to. But when on a visit to Rosings he was rudely reminded of his responsibility to her future.

Lady Catherine de Bough had compared his sister to a street child, left to run free and without restraint in her manners and actions. It had wounded him to hear Georgiana described so when she was nothing of the sort. But taking Lady Catherine's reproof to heart, he immediately set about finding her a companion.

As they continued along the lane in silence, Mr Darcy's thoughts once more turned to his last conversation with Elizabeth's mother. Decided he must dispel any fears Elizabeth might have on that subject, he said,

"Elizabeth, when we are married, I intend to be a kind and loving husband. I do not condone the use of violence in any form, especially against women." Unfortunately, he did not stop there, going on to say,

"As they are the weaker sex, how could I?"

Elizabeth's steps faltered, but she somehow managed to continue along the track. She was about to argue the point with him, pointing out that only a man, who suffered no pain as severe as childbirth, and who was nursed, raised and tended to by women, could think women the weaker sex. She could have sourced the feats of such women as Boudicca and Joan of Arc in her argument, but as their courtship had already survived one hiccup, she was not willing to rock the boat again quite so soon. Perhaps she should save this discussion for another day.

"Thank you, Mr Darcy. It pleases me to know that my physical well-being will be safe in your kind and capable hands." She replied.

Satisfied with her acknowledgement of his declaration, Darcy took her hand and gave it a reassuring pat, then placed in on his arm.

Oblivious of how condescending his last action appeared, Elizabeth thought, *and now I feel like the weaker sex*.

They walked for a little longer before turning back to meet Lydia, managing to converse with each other without further insult or misunderstanding.

When they returned, Lydia was waiting for them, and Elizabeth couldn't help but notice that her mood had lifted and she seemed quite cheerful.

All attempt to act in an adult fashion seemed to have been forgotten by Lydia, as she skipped along in front of them, humming a nondescript tune.

"Your visit to Maria went well, Lydia?" Elizabeth asked,

"Maria? Oh, yes, Lizzy, everything went very well," she replied gaily.

Chapter Thirteen

Darcy woke with mixed feelings the next morning. On his return to Netherfield yesterday, there had been a letter waiting for him. It was from Georgiana. In it, she expressed her happiness at being invited to join him for a visit and indicated that she would hopefully arrive sometime the next day.

Naturally, he was looking forward to seeing his sister again. It would give him the opportunity to introduce Georgiana to Elizabeth. The downside to Georgiana arrival was it meant he would have to forgo seeing Elizabeth for the day. Instead, as this was Georgiana's first visit to Hertfordshire, he would be obliged to remain at Netherfield and see her settle in.

Neither could he disappoint, Elizabeth.

Darcy dashed off a brief note to her, explaining the situation. It read,

Dear Miss Elizabeth Bennet,

Do not be alarmed at receiving this note, as I am quite well. However, I must cancel my planned visit to Longbourn today. My sister, Georgiana, has accepted my invitation to visit Netherfield and her letter denotes her arrival is imminent. Once settled, I would very much like to introduce her to you.

Your servant,
Fitzwilliam Darcy

Darcy, too impatient to wait inside, had stood on the front steps for almost fifteen minutes before the carriage came into sight. He watched as it turned onto the gravel drive and advance towards Netherfield House.

The wheels had barely stopped rolling before Georgiana swung open the door and jumped down, running into the outstretched arms of her slightly surprised brother.

He could not scold her for the unladylike behaviour, for he was as pleased to see her as she was to see him.

"Oh, brother, how I have missed you," Georgiana cried.

Darcy wrapped his arms around her waist and placed a soft kiss on her brow.

"It has barely been a fortnight Georgiana, no time at all. Besides, you had Mrs Annesley for company," he playfully chided her.

"Yes, I know," Georgiana said, leaning in further and tightening her grip around his neck, "but she is not you, brother."

Darcy smiled broadly at her compliment

While he understood and shared her sentiment, her words also made him felt guilty. His neglect meant that she had not reaped the benefits of mixing in a wider society. The fault was his. While Georgiana appeared content to remain at Pemberley, or wherever he took her, Darcy knew he had been neglectful in advancing her social skills, leaving her unprepared for her coming out of the school room, which was in only two years' time. Briefly, he had toyed with the idea of asking Miss Caroline Bingley if she would consider instructing Georgiana in the finer points of entertaining, deportment, etc. but had just as quickly rejected the idea. While her brother, Charles was everything affable and charming, the same could *not* be said of Miss Bingley.

Raising herself up onto her tiptoes, Georgiana whispered in Darcy's ear,

"I do not arrive alone, brother."

Georgiana looked over her shoulder. Observing that the second occupant had yet to alight the carriage, she said in a hushed voice,

"Miss Bingley has been beastly and boring. She finds fault in all that I do, and all that I say. She is worse than a governess. When she is not calling me a delightful *child*, which she does not mean as a compliment, she is questioning me about you."

Before Darcy could enquire further to her meaning, a woman's shrill voice called out,

"Mr Darcy, your assistance if you please."

Darcy looked over, only to see Miss Bingley slap away the outstretched hand of the footman, who was already waiting to help her down from the carriage.

"I fear I might fall without your assistance, sir," Caroline continued.

With a sigh of resignation, Darcy released Georgiana from his embrace and walked over to the equipage. As propriety dictated, Darcy offered his hand to, Miss Bingley.

Caroline eagerly reached out and grasped at Darcy's ungloved hand, holding it a little tighter than was strictly necessary. As the heat from his naked hand penetrated her glove, Caroline simpered,

"My, it is unseasonably warm today, is it not, Mr Darcy?"

Darcy smiled and gave a humouring nod.

Turning to follow the ladies inside the house, Darcy then heard a man call his name.

Recognising it instantly as the voice of Charles Bingley, Darcy turning to greet his friend.

"Darcy," exclaimed Charles, "how good to see you again." He dismounted his horse and bowed.

"Charles," Darcy exclaimed in acknowledgement of his friend's greeting, and then said,

"This is a surprise. I was only expecting Georgiana and her companion. How was your journey? Is it business that brings you back to Hertfordshire, my friend?"

Charles pursed his lips into a thin line, then said,

"Yes, our journey was uneventful but very tedious. For the first half of the trip, I travelled inside with the ladies, but Caroline's continuous comparing between the comfort of my carriage and your Landau, well Darcy, it was relentless. The seats are too hard, the windows too small, the curtains are not thick enough, and would you believe it, the springs are not springy enough. Her whining was sufficient to drive me outside and to mount my horse at the first inn we stopped at."

Although Charles smiled and laughed as he told the tale, Darcy knew from first-hand experience how trying it was to share a carriage with Miss Bingley.

Darcy could not help thinking, *how very typical of Caroline to be so critical.*

"So, what brings you back?"

"Why, the shooting, of course, Darcy, what else could it be?"

Though it was a valiant effort, Darcy knew Charles was lying.

If he was not mistaken, it was the allure of Miss Jane Bennet that had seen the return of his friend.

Once the newcomers had refreshed themselves, they regrouped in the drawing room to take of afternoon tea.

What should have been a refreshing and convivial meeting of friends and family was fraught and uncomfortable due to one person. Caroline Bingley.

Even though she was newly arrived and in need of rest, Miss Bingley put herself forward to act as hostess.

"I, unlike Miss Darcy, am not a novice at being a hostess," she commented loudly as she moved towards the tea tray, "With Charles being a single gentleman of independent means, it is my duty to act as his hostess until he takes a wife."

"But we are Darcy's guests Caroline. Miss Darcy should…,"

Darcy interrupted,

"No Charles, Miss Bingley is quite right, Netherfield is your house, and now you are in residence, we are your guests."

"But Darcy, I said you could use Netherfield, and we are unexpected additions to the party. I would be happy to have Miss Darcy act as hostess, very happy indeed." Charles said, generously.

A gloating Caroline could not hold her tongue.

"You see Charles, Mr Darcy understands. Besides, Georgiana is not yet out, and her hosting skills are far from polished. No, it is better if she continues to practice with Mrs…whatshername, for now."

Darcy looked over at his crestfallen sister, her face fierce with humiliation.

Although part of him did agree with Miss Bingley, Darcy wished she would keep her demoralising comments to herself. Could she not see the effect her harsh words were having on Georgiana?

As he had spent most of his life being a father, a mother and a brother to his sister, he could not stand by and see her treated so.

Walking round to stand behind Georgiana's chair, Darcy place a reassuring hand on her shoulder, and said,

"While your sentiments are admirable, Miss Bingley, might I ask, how is Georgiana ever to acquire the skills she needs, if you do not allow her to practice? As we are such a small party, where is the harm in letting Georgiana serve us a cup of tea, mmm?"

Fighting to conceal her annoyance, Caroline said,

"To be sure, Mr Darcy I am happy to oblige. I merely sought to save Miss Darcy from the humiliation of some calamity."

Caroline placed the teapot back on the table and made a great display of turning the handle to face Georgiana, but she was far from happy.

For the whole fortnight that Darcy had been away, Caroline had visited Georgiana at Darcy House with determined regularity. Every day, she had endured the shy girls' inane conversation, while gaining very little information on her preferred subject, which was Fitzwilliam Darcy. In fact, the pretext of keeping Georgiana company had been exhausting. And in return for her efforts, the only information Caroline had managed to glean from the girl, was that Darcy had invited her to visit him at Netherfield Park. Needless to say, it was an opportunity not to be missed, and she instantly invited herself to join them. The only bugbear in her plan was that when Charles heard of her plan to accompany Georgiana to Hertfordshire, he had insisted on joining them.

Georgiana nervously poured everyone a cup of tea, but when she handed Caroline her cup, only then did her hands began to tremble.

With very little grace, Caroline took it, though, after only one sip, she replaced the cup on its saucer and the saucer back on the table. As intended, it did not escape the notice of Darcy, Charles and most definitely not Georgiana that Caroline did not touch her tea again.

Caroline's foul mood did not abate, and soon she found it too difficult to hide her displeasure. With no Louisa to share her spite with, and not wishing to appear a shrew in front of Mr Darcy, she feigned a headache. Begging to be excused from supper Caroline hope that Darcy would miss her.

"I will take a tray in my room, though I doubt I will be able to eat a single morsel. The exertion of enduring such a long journey in inferior equipage, well, it is quite exhausting on the delicate female constitution."

Darcy had to suppress a roll of his eyes. He viewed Miss Bingley as anything but delicate.

Still, whatever their thoughts, all three of her companions made solicitous comments wishing her speedy recovery, while in truth, their repast was more enjoyable for the lady's absence.

As the group broke up, with the ladies going to rest for the afternoon, Bingley found himself alone with Darcy.

Although they had been friends for some years now, Charles Bingley still looked upon his friend with a degree of awe.

Darcy was one of the most powerful, wealthy, and respected men in society, not to mention the most eligible. Sometimes, Charles couldn't help but wondered why Darcy had chosen to befriend the son of a merchant, such as him? Though he had been left a considerable fortune upon the death of his father, Bingley still lacked self-confidence. And though he possessed an amiable nature and was considered a handsome man, he was not in the same league as Darcy, either in wealth or looks. Yet Darcy had taken him under his proverbial wing after their first meeting at university. Darcy certainly reaped no benefit from counting Bingley as his friend, either sociable or financially, yet he had been a genuine and sincere friend.

Darcy was familiar with most of Bingley's idiosyncrasies, and as he watched Charles wander around his own morning room, touching this, and straightening that he knew something was troubling him.

Finally, he could bear it no longer.

"You have something on your mind, Charles?" Darcy asked.

"No...well, yes, actually," Charles replied without elaborating.

"Then out with it man, I am not a soothsayer!"

Charles stopped fiddling with the furnishings and in an effort to appear more like his mentor, adopted a mirror pose to Darcy.

"As we are back in the district, do you think I should call on my neighbours, purely as a courtesy, of course?"

Though no name had been given, Darcy instantly knew to which family Bingley was referring.

Only a few short weeks ago, Darcy had been congratulating himself on extracting his friend from the clutches of Miss Jane Bennet.

Now, he could no longer feel so proud of his actions. Not only was he engaged to the lady's sister, but on closer acquaintance, he had found to his utter surprise that Jane Bennet was the personification of a genteel and virginal young woman, an ideal wife for his friend.

Swallowing humble pie was a new experience for Darcy, but swallow he must.

"Is it the Bennet family you are referring to, Charles?"

Bingley gave a nervous grin and said,

"Well, they were very hospitable to us when we first arrived in the Shire."

It was as Darcy suspected, Charles' feeling towards Miss Jane Bennet had not wavered during his brief absence from her side.

"Yes, I think you should pay a call on the residence of Longbourn, Charles. And, if a certain Miss Bennet is still of a mind, I would propose to her with alacrity."

Bingley's mouth dropped open. He was expecting Darcy to pour scorn on his idea, point out all the reasons why she was not suitable, how awful her family were, but to have him suggest the very thing he longed for, seemed like nothing short of a miracle.

"You do?" he asked with astonishment.

"Charles, I thought I was acting in your best interest when I encouraged you to sever all your connections within Hertfordshire, especially the Bennet family. However, I was wrong. Not only is it none of my business whom you marry, but it was hypocritical of me too."

"Hypocritical, Darcy? How so?"

Stiffening his back, resolved to be completely honest, Darcy took a deep breath, and said,

"My sole purpose in returning to Netherfield was to initiate a courtship with Miss Elizabeth Bennet. Then, if things went well, I would ask for her hand in marriage. So, you see, how could I condemn you for loving one sister, when I loved the other?"

Charles shook his head as if trying to untangle his muddled thoughts.

"You...love Miss Elizabeth Bennet, Darcy?" he asked.

"I do," Darcy replied with tender sincerity.

"Since when, man? How long have you loved her?"

Darcy took a moment to think. He could place no time on when his affections had become engaged. Indeed, he had been fighting against it so long, there did not seem a time when he did not love her.

"I believe it started that first night, at the Meryton Assembly..."

Charles interrupted.

"I remember. You refused to dance with any of the young ladies, especially Miss Elizabeth. You said she was tolerable, but not handsome enough to tempt you."

"Don't remind me," Darcy said and then had the good grace to colour at this reminder of his arrogance. "She walked passed me and went to stand with her friend, Miss Lucas. They spoke a few words together, and then they laughed. Well, Elizabeth laughed, Miss Lucas suppressed her mirth as all young ladies of good breeding are expected to. But Charles, I envied and admired Elizabeth's freedom, her confidence to express her emotions and show her happiness, with no fear of censure. That is when I first knew Elizabeth was different, so different to any other woman I have known."

Charles had never seen his friend, his very proud and correct friend, so animated before, about anything.

"Well, well." Bingley said in a jovial tone, "As I live and breathe, Fitzwilliam Darcy is in love, who would have thought?"

"Bingley," Darcy said in a severe tone.

"Oh, very well, but you must admit, Darcy, this information is newsworthy. You will have all the single young women of the Ton rending their clothes and throwing themselves on pyres, while their mothers stand by and wail like a banshee."

Darcy immediately saw the error of being so honest with his friend, and said,

"That is quite enough, Charles. I think you exaggerate my attraction to the opposite sex. Now, may I suggest we send your card to the Bennet's today, and then you and I will ride over and pay a call first thing tomorrow."

It suited Charles very well.

Chapter Fourteen

Caroline was still furious the next morning.

No-one had bothered to enquire after her health all evening. She had been left to stew on Darcy and Charles' lack of support until she finally fell asleep. This time with a genuine headache.

On entering the breakfast room, and seeing only Miss Darcy seated at the table, Caroline sat down and brushed the footman away when he tried to place her napkin on her lap. Instead, and with slow, deliberate movements, she flicked the cloth in the air and then put it on her lap.

Georgiana tried not to make eye contact with Caroline and pretended to be absorbed in her food.

"Are the gentlemen not joining us this morning?" Caroline asked.

It was with some trepidation that, Miss Darcy raised her eyes and made her reply.

"Fitzwilliam and Mr Bingley have already eaten, Miss Bingley. They left some time ago." Georgiana then lowered her gaze and again studied her hot buttered roll most diligently.

"Left? To go where, Miss Darcy?"

Georgiana was well acquainted with the steely tone of Miss Bingley's voice, and it did not bode well for her that she was alone with Caroline while she was using it.

With hesitation, Georgiana replied,

"I…I believe they have gone to make some calls, Miss Bingley."

Exasperated with the girl's evasive answers, Caroline made her question more specific.

"On whom have they gone to call, Miss Darcy?"

"The…the Miss Bennet's," Georgiana whispered.

Caroline flung down her napkin and screeched,

"The Bennet sisters! We have barely been back in the country twelve hours, and he is sniffing around the skirts of that Bennet girl already. And Mr Darcy, if he had gone with Charles it can mean only one thing. He has given Charles his blessing. The fool! This is all her vulgar mother's doing. Jane is pleasant enough when in her own setting, but she is not of our sphere, and I cannot be related to that dreadful family! I will not. If Charles marries her, we will be the laughing stock of all polite society." Caroline stood so abruptly that her chair toppled backwards and crashed to the floor.

Rushing forward to pick up the fallen chair, the young footman also came under attack.

"At least wait until I am out of the way, you imbecile," Miss Bingley said unkindly, before storming out of the room.

Such was her relief that Caroline had gone, Georgiana's shoulders visibly sagged from their hunched-up position around her neck.

Miss Bingley exuded a formidable presence when in the company of others, but when alone with her, Georgiana was just plain terrified. She hoped, no she prayed that Fitzwilliam would not marry her.

Her brother had always taught her to treat their servants well. They enjoyed the lifestyle they did, because these people were willing to serve them.

Georgiana turned to the footman, and said,

"I am sorry, I think Miss Bingley is a little unwell."

The footman knew Miss Darcy need offer him no explanation, but he gratefully acknowledged the sentiment behind her words.

"No harm done, Miss," he said as he righted the item of furniture.

Even before the two horsemen had dismounted from their steeds, or had time to hand their reins to the stable hand, Mrs Bennet had been informed of their imminent arrival.

Banishing her three youngest daughters upstairs, she was now fussing over Jane's appearance.

"Pinch your cheeks, Jane. You are looking excessively pale today. No, not like that, like this," Mrs Bennet said as she pinched at the small amount of excess skin covering Janes' cheeks.

"There, that's much better," Mrs Bennet cooed as she took her seat opposite her girls before the gentlemen were shown in.

Jane barely had time to rub her cheeks to ease the pain before Mr Darcy, and Mr Bingley entered.

Jane needed no artificial aid to make her skin flush. The tender look in Mr Bingley's eyes as he made his bow, had worked quite well enough.

It was Mr Darcy who took the lead.

"Mrs Bennet, Miss Bennet, Miss Elizabeth, you remember my friend, Charles Bingley."

"Oh, yes, we remember Mr Bingley, don't we girls. How very good it is to see you again, sir. Do you intend to stay long? Perhaps you will remain until after the New Year? Meryton boasts many dances and parties, particularly during the festive season. Indeed, we hold a large gathering ourselves. All our friends and acquaintances come. It would be a great honour if you consented to attend."

Darcy saw the flustered look on Charles' face as Mrs Bennet fired a barrage of questions at him, with no pause for breath.

Not for the first time, Darcy came to his rescue.

"Mrs Bennet, I wonder if I might trouble you for a moment of your time. I believe Miss Elizabeth and I would like to discuss some of the more general wedding details with you." Darcy glanced over at Elizabeth, only to see her raise her brows as she silently questions his words.

"Perhaps we should join Mr Bennet? He may also wish to contribute to the conversation?"

Darcy's request was asked not as a question, but more as a polite command, but to Mrs Bennet, it was like the proverbial carrot dangled before the donkey scenario. Besides, Mrs Bennet was more than happy to leave Jane alone in the company of Mr Bingley.

An excited Mrs Bennet ushered Elizabeth from the room and then hurried to overtake her along the corridor. Mr Darcy, who followed behind the ladies, winked at Charles as he closed the door.

Elizabeth was not quite so eager to formalise any of the wedding arrangements. Somehow, by putting things into place, it made the whole thing seem…real, rather than just play acting.

It was precisely at that moment that Elizabeth realised that was exactly how she had been viewing her engagement to Mr Darcy; as though it were a fantasy, a work of fiction. But it wasn't. She was engaged to Mr Darcy and would, in just a few short weeks become his wife.

Feeling a little dazed by her revelation, Elizabeth followed her mamma into Mr Bennet's study silently, suddenly very aware of Mr Darcy presence behind her.

Putting his book to one side, Mr Bennet looked at the trio of visitors and feared the worst. Only a catastrophe could have brought the three of them into his sanctuary at the same time, and no doubt it was instigated by his wife.

"Well, well, what's going on here then? No, my dear, let Mr Darcy speak, for I doubt I will get any sense from you, Mrs Bennet."

Though she was about to challenge her husband's command, Mrs Bennet remembered the presence of Mr Darcy next to her. Closing her open mouth, and smiled at Mr Bennet and took a step back.

Mr Darcy moved to the front of the group.

"I would very much like Mrs Bennet to update me on the wedding preparations, sir."

Uninterested in being involved or consulted on the running of his house or the lives of his children, Mr Bennet could not help but ask,

"And you decided to include me why?"

Unlike Mr Bennet, Darcy oversaw every aspect of his life, as well as his sister's. His assets and holding, his engagements and houses, Georgiana's schooling and his finances, there was nothing he was not fully abreast of.

Abhorred at the older man's lack of interest in his family and their well-being, Darcy felt no compunction whatsoever in making his future father-in-law feel guilty.

"Forgive me, sir, but you do intend to give your daughter away, do you not?"

"Yes, of course," said Mr Bennet.

"Then at some stage, you will have to attend a wedding rehearsal, will you not?"

"Yes, a rehearsal is what I expected, but as for any other arrangements I..."

Darcy interrupted Mr Bennet mid-sentence.

"Then I assume you also need to know the date, and the time of said rehearsal, as well as the actual wedding, sir. I understand as the head of the household, you will also need to oversee the number of carriages your family will have to hire, providing adequate stabling and accommodation for the wedding guests and their horses. Have you spoken to the local innkeeper to reserve any rooms? And I assume you have set aside a special fund for Mrs Bennet to draw on, to cover expenses?" Darcy began to reel off a list of items that Mrs Bennet would need the money for.

"The wedding breakfast, flowers, additional servants, the Church and organist, the bell ringers, need I go on? Though, I believe

Elizabeth's trousseau, is one aspect of the arrangements the ladies would rather we left to them. I assume you did not expect Mrs Bennet to deal with *all* these arrangements single-handed?"

Humiliated by his own neglect and ignorance, Mr Bennet felt the full force of Darcy's contempt.

Looking at his wife, a shamefaced Mr Bennet said,

"I am at your disposal for the rest of the day, Mrs Bennet," and for once in his life, he actually meant it.

Looking down at Jane, Charles thought she had never looked lovelier than she did right now. The glow in her cheeks complimented the red bow of her cherry lips, as her blue eyes stared up at him adoringly.

Having prepared no speech or fancy words, Charles Bingley made his proposal with words straight from the heart.

Confident that Jane's affection had not changed, Charles, dropped to one knee, took Jane's hands in his own, and said,

"Dear Miss Bennet…Jane, I can no longer deny the strength of my feelings for you. You are not only beautiful, but you are kind and considerate and caring. You are gentle and honest and loyal. You possess every attribute that is admired and desired by a man in his wife. You can be in no doubt as to my intentions since I arrived in Meryton. You alone possess my heart and my admiration, Jane. I have loved you since the very moment we met, and I wondered if you would do me the inestimable honour of agreeing to be my wife?"

Jane had quite given up on ever seeing Mr Bingley ever again.

After reading Caroline Bingley's letter, which had arrived the day after they left Netherfield, Jane was sure the next time she heard Mr Bingley's name was to read that he had married Georgiana Darcy. Miss Bingley had intimated as much in her letter, and why would she doubt the word of his sister. Miss Bingley had even gone on to explain that it was the dearest wish of both families to see the young couple united.

Only now, Jane knew that it was a combination of spite and wishful thinking on Caroline's behalf. Had Charles married Georgiana Darcy, Caroline had clearly hoped it would bring her one step closer to becoming Mrs Fitzwilliam Darcy herself.

Pushing the defects of her future sister-in-law's character to the back of her mind, Jane said,

"Oh, yes, I accept, with my all heart I accept."

Charles Bingley stood up, still holding Jane's hands in his own, and raised her up with him. They shared a deep and meaningful look. One that spoke volumes without words. A future that promised to be full of love and happiness, bliss and adoration, longevity and contentment. Then, they exchanged their first, chaste kiss.

Darcy and Elizabeth had left Mrs Bennet explaining to her captive husband, about all the extra work involved in planning a wedding, though with a slight exaggeration of the strain it was putting on her already fraught nerves.

With Mr Bingley and Jane still closeted in the morning room, Darcy and Elizabeth found themselves again sitting in the music room.

Besides the pianoforte and stool, there was a harp, which only Mary played, a violin and a flute hidden from view in a cabinet, which no-one played and a small table and several chairs.

Darcy sat on the ornate chair again, which was still where he had left it, facing the pianoforte. Elizabeth once more sat on the piano stool.

"Would you play for me, Elizabeth?" he asked.

Though it was a request, Elizabeth felt compelled to oblige.

Selecting a familiar piece of music, Elizabeth began to play.

For the first few bars, Darcy sat and listened politely. Then, he rose from his seat and moved to stand in front of her, resting his arm on the instrument.

Elizabeth felt a burst of heat rise up to stain her cheeks, as Darcy, unwavering in his gaze, scanned her face. His piercing blue eyes seemed to be absorbing every characteristic and trait of her features, committing them to memory.

Her fingers moved effortlessly over the keys, and all the while, Darcy watched her. Soon, it became apparent to Elizabeth that Darcy had not asked her to play in order to admire her musical skills, but to admire her.

At length, the piece came to an end, and Elizabeth rested her hands in her lap, again looking at Darcy.

Darcy raised a single eyebrow and nodded towards the instrument.

Apparently, Darcy had not yet finished with his observations. Selecting the next sheet down, Elizabeth resumed playing.

Darcy straightened and came to stand at her side.

His continued scrutiny was discomforting, and though she had often felt his constant gaze on her in the past, the duration and intensity of his inspection today were unnerving.

Elizabeth thought he might join her on the piano stool, or perhaps choose another tune for her to play. Instead, he reached out a hand and cupped it around her neck.

His hand felt warm against her soft skin, and she thought she might falter, but with determination, she played on.

With a delicate touch, his fingers caressed the nape of her neck, moving up slowly to caress and explore the texture of her hair.

Now, the intimacy of his touch did make Elizabeth falter, but she quickly recovered her fumble and resumed playing.

As he continued to stroke her neck with his thumb, Darcy entwined his fingers ever deeper into her loose tendrils, feeling the softness of each curl with his fingers.

Elizabeth became aware that her breathing felt constrained and her pulse had begun to race.

As the piece came to an end and the last note died away, Elizabeth let her shaking fingers rest on the cold ivory keys.

Soon, Elizabeth became aware of his warm breath on her, close enough to rouse the fine hairs that covered her skin.

Drinking in her fragrance, Darcy began to smell Elizabeth. Her dress, her hair, her skin…her essence.

Then, his voice low and barely audible, he whispered,

"I'm sorry, Elizabeth." His voice was thick with emotion.

With her eyes firmly fixed forward, Elizabeth waited, expectantly.

She had no doubt that he meant to kiss her now, but how?

A chaste kiss as when she had first accepted his proposal? Or the savage assault he had inflicted on her a few days ago. Having only ever been kissed twice, they were Elizabeth's only reference.

From his position, Darcy reached out and took Elizabeth's hand, raising her up and turning her to face him.

Cupping her cheeks in his hands, Darcy brushed her still tender lips with his thumb, and quietly said,

"Forgive me, Elizabeth?"

With her face now only inches from his, Elizabeth closed her eyes and surrendered to his apology.

With her capitulation, Darcy lowered his head and placed a feather light kiss on her parted lips. It was a kiss of remorse, and regret and repentance, but it quickly changed to one of purpose and passion.

As Elizabeth accepted his first kiss, Darcy knew she had forgiven him. Her soft, pliant lips remained motionless and unsure as he kissed her again.

Darcy withdrew, and Elizabeth thought he had done with kissing her, but he had not.

Tilting his head slightly, Darcy placed his lips only a hair's breadth from Elizabeth's mouth, and then, as if in slow motion he teased her lips. Each time he pursed his mouth, and let his lips brush against her mouth, Elizabeth thought he was about to resume kissing her.

After several teasing tastes of his mouth, Elizabeth found herself wanting to be kissed, longing to be kissed. Her bruised lips ached to be possessed, to be rewarded, until finally, she could bear it no more.

As Darcy moved in to brush her lips again, Elizabeth leant in to meet him.

It was strange, Elizabeth thought afterwards, to return a man's kiss. It was more pleasurable than she had anticipated, and once she had learnt the rudiments, easily executed. Though the sensation seemed not confined to just her mouth. It had radiated through her whole body, alerting areas of her being to a yearning she had never experienced before. Of all Darcy's kisses, this was the one she preferred. If each time they kissed it was as agreeable as this, she would not be unhappy.

Darcy was overjoyed to have extracted a naïve response from his intended. Within a few minutes of coaxing, Elizabeth had learnt to return his kiss with a gentle, butterfly touch of her own. Slowly she overcame her shyness and relaxed her body against his as he lovingly caressed her mouth with his lips while softly stroking her back. He hoped this was a sign that Elizabeth's opinion was thawing towards him, accepting of his love, and dare he hope, a budding of her own love?

Darcy stroked Elizabeth's cheek, about to resume their activity, when the shrill voice of Lydia resonated through the house, demanding to be allowed downstairs.

The mood was broken, and reluctantly, Darcy brought their pleasurable encounter to a close.

Chapter Fifteen

Darcy and Bingley returned to Netherfield for the afternoon. They had all be invited to dine at Longbourn, and both men knew the ladies would need some time to rest and then change. But first, each eager to share their happy news, the gentleman took their own sister aside and spoke to them privately.

Mr Darcy led Georgiana to the music room, a place she felt comfortable in, while Mr Bingley and Caroline remained in the drawing room.

Having seen Georgiana comfortably settled, Darcy pulled up a chair and sat before her.

Taking hold of one of her hands, Darcy began,

"Georgiana, I have some joyous news to share with you. It is the reason I returned to Hertfordshire with such haste."

Georgiana inclined her head slightly and gave a cautious smile.

"Well," Darcy paused, "...the truth is; when I first arrived in Hertfordshire at Michaelmas, a particular young lady caught my attention. Being as stubborn as I am, I tried to fight the attraction I felt for her. So much so, I returned to town to aid the process. But, as I expect you have already guessed, that is one fight I am honestly elated to have lost. My sole purpose in returning to the Shire was to first speak to the young lady's father and then to Elizabeth. Having been given Mr Bennet's permission to approach Elizabeth, I then ask her if she would do me the honour of becoming my wife. She has accepted, Georgiana, Elizabeth has consented to be my wife, and we are now engaged."

Darcy waited nervously for Georgiana's reaction, but he need not have worried.

Georgiana welcomed the news that at last, she was to have a sister. Not that she did not love and adore her brother, but she had always longed for a sister.

Forgetting all of Mrs Annesley's advice and training on how to conduct herself, Georgiana flung her arms around Darcy's neck and hugged him in a most unladylike fashion.

"Oh brother, is it true, you have found a wife? And a sister for me? I am so happy for you, Fitzwilliam."

For a long moment, Darcy enjoyed his sister's jubilation, then gently untangled himself from her embrace.

"Yes, a sister for you, Georgiana, but I do not expect you to join together against me," he teased.

"You must love her very much, William, to offer her your name and protection. So, she is one of the Miss Bennet's you wrote to me about? Will, I meet her soon?"

"Yes, and yes," Darcy said. "Miss Elizabeth Bennet. There is still more good news, Mr Bingley is to marry Elizabeth's sister, Jane. Now, Mr and Mrs Bennet have invited us all to dine with them this evening, so run along and get ready. We must leave at six-thirty sharp."

With a childlike skip, Georgiana hurried upstairs, happier than she had been for over a year. But today she would not think of George Wickham or his betrayal of her affections. Today was a day of celebration.

A similar scenario was being played out in the Netherfield drawing room, but with a very different outcome.

Mr Bingley had asked Caroline to make herself comfortable. He wanted to share some good news with her.

However, unbeknown to Charles, Caroline had already guessed his secret and was not at all happy about it.

If Charles was expecting felicitations from his sister, he was about to be sadly disappointed.

"Caroline," he started, "After much consideration, and believe me I did try to heed your advice, I have concluded that I will only ever love one woman. That woman is Jane Bennet. Therefore, today, I asked her to be my wife, and she has accepted me. I am to be married, Caroline, and you are to have another sister."

Caroline's unwavering stare and silence began to unnerve Charles, and as his courage began to fail him, he nervously asked,

"Are you not happy for me, sister?"

It was as she expected. Her weak-willed brother had returned to the doe eyes Jane Bennet and thrown his heart and his fortune at her feet.

With no effort to disguise her contempt, Caroline sneered,

"One sister, Charles, don't you mean five sisters. Jane herself is bearable, but she does not come alone, does she, Charles?"

Standing, Caroline began to pace to and fro before her brother, knowing her actions would intimidate him.

"Do you expect me to wish you joy, to be happy for you? To rejoice, knowing that your childish infatuation will bind us to that dreadful family forever. To think I will be associated with that ridiculous mother, the idle father and unbearably common sisters. It is beyond contemptible, Charles, how could you do it? Have you no regards for the feelings of your sisters? Do not fool yourself, for Louisa will not be happy for you either. She and I are of a mind where the Bennet family are concerned."

Caroline ceased her pacing for a moment, standing before her brother.

"I insist you break with her, Charles, it's not too late. You cannot expose your family to such ridicule, and your marriage will make us the laughing stock of society. And for what... to satisfy your male cravings?"

"But Caroline, I love Jane, and she loves me. Besides, I can't break it off, I have already spoken to her father, and Jane has told her mother."

"Have you exchanged contracts?"

"Well, no..."

"Then there is no breach of promise." Caroline resumed her pacing.

"I love Jane, Caroline, and I want to marry her," Charles said with determination.

Through experience, Caroline knew if she browbeat her brother for long enough, he would capitulate.

"Oh, Charles," she said in a derisory and dismissive tone, "You fall in love with a new face every season. This time next year you won't even remember her name."

"I think Charles will find that harder than you imagine, Miss Bingley."

Even before turning to trace the deep baritone voice, Caroline knew it was Mr Darcy that stood behind her.

Turning to face him, Caroline said,

"I see no reason why not, Mr Darcy. Once Charles has returned to town, attended a few balls and recitals, Jane Bennet will be banished from his affections for once and for all. His broken heart, if indeed it is broken, will soon mend. And perhaps...in a year or two, Georgiana and Charles..."

"Georgiana and Charles are not suited, Miss Bingley, and I have promised her she may marry for love, not convenience. Now, unless it is your intention to sever all contact with me too, Miss Bingley, I do not see how you can avoid an acquaintance with the Bennet family."

Caroline furrowed her brow and stared at Darcy.

"Why should that be, sir? We hardly move in the same circles, thank goodness."

"No, but once Miss Elizabeth Bennet is my wife..." Darcy paused, allowing Caroline the time to understand his meaning, "You will find it almost impossible not to meet one, or perhaps all the Bennet at any number of social occasions."

Caroline blanched as she realised her prize had been torn away from her, and by the one person she despised the most, Miss Elizabeth Bennet.

"You cannot be serious, sir, say it is not so."

"Oh, but it is so, Miss Bingley, I am deadly earnest," Darcy replied with a single raised brow.

Then a soft voice from behind Darcy said,

"I am very happy for my brother, Miss Bingley, and I will welcome his wife as my new sister," Georgiana said bravely.

Caroline then made another disastrous mistake. She rounded on Georgiana.

"What do you know of the world, you are only a child, with childish fantasies about love and happy ever afters. Life is not like that Georgiana, if it was, do you think I would still be a spinster?"

Georgiana saw her brother stiffen and his jaw clench as he fought to maintain his composure.

"Georgiana may still be a child in your eyes, Madam, but at least she is a kind child. She does not spread her vitriol on others just because things have not gone her way. And, as far as I am concerned, she is everything I could wish for in a sister, unlike some people I know." The icy tone in which Darcy delivered his rebuke, saw Caroline blanch.

Charles had sat in a stunned silence at his sister verbal attack on Miss Darcy, but now he found his voice.

"That is quite enough, Caroline. I will not have you insult my guests under any circumstances, and especially not under my own roof. You will apologise to both Darcy and Miss Darcy."

Caroline stared back at her brother, the glint of defiance clearly visible in her countenance.

When no apology was forthcoming, Charles raised the stakes.

"Very well, Caroline, I will make arrangement for you to return to town first thing in the morning, until then, you will confine yourself to your rooms."

Caroline quickly realised, if she was to work on both Darcy and Charles, to either force or cajole them into breaking their engagements, she must hold her tongue…for now anyway.

So, it was with more than a resentful lump in her throat, that Caroline said,

"You are quite right, Charles. I don't know what came over me; it must have been the shock of hearing you were both engaged. I apologise, Miss Darcy, Mr Darcy." Then Caroline attempted to smile sweetly, but such was her mood that it looked more like a grimace than a smile.

Georgiana managed a faltering smile, while Darcy inclined his head in the briefest of acknowledgements at her words.

Miss Bingley's apology did not fool Darcy. He suspected she had an ulterior motive for her words of excuse, for that was what they were. There must be another reason she had capitulated so easily. From now on, they must both be more circumspect when dealing with Caroline Bingley. Today's paroxysm confirmed what he already suspected. Caroline Bingley was capable of great acts of spite, and mischief-making, if the purpose suited her.

Darcy assisted his sister from the carriage and then offered Miss Bingley the same courtesy.

This time, Caroline ignored his outstretched hand, making a great show of alighting from the equipage without any assistance.

"I am quite capable of managing two steps unaided, Mr Darcy," she stated.

Having entered Longbourn, Mrs Bennet went to great lengths to make her guests welcome. From fussing over their seats and plumping up the cushions, to offering to move everyone's chairs either closer to the fire or further away from the heat. Nothing was too much trouble, she assured them.

Finally, just when Mrs Bennet seemed happy that everyone was settled and reasonably comfortable, dinner was announced.

The consumption of the first three courses of soup, fish, and lamb had been uneventful, passing with benign conversation from all present.

Relieved that Caroline appeared to be behaving herself, Darcy and Bingley began to relax.

Caroline had smiled and nodded when complimented on the beautiful quality of her couture by Mrs Bennet.

In return, Caroline had then praised Mrs Bennet on the delicious repast, saying how her hostess must treasure such an excellent cook. She had even borne Lydia's impertinence with a smile when the young girl commented on how unfashionably tall Caroline was, and what an inconvenience it must be for Caroline's modiste to have to use extra cloth for all her gowns. Her fixed smile gave no hint of what was to come.

Finally, as the meal came to an end with the cheese board being produced, along with the fruit and dessert wine, Caroline's mood visibly changed.

Having lulled everyone into a false sense of security, and comfort, she now unleashed her vitriol.

Turning her attention first to Jane.

"I have been remiss in wishing you joy, my dear sister to be."

Jane smiled shyly, and said,

"Thank you, Miss Bingley. I am so pleased you approve."

"Oh, I don't, but Charles won't listen to reason," Caroline said with a superior air. Then, before any of her shocked fellow diners could respond, she turned to Elizabeth, saying,

"And Miss Eliza, I understand you are to marry Mr Darcy? A surprise, I must admit, for these many weeks now you seemed to prefer, and yes, I must say enjoyed, the attention of Mr Wickham. Now, if you had announced your engagement to that gentleman, no-one would think you were setting your sights above the station you now occupy."

"George has never like Lizzy half as much as he likes me!" Lydia declared loudly, as she slammed her cutlery onto the table.

"Go to your room this instant," hissed Mrs Bennet, for once in no humour to indulge her youngest child.

Together, Mr Bennet, Mr Bingley and Mr Darcy all rose. Mr Bennet looked at the young men in turn, and Charles looked to Darcy, and Darcy looked at his sister.

Georgiana was staring down at her untouched fruit, her trembling hand rattled the fruit knife against her plate.

Cursing himself for relaxing his guard on Miss Bingley, Darcy raised his hand to silence the room.

"I think you have said quite enough, Miss Bingley. You already made your sentiments know to Charles and me at Netherfield, Madam. Your rudeness to our hosts is inexcusable. You will apologise this instant, and then you will return to the Park forthwith."

All eyes turned to Caroline.

Her boldness and rudeness had been unleashed, and if she could not have Darcy as her own, she would do her utmost to make sure no-one else would have him, especially Eliza Bennet.

She rose and dabbed at the corners of her mouth with her napkin, as if she had all the time in the world, before throwing the cloth onto the floor, and saying,

"Why do you act so surprised, sir? I have heard you pour scorn on this wretched family many times. Did you not say that Miss Eliza was no beauty? That you would sooner call her mother a wit than admit, she was handsome? And not two weeks past, you told Charles that an alliance with such a family would be insupportable?" Then Caroline turned her attention solely onto Elizabeth, "Mr Darcy not only convinced Charles to return to town, Miss Eliza, but he also advised him to sever all connections with your family, saying such an acquaintance would not only be insupportable, but also a degradation to his reputation. Is that the kind of man you wish to marry? One who secretly despises you and all your relations?" Next, she turned to the open-mouthed Mrs Bennet. "Is Mr Darcy really the man you want as your son-in-law? A man that does not esteem you or your daughters in any way whatsoever?"

Mrs Bennet was torn. Her indignation on learning Mr Darcy true opinion of her family had hurt, there was no denying, but then he did have ten thousand a year.

"I…well…," she wavered.

"Of for goodness sake, woman, where is your pride?" Caroline spat with venom at the stuttering Mrs Bennet.

"And where is your pride, Miss Bingley?"

All eyes now turned to Elizabeth, who had risen from her seat.

"You have insulted my family and me in every way possible, and I must now ask you to importune us no further. Hill will see you to your carriage."

Caroline felt the force of Elizabeth's words, more so than any others. Compared to her own behaviour, Elizabeth's breeding had stood out, whereas she had appeared sadly lacking in all the essentials. It made her despise her even more.

Up to this point, Charles had been frozen with horror at his sister's outburst, but suddenly, through the emotional fog he finally found his voice and acted. Moved forward, Charles took hold of Caroline's arm and propel her out of the dining room door.

"Get out!" he said, annunciating his words with force and clarity.

Try as she might, Caroline could not shake free from his grip.

Propelling her along the corridor and out the front door, Charles did not stop even to collect her cloak.

Charles waited in silence with Caroline, not trusting her alone for even one minute.

The door behind them opened, and as they both looked round, they saw Mrs Hill walked out with Caroline's cloak and reticule.

Having given them to Miss Bingley, Hill then gave a derisory sniff, put her nose in the air and walked back in inside, closing the front door with a resounding thud.

Within minutes Darcy's carriage was brought round, and Charles, still the gentleman, opened the door for his sister.

"I will deal with you later," he said, and then without a second glance or another word to his sister, Charles Bingley closed the door and nodded for the driver to walk on.

Charles watched as the carriage rolled through Longbourn's gates, despairing of ever being able to rectify the damage his cruel and heartless sibling had inflicted tonight.

The silence in the dining room at Longbourn was palpable.

Kitty sat wide-eyed looking around at her elders. With bated breath, she waited for one of them to speak while hoping no-one would remember she was present and send her to her room. She sensed that now was not the time to express an opinion or ask any questions.

Mary had pulled a small volume of sermons out from her pocket; intent on scanning the pages for a passage that would fit the event.

Mrs Bennet was understandably flustered, and had absently began to wring her handkerchief in her hands, wrapping it first this way, and then twisting it that way until it was in a sorry state. Once again, the question of what was to become of them when Mr Bennet died had reared its ugly head.

Mr Bennet cast his eyes over all who were seated at his table and sighed. He knew no good would come of having five daughters.

How was he ever to sort this mess out, when all he really wanted to do was sit in his library, read a good book, and indulge in a nice glass of port?

Jane's eyes were cast down, and if the truth be known, they were a little moist.

Only Elizabeth showed any resilience and was defiant in the face of adversity. She walked round to where Jane sat and took the now vacant chair next to her.

Putting a consoling arm around her sister's shoulders, Elizabeth said,

"You cannot rely on Miss Bingley's account for any other's words or deeds, Jane. You must judge them for yourself."

From her first encounter with Miss Bingley, Elizabeth had mentally marked her as a thoroughly unpleasant woman. A woman that felt little compassion or regard for those she considered below her notice. Often compelled to compliment others in a tone blatantly dripping with insincerity and derision.

Elizabeth had to admit she was surprised at the lengths Miss Bingley was prepared to go to ensure Jane did not marry her brother.

At first, Mr Darcy was torn. Should he go to Elizabeth and defend himself against Miss Bingley's accusations, or first comfort his sister? Hearing Elizabeth's words of encouragement to Jane, Darcy's decision was made. Though he was not ignorant to the fact that they might never now marry, Elizabeth's defiance and resolve not to be influenced by Caroline's vitriol, only made him love her more.

Darcy went to Georgiana.

"Come, dearest, we must go now."

Georgiana always knew there would be a time when George Wickham would once more come into their lives, whether in name only or in person, but she had thought herself quite safe from him in Hertfordshire. It was a long way from both Pemberley and Ramsgate, and Georgiana was unaware that Miss Bingley had even met Mr Wickham. Yet, in a way, she was pleased this first reference to him was over. It had made her realise she no longer harboured any feelings towards Mr Wickham. No residue of love or devotion or admiration remained in her, just a tremendous sense of relief. Finally, she had left the school room behind, and with it, her adolescent crush

In the light of this revelation, Georgiana realised there were other bridges to be mend. Displaying her newfound maturity, she turned to her brother, and said,

"First, you must speak to, Miss Elizabeth."

Darcy looked over to Elizabeth, and as their eyes met, he said, "Tomorrow, my love."

Elizabeth understood his meaning, and with a slight inclination of her head, agreed.

Darcy helped Georgiana from the table and then he both apologised and thanked Mr and Mrs Bennet for inviting them.
Mrs Bennet gave an awkward curtsy.

It was with a great deal of trepidation that Charles Bingley returned to the dining room at Longbourn. Half expecting to be ordered from the house, he was undeniably surprised to be ushered in, and to find everyone still present.

"Jane...I..." he faltered.

Jane was being comforted by Elizabeth and had not cast even the slightest glance in his direction.

Embarrassed, humiliated and angry, he felt everyone wished him gone.

Straightening his back and inhaling deeply, Charles said,

"Mr Bennet, Mrs Bennet, words cannot express how very sorry I am for my sister's behaviour. I had no idea she intended to vent her ire on us in such a public and offensive outburst. I think you have long been wishing us gone. However, with your permission, I would like to call tomorrow?" Charles asked, though his voice began to wane at the end.

Mr Bennet raised a single quizzing eyebrow in Janes direction.

The nod of Jane's head indicated she would permit Mr Bingley to call on her.

Mr Bennet eyed Charles Bingley for a full ten seconds before he said,

"You would, would you? Very well, come back tomorrow, both of you. Now, you had better take my carriage to see you all home, good night."

Chapter Sixteen

Having accepted the loan of Mr Bennet's dated, yet surprisingly comfortable carriage, Darcy, Charles, and Georgiana made their way back to Netherfield Park. Upon arrival, Darcy took his sister into the drawing room with the intention of administering a small restorative to her, while Bingley went to speak to his sister.

Somewhere, though he was not sure where, Darcy recalled hearing that a sip of brandy should be administered when someone had suffered a shock.

Georgiana looked at the proffered glass in her brother's outstretched hand. She had never tasted hard liquor before and saw no reason to start now.

"What is this, brother? I am not ill."

"It is for the shock, Georgiana," Darcy stated, his voice heavy with concern.

"The shock? Yes, it was a shock to hear Miss Bingley mention, Mr Wickham. I was not aware they shared an acquaintance," she said, in her usual soft voice.

"Are you sure, Georgiana? There is no shame in admitting you have been affected by the incident."

With another unexpected display of maturity, Georgiana placed her hand on Darcy's arm, and said,

"I am quite well brother, truly. In fact, I should thank Miss Bingley. Though she is ignorant of my foolishness over Mr Wickham last summer, it has made me realise that he has no power over me. My childish infatuation with George Wickham is quite in the past, and that is where I intend for it to remain, in the past."

"Darcy, I say, Darcy, Caroline has gone. The butler told me she stopped only long enough to collect her maid, instruct the housekeeper to have her trunks sent back to town, and then she left."

Darcy looked over at the befuddled features of his friend, who had burst into the drawing room and was now standing in the open doorway.

"No doubt she will stay with the Hursts," Darcy said pragmatically.

Bingley, still standing in the doorway, looking as though he was unsure of what to do next. He had intended to have things out with Caroline, but that meeting, due to her flight, must now be postponed.

"You have been reprieved from dealing with your sister tonight, Charles, but it is a matter that still has to be addressed. But now, you must pour all your efforts into healing the rift Caroline's outburst has opened between you, and Miss Bennet. Perhaps you should retire and think about how you can do that?" Darcy advised him.

"Yes, of course. And you, Miss Darcy, are you well?"

"Thank you, Mr Bingley, I am quite recovered," Georgiana said, and made a point of looking at her brother as she spoke.

The candles at Longbourn were still burning brightly long after the midnight hour. Mr Bennet had removed himself from the fray and taken cover in his favourite room.

"I have no doubt you will all make your decisions better without me. Though, if you should need me, I'll be in my study," he said.

Mrs Bennet dismissed him with a wave of her battered handkerchief, and when Kitty yawned, she waved her away to bed too.

Moving into the small back parlour, Elizabeth asked Mrs Hill to bring some hot tea and plenty of sugar. Then, she gently steered Jane and her mother to the divan nearest the fire.

It was typical of her father to abscond during a crisis. Too often she had observed this pattern of behaviour from him. It was no wonder her poor mamma had finally given up trying to discipline her youngest children. After raising five daughters, almost single-handedly, she was understandably exhausted. And although she knew her mother would offer her no thanks for helping, Elizabeth stepped into the breach left by her father's absence.

"Mamma, I do not think we can put any credence on what Miss Bingley said tonight. I believe it was a combination of the wine and her imagination talking. I don't think her words reflect either Mr Bingley's or Mr Darcy's true sentiments. I certainly will not be jumping to any conclusions merely on her word. And, I suspect neither will Jane."

Jane turned her tear stained face to Elizabeth, and whispered,

"But what if she is right? What if Mr Darcy did try to turn Mr Bingley away from me? If Mr Bingley's love for me is so shallow, his heart so easily swayed once, might he not be easily persuaded again? Could I marry such a man, Lizzy, could you?"

The points Jane made were valid, and under any other circumstances, they might have warranted further investigation. However, they were said with bitterness and anger, frustration and malice, borne out of Caroline's disappointed hopes. Elizabeth was sure Caroline Bingley's sole intention had been to drive a wedge between Mr Bingley and Jane, and Mr Darcy and her.

Well, Elizabeth thought, Miss Bingley will find us Bennet's are made of sterner stuff than the soft town folk she usually deals with.

Besides, Elizabeth had already decided she would not let Miss Bingley's obvious infatuation with becoming Mistress of Pemberley, deter her from marrying its master.

There was too much at stake. Not only Elizabeth's future but the future of the entire Bennet family rested on either Jane or her marrying well. One of them must make a good match. She was also under no illusion that neither Jane or herself would be sought out and courted by any other wealthy gentlemen. Elizabeth would not be the one to jeopardise her family's future comfort.

"But Jane, you seem to forget that I am not in love with Mr Darcy. I admire and respect him, but unlike you and, Mr Bingley, ours is not a love match. Now, are you going to turn away from a man who adores you, and whom you love in return, merely because of an angry tirade by his spinster sister? Or, are you going to marry your prince charming and give mamma a dozen grandchildren?"

Jane could only manage a weak smile in reply.

Lizzy was right. There had been several times since that first night in Meryton, that Miss Bingley and Mrs Hurst had made sly and unkind comments about members of her family, but Jane had dismissed them all, thinking herself too sensitive and provincial. However, tonight's debacle had made Jane realise they were not said in jest as she thought, nor was it a misunderstanding on her part. No, both Miss Bingley and Mrs Hurst were serious in their dislike for her and her family. They had been laughing at her behind her back. Laughing at her family.

So, how could she marry Mr Bingley now? Caroline and Louisa were his sisters, his family. She could not expect him to choose between his family and hers! Jane's tears began to fall again.

Mrs Bennet could not bear to see Jane cry. All those tears would cause her eyes to swell, and tomorrow, if he should come, Mr

Bingley would have second thoughts himself about taking her as his bride.

This was finally enough to goad her into action.

Taking what remained of her shredded handkerchief, Mrs Bennet dabbed at Jane's eyes, saying,

"Come now, Jane. How could Mr Bingley not love such a sweet girl as you? You have the kindest nature, a pleasing figure, and the prettiest face in the county. Of course, Mr Bingley wants to marry you," she cooed.

Elizabeth was just about to commend her mother for supporting Jane, when she ruined it by adding,

"But if you keep crying you will inevitably end up looking like a tomato, all swollen and red faced, and then no-one will want to marry you."

"Mamma!" Elizabeth exclaimed, before turning back to sooth Jane again, "Come, Jane, let's get you to bed and put a cold compress on your eyes. The hour is very late, and if I am not mistaken, Mr Bingley intends to be here very early."

Caroline flung the carriage door open and rushed up Netherfield's front steps. Pushing open the front door she bellowed for her maid.

"Rose! Rose, where are you?" turning to a startled footman she ordered him to find her maid and to be quick about it.

Rose, who had been dozing by the kitchen fire while she waited for her mistress to return, hurried upstairs when she heard her name called. From experience, Rose knew it was not wise to keep Miss Bingley waiting.

Rubbing her eyes, she sleepily said,

"Yes, Miss?"

"Get in the carriage; we are leaving."

"Now, Miss? But it's the middle of the night? It's not safe…"

"Yes, now Miss! Don't argue with your betters and get in the carriage!" Caroline shouted.

Then, turning her attention to the housekeeper who had hurried upstairs behind young Rose, Caroline ordered,

"Have all my things packed and sent to my sister's house."

"Begging your pardon, Miss, but I don't have the address," said the startled housekeeper.

"Ask my brother! I am sure he will be more than pleased to supply it."

Then she gave Rose a push in the back, propelling her out of the front door.

Rose stood to one side and watched as Caroline climbed into the carriage, who then waited impatiently for Rose to join her.

With a resounding thud, the front door to Netherfield Park closed.

Rose looked over her shoulder at the closed door, and wailed, "But, miss, my things...my coat...."

Caroline was in no mood to deal with whining servants. Concerned only with her own comfort, she snapped at the girl mid-sentence,

"Get one of the horse blankets from the tack box. If it's good enough to keep a valuable animal warm it's more than good enough for you!"

Shivering, and snivelling, Rose walked around to the back of the carriage and lifted the heavy wooden lid of the box. Feeling inside, she pulled out the top blanket, and then let out a scream.

Caroline had no intention of being anywhere near Netherfield when Mr Darcy and her brother returned from the Bennet's. Taking her frustration out on Rose for their delay, she looked out of the carriage window, and hissed,

"Get a blanket girl, and get in here before I change my mind and make you ride up top."

"But...Miss, there is something I think you should see," her voice quivered as she defied her mistress.

Caroline climbed out of the carriage and walked to where the frightened girl stood.

"If this is a ruse to make me feel sorry for you then you are sadly..."

For the briefest of moments, Caroline Bingley was speechless, but it did not for long.

"Why, what do we have here? It appears we have a stowaway on board, Rose. Or should I say a runaway."

Caroline looked down at the curled-up form squashing into the blanket box.

Holding out an inviting hand, Caroline smiled, and said,

"I think you will find it much warmer inside the carriage, Miss Lydia."

Chapter Seventeen

Elizabeth rose early the next morning. She wandered into the breakfast room and was not surprised to find only her father there. Kissing him on the cheek, she then took her usual seat.

"Well, Lizzy, if I had known we were to be witness to such a show last night, I would have invited more of the neighbours around," Mr Bennet said, trying to make light of the situation.

Elizabeth pursed her lips in a slight smile and continued buttering her roll.

Mr Bennet looked at his favourite child. Her disappointment in his lack of intervention last evening was evident in her expression. If he had been more so inclined, he would have been disappointed in himself, but he was too old to change now.

Nevertheless, he must try to redeem himself in Elizabeth's eyes; he could not bear for her to think badly of him.

Resting his cutlery on the side of his plate, Mr Bennet leant back into the curve of his chair, and said,

"What do you make of it all, Lizzy? Is there any truth in what Miss Bingley said?"

Elizabeth now raised her eyes up to look at her father, studying his features to see if he were really interested or merely trying to cover his previous indolence. The seriousness of his countenance told her that he was indeed, in earnest.

"I have long held the belief, Papa, that Miss Bingley is capable of great acts of spite. Both Jane and I have been the recipient of her malice in the past. Also, I think when the cause suits her, she will use all methods at her disposal to get what...or whom, she wants."

"You mean Mr Darcy? Oh, I don't think you have any worries in that department, Lizzy. Mr Darcy only has eyes for you." He paused, before saying, "Don't think I have not seen how he watches you, my dear. There is a man who despite his best efforts, cannot hide his love and admiration for you."

Elizabeth smiled. It had not escaped her attention either that Mr Darcy's eyes had a habit of following her every move. One time, when talking to her dear friend Charlotte Lucas, she had expressed her annoyance at Mr Darcy's furtive observations. Charlotte had berated her, saying 'do not allow your fancy for Mr Wickham make you appear unpleasant in the eyes of a man ten times his consequence.'

Ten times his consequence? Yes, he probably was. Wickham certainly was not the man he pretended to be. His deplorable behaviour in Meryton had proven that. Mr Darcy would never have behaved so towards her, or any woman for that matter. Ten times his consequence? Indeed, he was.

"So, Lizzy, should I run the young pups off when they arrive? Is it possible there are other rich men waiting to sweep you and Jane off your feet?"

"I wish you would not do so just yet, Papa." Elizabeth looked at her father with a playful smile. "To do so would certainly fulfil all Miss Bingley's desires. Besides, I am sure there would be no living with Mamma if you did. No, there is always two sides to every story, and I am extremely interested in hearing what the gentlemen have to say."

Mr Bennet smiles. Elizabeth was wise beyond her twenty years, and sometimes, guided even him by example.

"The constable came to see me yesterday. He informed me there is no sign of Mr Wickham. I have heard many rumours about Mr Wickham and what he's been getting up to since he arrived in Meryton. I am told he has run up debts with almost every shopkeeper in town. And now, it appears he had deserted the militia and gone who knows where. I can't be unhappy about it though, Lizzy,"

Elizabeth was not surprised to hear this. Although it was probably for the best, she knew Lydia would be sad to hear this news.

"Oh, I thought Lydia might be in here," said Kitty as she burst into the breakfast room. Her disappointment at finding only Elizabeth and her father present was evident on her face, and in her tone.

"Lydia never joins Papa and me for breakfast, Kitty. Have you looked in her bedroom, all the bedrooms? Perhaps she is talking to Jane or Mary?"

"No, I have checked. Jane is waiting for Cissy to dress her hair, and Mary is writing in that diary she thinks no-one knows about."

"And Mamma?" Asked Elizabeth.

"Mamma is still asleep. I could hear her snoring."

"I expect she is exhausted from wrestling with her nerves all night," Mr Bennet said, feeling the need to defend his wife's unladylike emissions.

"Do you want me to help you look for her, Kitty?" Elizabeth offered, as she rose from the table.

Kitty nodded.

And so, they left Mr Bennet to finish his breakfast in peace.

After checking and rechecking every room in the house, and questioning all the servants, Elizabeth realised Lydia was no longer at Longbourn.

Knowing her father had returned to his study, Elizabeth made her way there to share this information.

"Gone! What do you mean gone? Speak clearly, child. Have you looked everywhere? All the rooms in the house? The bedrooms, the kitchen, the stables, the attics?" Mr Bennet asked with agitation.

"Yes sir, Lydia is nowhere to be found. Kitty and I have conducted a thorough search of all the house and gardens. Lydia is not to be found anywhere! I can only surmise she left either last night or early this morning. But judging by the tidiness of her bed, I would say she left last evening."

"And where would she go in the dark? She must know that our nearest neighbours or the Lucas's would send word of her arrival. Has there been such a note?"

"No, Papa, but..." Elizabeth paused, reluctant to put her thoughts into words.

"But? But what, Lizzy?"

"Two carriages left Longbourn last night, sir. Could she have been in one of those?"

"You think she has gone to Netherfield Park? For what purpose, may I ask?"

Before Elizabeth could answer, Hill knocked on the door and informed them that Mr Bingley and Mr Darcy had arrived.

"Begging your pardon, sir, but as the mistress is indisposed, and Miss Bennet is still not down, I thought Miss Elizabeth..."

"Yes, of course, Hill. Tell them I will be there directly," Elizabeth said. Then, turning back to face her father, she asked,

"The gentlemen may have news of Lydia. Will you come too, Papa?"

"Am I to understand that no-one had seen Miss Lydia since dinner last evening?" asked Mr Darcy.

"That is correct," confirmed Mr Bennet.

"And you say her bed appears unused?"

Elizabeth nodded.

Darcy looked at Charles, who returned his gaze, their faces etched with both worry and realisation.

Together, they said,

"Caroline!"

"You think Miss Bingley took Lydia to Netherfield? For what purpose, sir?" inquired Mr Bennet.

With Mr Bingley suddenly becoming reticent, while managing to flush scarlet, Darcy stepped forward to fill the breach.

"Not to Netherfield, sir, but to London.

"London!" squawked Mr Bennet.

"I fear so, sir. On our return to Netherfield yesterday, the butler informed Charles that Miss Bingley had returned only long enough to collect her maid. She then left instructions for her trunks to be forwarded to Mrs Hurst and then she left, taking my equipage. I think it entirely possible that Miss Bingley took Miss Lydia with her, but the only way to know that for sure is to go to London."

Mr Bennet could hardly believe what he was hearing. This time yesterday he was enjoying a friendly gossip with the constable and looking forward to the prospect of an excellent meal with their new acquaintances. Now, he had two daughters with possible broken engagements, the prospect of a distraught wife and a daughter run off to the city. How could everything change so rapidly?

"I suppose I must go with you?" Mr Bennet asked, hoping someone would say it was not necessary.

Instead, Mr Darcy not only agreed with him, but he asked if Elizabeth might accompany them too."

"Surely it would be better if Kitty went? Lydia is much closer to her than to me?" Elizabeth said practically.

Darcy turned to his betrothed.

"Perhaps so, Miss Elizabeth, but I cannot leave my sister alone at Netherfield while we search for Miss Lydia. Georgiana must return to London with us. Once there, I will prevail upon the kindness of our Aunt Matlock to care for her until this matter is resolved. She loves Georgiana like a daughter so it will be no hardship for her. Also, Georgiana told me that she likes you very much, Miss Elizabeth. With so little time remaining before our wedding, am I being selfish wishing to see you and Georgiana become better acquainted?" Darcy paused to let his words sink in, before adding, "It is for this reason, as well as your mature attitude, that I think it wiser if you, and not, Miss Catherine accompany us to town."

Elizabeth could not fault his reasoning.

Looking to her father, she asked,

"Papa?"

Mr Bennet could find no viable excuse why either he, or Elizabeth should remain at Longbourn. Reluctantly he agreed with Mr Darcy's Proposal.

From Darcy's point of view, any time spent with Elizabeth was time well spent. With their impending nuptials approaching ever nearer, he must indulge himself in Elizabeth's company at every opportunity.

Mr Bennet had no doubt they would find Lydia at Mrs Hursts. Having made her point, he hoped she would come home quietly and not make a scene

"Very well, you have my permission to join us, Lizzy. I had better send an express to Mr Gardiner and ask if we can impose on their hospitality."

"You must stay at Darcy House, sir. It will be no inconvenience, I assure you." Darcy offered.

It appeared all was arranged. Mr Bingley, Mr Darcy, Mr Bennet, Miss Darcy and Elizabeth would leave for London after luncheon.

"You think Mr Wickham is involved, sir?" asked Fletcher as he changed Darcy into his travelling outfit.

"You doubt it, Fletcher?" asked Darcy "The fifteen-year-old sister of the woman I am engaged to marry, goes missing, just days after being caught lying to her father, prompted by her association with Wickham. In my mind, there is no doubt that these events were put into motion, or at the very least suggested by, George Wickham. Miss Lydia is exactly the kind of stupid, ignorant and self-absorbed girl Wickham prefers. She is gullible and pliable, and will believe all the lies he feeds her, while blindly doing his bidding."

"I have not met the young lady, sir, but by your description, she sounds just the sort of girl Mr Wickham prefers to take advantage of."

Then, more to himself than to Fletcher, Darcy muttered,

"What I cannot fathom, is how Miss Bingley and Miss Lydia made the arrangements to meet. Lydia has not been allowed out of the house unaccompanied for days, and Miss Bingley learnt only yesterday of our engagements? When did they have time to plan this shenanigan?"

Then looking at Fletcher, he asked,

"Could it possibly be by chance that they met up?" then, shaking his head, he concluded, "Whichever it was, they both have a lot of questions to answer."

No-one was willing to admit that they had conveyed the news of Lydia's disappearance to Mrs Bennet, but the entire Bennet household was now privy to her lamentations.

"Oh, my baby. My dear, sweet girl, gone. Why would she do such a wicked thing? Oh, Lydia, you are breaking your mother's, heart. Not to mention the state of my poor nerves. I am frightened out of my wits for her safety, and I have such trembling's, and fluttering's, all over me. Spasms in my side and pains in my head and my heart is beating at such a rate that I am sure to get no rest by day or by night until Lydia is safely returned home. Oh, Lydia, my baby."

As objectionable as a trip to town was for Mr Bennet, on this occasion, he could not wait for the carriage to be brought round.

Chapter Eighteen

With Mr Darcy's carriage taken by Caroline and used to return her to London, Mr Darcy's party were forced to use Mr Bennet's old carriage to convey them to town. Though his horses were slower, the carriage was comfortable and spacious. However, not spacious enough to accommodate five adults. Therefore, Mr Darcy and Mr Bingley elected to follow the carriage on their own mounts.

For the entirety of the journey, conversation between the occupants of the vehicle was minimal. Everyone had much on their minds.

Georgiana's shyness at sharing a carriage with Mr Bennet forced her to bury her head in a book, and while Elizabeth had tried to engage the young girl in conversation several times, she abandoned her attempts when Miss Darcy managed to return only a smile.

Mr Bennet stared out of the window, lost in his own thoughts. Wondering how he was going to deal with Lydia when they met again. There was no doubt in his mind that Mrs Bennet would dismiss any attempts he made at chastising his wayward daughter or curtailing her freedom. Besides, that had already proven ineffective, as their journey today testified.

Occasionally, when his own thoughts let him, Mr Bennet would cast a sidelong glance at Elizabeth. To a less observant eye, it appeared she too was reading, but on closer inspection, Mr Bennet knew the page number had not altered for the last five miles.

Meanwhile, Elizabeth had decided if Lydia was safe and well when they found her, she was going to give her the scolding of her life.

Lydia was wilful, disobedient and argumentative, and their mother's continued adoration of her youngest child did nothing to curtail this behaviour.

In Mrs Bennet's opinion, Lydia could do no wrong. Yet, her other children were hard pressed to gain a compliment that was not somehow sullying with a caustic remark.

Jane was beautiful, but would never catch a husband if she did not show more affection than she truly felt.

Mary's sermonising would someday save many lives, she was sure, but as for a husband...well, maybe a convent.

Kitty was a nice enough child, with nice enough manners, but she must learn to shine more or she would end up an old maid.

And Elizabeth, well Elizabeth had long ago given up on her mother being pleased with anything she said or did. That was until Mr Darcy turned up on their doorstep with an offer of marriage. Of that she was ecstatic, but the complaining still did not abate. *Elizabeth, you must find out if Mr Darcy prefers cake or trifle? Elizabeth, ask Mr Darcy if he likes meat best or fowl? Elizabeth, why haven't you put the blue dress on, Mr Darcy said the colour particularly suited you?* In her mother's eyes, she could do no right. Only Lydia escaped the critical eye and opinions of their mother. And now, when her time should be spent getting better acquainted with the man she was to marry, they were chasing over town looking for her runaway sister.

The gentlemen had all agreed it would be prudent to see the ladies safely inside Darcy House before they continued to Mrs Hurst's residence. Once there, they would all confront Caroline and Lydia together.

Mr Bennet helped Elizabeth alight from the carriage, and then Darcy handed his sister down.

"Tomorrow, you will go to stay with Aunt Matlock, but until then, perhaps you could give Miss Bennet a tour of the house, and show her to her room?" he asked Georgiana.

Georgiana smiled at her brother and nodded.

"Of course, Fitzwilliam."

Darcy looked over to where Elizabeth waited on the path for Georgiana. They shared a look of mutual understanding, and then Elizabeth gave him a faltering smile.

A momentary feeling of elation touched Darcy's heart, warmed by the thought that Elizabeth had smiled at him. It was nothing, and something and he rejoiced in this small and simple gesture from his beloved Elizabeth.

The ladies disappeared into Darcy's London residence, and then Darcy and his companions climbed into the carriage.

Soon, it was winding its way through the streets of London, the atmosphere inside was sombre and silent.

Mr Bingley fidgeted in his seat, turning this way and that until finally, Mr Darcy felt compelled to ask,

"Do you wish to change seats, Charles?"

Bingley stopped moving, pursed his lips and looked to the floor.

"My seat is quite comfortable, thank you, Darcy."

"Then what is it?"

Relieved that he could unburden himself, Bingley twisted to face the other gentleman, and said,

"It's Caroline. You know how she is, Darcy. She never listens to anything I say, and can be quite intimidating."

Darcy sighed. Caroline, as the youngest of the Bingley siblings, had apparently always managed to get her own way, even from an early age. Now, as an adult, she still expected to have her every whim catered for, and ever idea approved of and acted upon. She often talked over people, ignoring their words and advice, and did virtually as she pleased. Only he, it seemed, held any sway over her. But that was before he had become engaged to Elizabeth.

Darcy knew he should not interfere between Bingley and his sister, but he also knew Charles was too weak to reel Caroline in alone.

"I can help if you like, Charles?" Darcy offered.

"Oh, would you, Darcy? Caroline always heeds your advice."

"Mmm," was all the reply Darcy could offer.

Their visit to forty-two Briar Crescent was relatively brief. The butler showed them into the drawing room and then went to inform his mistress of their arrival.

Mrs Hurst walked in first, entering in a dignified manner, and greeted her guests politely, before seating herself in a chair by the fire.

Caroline, on the other hand, swept in like a hurricane. Flinging open the door and then pausing in the portal for dramatic effect, before entering the room fully.

No-one knew quite what to expect or where to begin, but Caroline's voice was both aggressive and defensive, while her manner was unrepentant and defiant.

"If you think I am going to apologise you have had a wasted journey," she said haughtily.

Caroline's anger was evident, not only in her words and actions but by the fierce flush that covered her cheeks, which clashed with the burnt orange dress she was wearing.

Darcy and Mr Bingley deferred to Mr Bennet, giving him the floor to first question Caroline about Miss Lydia's whereabouts.

"Miss Bingley, I am an old man and dislike leaving my manor to travel the city at the best of times, but you have managed to not only rouse me from my home, but you have also succeeded in being the first woman to arouse my anger. Where is my daughter?"

Caroline looked at Mr Bennet with the usual sneer of contempt she bestowed on everyone who was not Darcy.

"Why would I know where Miss Lydia is, I am not her keeper?"

Roused to go even further, Mr Bennet said,

"I did not mention Lydia by name, madam. Now, do you deny carrying my daughter off in Mr Darcy's carriage last evening?"

Caroline was on the verge of confirming her denial but realised there was no point. She had hoped Mr Darcy would come alone with her brother, but she knew by the set of his jaw and the steely cold glare in his eyes, that the likelihood of them ever being alone together again was minuscule.

"I do deny it, sir?" she said brazenly, "however, when I left Hertfordshire I did allow a runaway to ride inside my carriage rather than the storage box where I found them."

"And this runaway was Lydia, my daughter?"

"It was."

"So, where is she now? Bring her down at once so that we may be on our way." Mr Bennet said impatiently.

A slow smile spread over Caroline's face as she moved a few steps closer to Mr Bennet, and whispered,

"I cannot, she is not here."

"Not here?" echoed Mr Bennet, "Then where is she, madam?"

Caroline sauntered over to where Mr Darcy was standing. Leaning unnecessarily close to him, she lowered her chin and raised her eyes, trying to look coquettish.

Then, in her best come-hither voice, she greeted Mr Darcy,

"Fitzwilliam."

There was a sharp intake of breath from everyone present at Caroline's blatant breach of protocol, but this time, it was her brother who reprimanded her.

"Caroline! Have you no shame?" asked Mr Bingley, "Darcy is an engaged man."

"Mr Darcy's refined manners will be wasted on that country chit," Caroline said huskily, ignoring her brother's rebuke.

Sidling up even close to Darcy, Caroline raised her hand and softly caressed his cheek, saying,

"What Mr Darcy needs is a woman, a real woman, a sophisticated woman. What Fitzwilliam Darcy needs…is me."

No-one, least of all Caroline, saw Mr Darcy raise his hand, it was done so swiftly and so silently. Grabbing Caroline's wrist in a firm hold, Darcy purposely forced it away from his face.

"You forget yourself, madam," Darcy said, the coldness in his voice enough matched the steeliness of his eyes.

Caroline tried to break his hold, but Darcy had more to say.

"Elizabeth Bennet is no country chit, madam; she is ten times the woman you are. She is kind and caring and thoughtful. She is affable and honest and righteous. Intelligent and witty and generous." Pausing to draw in a calming breath, he continued thus, "Elizabeth is dependable and loyal and respectful. And moreover, she is beautiful both inside and out. Something which you can no longer lay claim to, Miss Bingley. The vitriol, anger, and malice you choose to rain upon others have damaged your beauty beyond repair. And you madam, are the last woman I would ask to be my wife!" Darcy finally released Miss Bingley's hand, thrusting it away with enough force to twist Caroline away from him.

The room was silent.

A wave of humiliation engulfed Caroline who instantly began to sob.

It was at this point that Mrs Hurst intervened. She hurried over to her sister and put a consoling arm around her shoulders.

"Come, sister, tell them what they need to know and then they will leave us in peace."

"Never!" spat Caroline through her ragged sobs.

Louisa Hurst had not always agreed with her sister's action, and indeed this was one of those times. However, she was still her younger sister, and although it was evident to everyone else that Mr Darcy had no interest in her, Caroline had just had her heart broken. Her actions could not be condoned, but they could be explained.

"Very well, I will tell them," said Mrs Hurst, wanting to bring this unpleasant meeting to a conclusion.

"Mr Bennet, Miss Lydia was not the only passenger my sister picked up last night. As the carriage neared the crossroads just outside Meryton, Lydia begged my sister to stop. Immediately the horses had come to a halt, a man in uniform opened the door and climbed in. Apparently, Miss Lydia was not running away, Mr Bennet; she was eloping."

Mr Bingley and Mr Bennet looked at each other and then at Mr Darcy, but Mr Darcy's eyes had remained on Caroline.

In a low, guttural voice, he asked,

"Who was it, Miss Bingley?"

Caroline shook her head and buried her face in her hands. She could not bear for any of them to look at her.

With some gentle coaxing from Mrs Hurst, Caroline's weeping momentarily subsided.

Seizing this opportunity, Darcy repeated his question.

"Tell me who climbed into the carriage, Miss Bingley?"

Raising her tear-sodden eyes just long enough to meet Mr Darcy's stare, she shouted,

"It was Mr Wickham. Miss Lydia was eloping with George Wickham."

Chapter Nineteen

The journey back to Darcy House was a sombre one, with each of the gentlemen lost in their own thoughts. It wasn't until they had closed the study door behind them that the issue was again raised.

Mr Bingley, who had never had to deal with anything so unsavoury as an elopement before, was at a loss to know where to begin looking for Miss Lydia. He felt all the weight of Caroline's behaviour and involvement on his shoulders, and desperately wanted to make reparation to Mr Bennet. After all, such a scandalous happening could jeopardise his chance of marrying Jane.

"I suppose we should inform the runners, and hope they locate Miss Lydia and Wickham before any damage is done?" Mr Bingley asked naively.

"I am afraid the moment Lydia met that worthless young man the damage was done," sighed Mr Bennet.

Until now, Mr Darcy had appeared to be listening to his companion's debate. Their suggestions of, send for the runners, scour the street, inform the magistrate, were all good ones, had it not been George Wickham they were dealing with.

He, however, knew exactly what to do next.

Darcy was no stranger to the baser instincts that George Wickham possessed. Having shared rooms with him at university, Darcy had witnessed first-hand how licentious and debauched Wickham's behaviour could be. If they were to rescue Lydia with her maidenhood intact, every second counted.

"Enough speculation, gentlemen. The runners are too slow and too few. They have no idea of what Wickham is capable of. I, on the other hand, know just the person to ask where Mr Wickham would hide with a young girl."

Mr Bingley and Mr Bennet looked at Darcy with anticipation, as they waited for him to elaborate.

"Due to the nature of her involvement with my family, I have for almost a year now had a certain, Mrs Younge's whereabouts relayed to me every month. The woman has moved around the country several times, but never too far from her accomplice. I propose to pay her a visit directly. Once I have ascertained the location of Wickham's hiding place, you may join me if you wish. Though I must warn you, George Wickham has a dark side to his nature, one which we are likely to encounter when we find him."

Neither Mr Bennet, being a man who liked to exert himself as little as possible, nor Mr Bingley, a young and somewhat unworldly gentleman, argued to accompany Darcy on his fact-finding mission.

And so, Darcy set on his own to confront the woman who had betrayed his trust and almost led Georgiana into ruin.

Darcy stood rapping on the door of the address his lawyer had supplied him with some weeks ago. Several flecks of old paint flake off as his silver topped cane made contact with the wood.

No answer.

Darcy knocked again, this time with increased force.

As he strained to catch any sound of habitation, Darcy could hear the faint sound of voices.

Knocking for the third time, Darcy shouted through the wooden structure.

"I know you are in there. I can hear you talking."

For a few seconds, all fell silent; then a chair could be heard as it was dragged across the floor.

Losing his patience, Darcy shouted even louder,

"OPEN THIS DOOR!"

Glaring at the door handle, Darcy was relieved to see it begin to turn.

The instant a crack appeared, Darcy thrust his foot into the opening and added some weight behind his shoulder to force it open.

What he found on the other side of the door, shocked him speechless for a moment.

Before him, in what could only be described as rags, were several young children. The tatters of clothes that hung from their emaciated bodies were covered in stains, of what appeared to be a combination of food, beer, and human fluids. Their faces and matted, hacked hair were almost as dirty as their bare feet. His heart lurched as the sight of such neglect.

The terrified children huddled together behind the half-open door, their saucer-like eyes peering up at the official looking gentleman who had just stepped in from the street.

Darcy cast his eyes over the group of children and then singled out a girl of about seven years of age.

"Are you the oldest?" Darcy asked.

The girl nodded.

"Where are your parents, child?"

His soft reassuring voice gave the girl confidence to speak, and she replied,

"Dead, sir."

As Darcy considered the face of the girl, he thought he saw something familiar, but instantly shook it off.

"Are *all* your parent's dead?"

"Yes, sir. That's why we live at the orphanage."

It was an answer Darcy had not expected. Apparently, Mrs Younge had found a more lucrative form of employment than that of a companion.

Before he could question them further, a young woman of about eighteen years walked in through the half open door.

Immediately, she began to berate the children for opening the door.

"What had the mistress told you? You are not to be seen and not to be heard. Now..."

She stopped mid-sentence as she finally realised they were not alone. Her eyes quickly assessed Darcy, who was standing fully in the hallway. She could see he was a gentleman, and obviously not pleased about something.

"I am sorry if these little beggars have been bothering you, sir. They all know better than to come out of the dormitory." She gave them a scowl, but the smile that followed told them her anger was not sincere. "They sometimes sneak out when the mistress goes out. Was she expecting you, sir?"

Darcy watched as the children scampered to the girl and cleaved to her legs, vying for her attention. They trust her. Some small ray of sunshine in what he could only surmise was a meagre and wretched existence.

His all-encompassing glance, though brief, missed nothing. Her face was scrubbed clean, and her cheeks were rosy from being out in the cold. Her hair was tied back with a brightly coloured piece of cloth, and pinned to her head was a straw hat that had seen better days. She wore a grey dress that was a little too big for her slender frame, and the black boots on her feet were scuffed at the toes and heels. A thin shawl rested on her shoulders, which would have afforded her little protection from the December air. Her hands were ungloved and chapped red, probably from manual labour. Resting in the crook of her arm was a wicker basket, its size exaggerated by its merger contents. Only a small loaf of bread and a trifling cube of cheese lay lost on the bottom of the carrier.

Deciding his tactics, Darcy quickly ascertained he would gain more information from this young woman if he befriended her, rather than browbeat her.

"I'm afraid it is my fault, they only opened the door because I was insistent. Your mistress, Mrs Younge, will she be very long...?" he asked.

Reassured by his soft, almost jovial tone, the girl replied,

"Sarah." She smiled shyly. "A while I would think. The mistress has gone to see her special friend. I understand he is just back from the country."

It must be Wickham, Darcy thought.

Intent on winning her trust, and wanting to inspect more of the premises, Darcy asked for a glass of beer, and then followed her through into what she called, the best parlour.

Every fibre of his being rebelled against sitting on the shabby and filthy furniture, but he forced himself to take the glass of beer from Sarah's hand, sit down and take a small sip.

Putting the glass to one side, he asked,

"Your mistress is thinking of getting married?"

"Oh, no, sir." Sarah laughed. "Apparently, they have been friends for years, ever since Mr Wickham was at university. The mistress said she was going to interview a new maid Mr Wickham had found for her. Then, if things work out, I will be promoted to Mrs Younge's assistant, and she might be able to give me a small wage."

The 'new maid,' must be Lydia. So, it appeared Wickham never had any intention of marrying the girl. His only plan was to use Lydia as a mean of extorting financial remuneration from Darcy.

Returning to the task at hand, and trying not to sound too eager, Darcy asked,

"You do not get paid at present, Sarah?"

"Lord, no sir. There's scarcely enough money to put food on the table for the little ones, never mind pay me a wage. I do the best I can for them, but there's no money left over for luxuries like soap, and

Lord knows they could all do with some better clothes. And as for their hair, well I have to keep it short because they keep getting lice."

"So how will getting a new maid make things better, Sarah?"

"Oh, the mistress said Mr Wickham is owed some money from an inheritance. Some rich man died and left him hundreds in his will, thousands I shouldn't wonder. If the mistress takes on the new maid, Mr Wickham has promised to pay her twenty pounds a year towards the orphanage."

"And the children, Sarah, where do the children come from? Are they all from one family? They bear a striking resemblance to one another, in fact, there is something vaguely familiar about them," he said, looking from one dark head to another.

"No, sir, not one family. The mistress sometimes goes away, maybe for a few weeks, or like last year, many months. But when she comes back, she usually has a new baby with her. We have seven now."

A rather unsavoury and shocking thought was evolving in Darcy's mind. Surely even Wickham could not sink so low.

"More beer, sir?"

Darcy shook his head and then smiled at the young woman

"Tell me, Sarah, where might I find Mrs Younge and her friend Wickham?"

She blushed, and then replied,

"Wickham has taken rooms down at the docks, sir. I think he is staying at The Wooden Peg Inn."

Having got the information he needed, Darcy made ready to leave. Taking Sarah by the arm, he moved towards the front door.

However, this young girl and her attempts to care for these poor unfortunates had touched him.

Giving her the only thing he could, Darcy reached into his pocket, he pulled out a gold sovereign.

"Sarah, you have been most helpful today. Here is a gold sovereign, do with it what you will, but do not tell your mistress I was here."

Mesmerised by the glint of gold, Sarah took the coin from Darcy's fingers and turned it over in her hand. She knew exactly what she was going to buy. Soap to wash the children and their clothes, alcohol to rid them of the lice, and enough beef and vegetables to make a stew to fill their bellies for days.

Remembering her manners, she breathlessly said,

"Thank you, sir." And she bobbed an awkward curtsy.

Darcy put his hat on, intending to leave, but then an idea stopped him in his tracks.

Pausing in the doorway, Darcy turned back to the girl.

"Sarah, do you like working here, looking after the children?" he asked.

"Oh, yes, sir, I like looking after the children very much. They don't have anyone else to love them, you see. No parent or brothers or sisters. No aunts or uncles or cousins or grandparents. Just me."

"And do you not have any relatives, Sarah? Someone who could take care of you?"

"No, sir. Mrs Younge took me from an orphanage too."

"Do you like the city, Sarah, or would you like to live in the country?"

"Oh, I couldn't leave the children, sir. I love them like they are my own brothers and sisters." Sarah said, putting her arms around the two nearest waifs.

"I meant you and the children. You could all have new clothes; the children could go to school, and you would all have plenty of food for the table?"

"Oh, sir, it would be like a dream come true."

Darcy smiled.

"Then I shall return, but remember, tell no-one I was here."

Chapter Twenty

Darcy had much to think about during the carriage ride back to his Grosvenor Square residence. An alarming thought was burrowing its way through his mind, and the conclusion it was heading towards was not one he wanted to believe. Could Wickham really sink that low, be that vile? Was it possible that Wickham had fathered all those children now in the care of Mrs Younge and Sarah? He obviously has no interest in marrying their mothers, or being a father to them, so why gather them all under one roof? Extortion? Blackmail? Could it possibly be the way Wickham had been funding his lifestyle? Sarah's information pointed towards Mrs Younge arriving on the scene of each girl's confinement, and then removing the unwanted child. No doubt to the relief of the families involved, who were probably still paying Mrs Younge for her silence and the child's upkeep, such as it was.

Too many questions, he did not know the answer too. But one thing he was sure of, having discovered the existence of these unwanted and unloved children, Darcy, being the man that he was, could not leave them in the care of a woman such as Mrs Younge.

Striding straight through the house to his study, Darcy expecting to find Mr Bennet and Bingley waiting for him, eager to be off. However, to Darcy disgust and annoyance, he found them both reclined on a chair and a sofa, asleep. No doubt having enjoyed a hearty lunch and a glass of his port, the rigours of the day had proved too much for them both.

Rousing Bingley with a kick to his boot, and tapping Mr Bennet firmly on the shoulder, Darcy informed his sleepy companions that he had discovered the whereabouts of Wickham.

Seeing their lack of response and enthusiasm, Darcy sternly reminded them that they should leave now, or risk Lydia's ruin.

Both gentlemen professed a need to refresh themselves before setting off, and so Darcy was left to cool his heels in his study while waiting for them return.

Some minutes had passed when a quiet tapping came on the door. Darcy, thinking it was Charles or Mr Bennet returning, barked, "Come."

Elizabeth cautiously opened the door and peered inside.

"May I join you?" she asked.

Jumping to his feet, Darcy cleared his throat and beckoned her to enter.

"Miss Darcy is resting, so I came to see if there was any news of my sister?"

A wave of emotion swept over Darcy as he saw his betrothed standing before him, her face etched with worry and concern for a sister who cared for no-one but herself.

Darcy could not bear for her to be in pain or to suffer anguish. When he had proposed to Elizabeth, he had promised to not only love her, but to protect her too. Yet, he had selfishly brought her to London to be at his side while he pursued Wickham and her sister all over the city. Embarrassed and ashamed of his selfishness Darcy felt the need to actually, physically, protect and comfort her.

Unconsciously acting on this urge, Darcy stepped forward and pulled Elizabeth into a tight embrace. Folding his arms around her back, pulling her body into the circle of his love and care, gently placing a kiss on her dark curls.

For some reason, Elizabeth accepted Darcy's embrace, welcomed his reassuring arms and comforting kiss. It no longer felt strange to be held by him, embraced by him or kissed by him. It almost felt…natural now.

"I think I have located them, Elizabeth," he said hoping to reassure her. "If my information is correct, there is hope we may return Miss Lydia to her family unharmed."

Darcy felt some of the tension leave Elizabeth's body as her shoulders slumped and she released a soft sigh.

"I have been to see a former employee of mine, one I knew had a long-standing association with Wickham."

"Did they know where Lydia was?" Elizabeth asked urgently.

"She was from home when I arrived, but her maid was very forthcoming. Apparently, Mrs Younge now runs an orphanage, although I suspect it only has one patron. Sarah, the maid, informed me her mistress was expecting Wickham to shortly be in the position to supply her with not only a regular, annual income of twenty pounds…but also a new serving girl."

Elizabeth now raised her eyes and looked questioningly at Darcy

"Though it is as I feared, Wickham does not intend to marry Miss Lydia, but only use her to extort money from me, we can act swiftly to foil Wickham's plans. We also have the element of surprise, so I am hopeful of a successful recovery, Elizabeth."

His words had the desired effect, and Elizabeth did feel reassured, and comforted.

With her head again resting on Darcy's shoulder, and his strong arms still wrapped around her body, Elizabeth could not help but feel safe and secure, insulated against any trouble that may come her way.

"It is hard to believe that a man who appeared so full of goodness and charm and kindness, could mask his true character so completely. How easily he fooled us all." Elizabeth said with both bitterness and humiliation.

Her previous treatment and harsh words which she had levied at Mr Darcy had been almost entirely fuelled by her belief in Wickham's lies. Lies she had been only too ready to believe. And all because Darcy had bruised her vanity. How she wished she had not been so vocal in her dislike of him, using her wit to malign and disparage him whenever the opportunity arose.

Humbled, she quietly said,

"We do not deserve such kindness from you, sir...I do not deserve such kindness from you. Mr Darcy...Fitzwilliam, I have not always been complimentary when your name arose in conversation. I am sorry. I did not know you as I do now."

"We neither perform at our best in front of strangers, Elizabeth. I can forgive you anything that occurred before we were engaged."

"But I said..." she began, but Darcy put his finger to her lips to silence her.

"My darling, you were free to express your opinion of me as you wished...before we were betrothed. Now, I just ask that you are more circumspect with your displeasure towards me in the future."

He moved his finger and let it run over her cheek, savouring the softness of her skin. He lifted her chin and lowered his face towards her face, testing to see if she shied away, but when Elizabeth remained open to his advance, he bent down to kiss her.

At that moment, Bingley and Mr Bennet entered, saying,

"Come, Darcy, no time to tarry." much to Darcy's chagrin.

Darcy rapped on the bedroom door at The Wooden Peg Inn with his cane.

Movement could be heard inside, but it was several minutes before anyone came to open it.

Peeping out of the three-inch crack, was Wickham, a look of incredulity on his face.

"Darcy!" he exclaimed.

"Open the door, Wickham, we need to talk," Darcy said stonily.

Instantly, the confident fraudster reappeared, and Wickham said,

"Do we, Darcy? Pray, what's on your mind?"

Keeping control of his anger, Darcy replied,

"Lydia Bennet, George. Is she in there with you? Let me speak to her?"

"Miss Bennet? Why yes, she is, Darcy. Unfortunately, Lydia is indisposed at present, and cannot come to the door."

"What ails her, George? Does she need to see a physician?" Darcy asked with concern.

Peering over his shoulder, Wickham laughed, then turned back to say,

"Sorry, old man, she's a little tied up at present."

Darcy stood silent for a moment, considering what his next move should be. Was Lydia really ill? Or was it a ruse by Wickham to get them to leave so he could move them?

Darcy concluded it was the latter.

"May I at least speak to, Miss Bennet?"

"No!" Wickham said and then tried to close the door.

Unfortunately for Wickham, Darcy had anticipated this move and had surreptitiously put his foot, and his cane in the opening, preventing it from closing.

"I really must insist, George," Darcy said, his voice as cold as ice.

Darcy began to push on the door with his free hand, but it did not give. Wickham must have something lodged on the other side.

Mr Bennet had done as Darcy asked. He had stayed back and let Darcy talk to Wickham alone. But now, with the prospect of them having to leave without even speaking to Lydia, it was too much for him.

Standing on his tiptoes, he called out to his errant daughter over the top of Darcy's head.

"Lydia, Lydia Bennet, are you in there, come to your father this instance?"

Darcy cursed under his breath, irritated that Mr Bennet has shown Wickham, their hand. The only consolation was that Wickham knew he was not alone.

If Darcy expected Wickham to capitulate and open the door fully, he was sadly mistaken.

"Papa, papa, don't leave me." Came a muffled cry.

Distorted, but clearly the voice of Lydia Bennet, it prompted her father into action.

Mr Bennet pushed forward and stood by Darcy's side.

Wearing his sternest frown and wagging his finger in Wickham's face, he said,

"Young man, I demand to see my daughter this instant."

"Get back, old man," Wickham scowled.

Deciding this toing and froing was getting them nowhere, Darcy moved Mr Bennet to one side, and now put his shoulder to the door.

Slowly, as the door began to inch back revealing more of the room behind, Darcy called to the others to help him.

"I wouldn't if I were you, Darcy," Wickham said in a menacing tone.

At first, Darcy was ignorant of his meaning, but some movement caught his eye, and he looked down. Wickham was pointing a pistol at him.

Darcy held up his hand to forestall the other gentlemen coming to his aid. If the pistol was loaded, Wickham only had one shot, but what if he had more than one gun?

Darcy took a moment to straighten his clothes.

"Very well, George, what is it you want?" Darcy asked in a bored tone.

Wickham thrust his face into the opening and hissed,

"I want what you owe me, what is due to me. The living your father promised me and an annual income."

Remaining calm, Darcy reasoned with him.

"But George, I have already compensated you for that living. Did you not declared that the life of a cleric would not suit you? You cannot expect me to pay you twice. Where's the fairness in that?"

"Fair, fair, you dare speak to me of fair. I have had to scratch out a living since your father died. I have had to do the vilest things imaginable to try and get by, and all because you would not give me a decent inheritance."

"First, George, let's not forget I compensated you with three thousand pounds for the Kympton living; plus, one thousand pounds from my father's estate, as stipulated in his will. Four thousand pounds in total, George. That should have lasted the son of a steward a lifetime. You have to agree, George, that is an awful lot of money."

"You *could* have given me more, but you *chose* not to. It's because you were jealous, jealous of the love your father showered on me," and then to add the final insult, he said, "He always did prefer me to you."

"Maybe so, George, but *I* am his son, and *you* are still only the son of our steward."

"Quite so, Darcy." Said the faint but clearly audible voice of Mr Bingley.

Bingley had stepped in at the wrong time.

As Darcy expected, Wickham slammed the door shut.

The three gentlemen were left standing on the other side of the closed door, no closer to retrieving Lydia than they were when they arrived.

The slamming of iron against iron told them that Wickham had bolted the door. Even if Wickham didn't have the pistol in his hand now, there would be no point in trying to break the door down. These old dockland inns were solidly built, meant to withstand time, tides and salt water for years to come.

As they turned to leave, the soft muffled sobs of the young woman filtered through the cracks of the beams and door frames.

Mr Bennet turned back, intent on rescuing his child, but Darcy put out his arm to forestall him.

"If we want to win the war, we must concede defeat in this battle, my friend."

Reluctantly, Mr Bennet let Darcy usher him out and back into the carriage.

Chapter Twenty-One

It had been a long day. On their return to Darcy's townhouse, Miller, the butler, informed them that the ladies had retired some time ago.

Bingley and Darcy had not realised that the hour had grown so late, but Mr Bennet, being twice their age, felt every year of his age. Country life was lived at a much slower pace than the city, and having been here only a few hours, it reminded Mr Bennet of just why he seldom ventured from his own patch.

The men ate a cold repast in relative silence, and when Darcy excused himself on the pretext of estate business to attend to, both Mr Bingley and a very grateful Mr Bennet retired for the evening.

With the door of his study firmly closed behind him, Darcy quickly despatched a footman to deliver a hurriedly scribbled note to his cousin, Colonel Richard Fitzwilliam.

Richard,
I am in need of your military expertise.
Please come to Darcy House as soon as possible.
It is a matter of urgency.
Your cousin,
FD

Darcy was not idle as he waited for Richard to arrive. Going to the bookcase to the left of his desk, Darcy pulled out a tatty looking leather-bound book. Returning to his chair, he opened the book, but not to read.

Inside, the book was hollowed out, leaving a secret compartment for the owner to conceal whatever they wished.

Carefully, Darcy removed several small sheets of paper, which were held together with a thin piece of red ribbon.

He spread them out over his desk. There were more than even he remembered, eleven piles in all, each of more than a dozen notes. They were promissory notes issued in lieu of payment, all wrote by Wickham.

Taking a clean sheet of paper and a quill, Darcy began to write.

Cambridge	£259 6s 8d	Complete
Oxford	£ 26 18s 7d	C.
Windsor	£ 34 9s 11d	C.
Aldershot	£ 43 16s 2d	C.
High Wycombe	£ 60 2s 3d	C.
Basingstoke	£ 63 3s 6d	C.
Rochester	£ 84 12s 8d	C.
Dartford	£109 11s 2d	C.
Harrow	£124 4s 10d	C.
Watford	£143 12s 8d	C.
Meryton	£188 7s 4d	amount to date
Total	**£1,138 5s 9d**	

The list went on and on. Everywhere that Wickham had lived, he had run up debts. Everywhere Wickham had run up debts, so Darcy had paid them off. There were debts for clothes and boots. For lodging, food, drink and gambling. Wickham had even paid for his pleasures of the flesh with an I.O.U. Apparently, Wickham paid for nothing with cash.

For three years now Darcy had been settling Wickham's debts and buying up his gaming markers and promissory notes. Not to save him from the debtor's prison, or even worse, deportation, but so that the honest tradesmen and merchants, the tailors, and cobblers, and blacksmiths could continue going about their business and feeding their families, instead of struggling to make ends meet when Wickham failed to pay his due.

Before him, Darcy spread out the map he had marked tracing Wickham's travels. Each marker was a testament to where Wickham had honed his ability to charm, trick and deceive innocent people into lending him money and goods in ever increasing amounts.

Starting at Cambridge, he had then skirted around the capital, staying in towns where the inhabitants would be more susceptible to his form of refined and polished charm. Each time he moved on, he appeared to have become bolder, and the level of debt rose accordingly.

The Cambridge debt, which included Wickham's time at the university had been the largest so far. Darcy had paid it to honour his father's wishes, who had died just days after he graduated with honours. Unsurprisingly, Wickham had failed to graduate.

"My God Darcy! Are *all* these Wickham's debts? There is enough money owed here to feed my men for a year!" exclaimed the colonel.

Darcy had been so intent on the task at hand, he had failed to hear his cousin arrive.

Moving to greet him, hand outstretched, Darcy said,

"Good evening, Richard. Yes, but these are only the ones I know about. I am certain there are many more out there that I do not know about."

"This must run into thousands, Darcy? Have you paid them all?"

Darcy nodded.

"Then you're a fool. Your father liked Wickham, but not to this extent. You have served your father's memory well, cousin, now let Wickham find his own fate. He will either tighten his belt or find himself in debtor's prison."

Richard was right, and Darcy knew this, but he still felt accountable for Wickham's foul deeds. As for Richard, he only knew the life of a soldier, responsible for his men and himself. Darcy's burden was much heavier, with the well-being of whole families.

Colonel Richard Fitzwilliam had spent his formative years growing up with Darcy and Wickham, although he was a few years older than them.

Being the second son of an earl, he had a choice of careers. Join the church, join the army or navy, or lead an idle life of frivolity and boredom. As there was already a bishop and a black sheep in the family, he had decided to join the army. So, at the tender age of fourteen, his father bought him a lieutenant's commission in the military. By the age of sixteen, he was in command of his own battalion of one thousand men, fighting a little know general called Napoleon Bonaparte on the Italian peninsula. Although commended for his bravery and promoted to Major, he had barely escaped with his life.

Undeterred, Major Fitzwilliam had badgered his commanding officer to send him to Egypt, where once again Napoleon was waging war.

Though the British troops initially pushed Napoleon's armies back to Switzerland, when Russian retreated from the fray, Bonaparte advanced once more.

Over the next few years, Richard's bravery and leadership were rewarded with two further promotions, until he attained the rank which he now held, Colonel.

With the Treaty of Amiens, signed in 1802, England enjoyed a small respite from the rigours of war, but all too soon the French and the English were again battling one another.

Then, Richard and a few of his best men were drafted into a small elite group of soldiers by the Duke of Wellington, splitting their time between England's shores and undercover trips to the continent. Fortunately, for Darcy, Richard was in the country at this time.

"So, what has he been up to now?" Richard asked.

Darcy filled Richard in on all that had occurred in the last three months, including his engagement to Elizabeth and Lydia's foolish elopement.

"I warned you that Bingley's sister had her eye on you," he joked.

"I rather think her eye was on Pemberley, cousin, not me. Besides, is that all you took from what I just said?" Darcy asked.

"Of course not. You are engaged, Bingley is engaged, and Wickham is up to his old trick. But Wickham must be the task we tackle first. So, what's the plan?"

Darcy had given much thought to what could be done about Wickham. He could buy him off and hope Lydia Bennet was unsoiled. Or, he could call in George's debts, the result being he would then be thrown into debtor's prison. Or, the most ungentlemanly choice of all, he could challenge Wickham to a duel, though Darcy knew that would be an unfair fight. He far outstripped Wickham in both shooting and fencing, in which case, it would be murder. Then there was the legal complication. Duelling was illegal, and he was a magistrate; both components rules fighting out in Darcy's eyes.

Relating all this to his cousin, Richard watched as Darcy fought against his emotions, fought against what he would like to do to Wickham, and what was the right and moral thing to do.

Richard put his arm on Darcy's shoulder, and said,

"Darcy, my friend, I can see the turmoil this causes you, feel the pain it gives you. Let *me* deal with Wickham. I can promise you he will trouble you no more. Just say the word."

"Thank you, Richard, but killing Wickham would not sit well with my conscience. I understand as a soldier you have seen, and done many things in the name of our country, but killing Wickham in cold blood? No, it would just be murder."

"I know your scruples would not allow me to harm him, Darcy, but let me remove him from your life, forever. I promise I won't harm a hair on his head," Richard said and raised his hand in mock horror.

"You could do that? With no injury to Wickham?" Darcy asked with hope.

"I promise. I will not harm a hair on Wickham's head." Richard repeated.

Darcy mulled Richard's offer over in his head. To be rid of Wickham forever was something he had wished many times in the past.

"Very well. But first I must rescue Miss Lydia from his clutches. Then, and only then, will he be yours."

"And how do you intend to do that?" Richard asked.

"Simple," Darcy answered, "Give him what he wants."

Elizabeth had tried to sleep, but her mind was in turmoil. As she paces to and fro in her bed chamber, she pondered the events of the last two weeks.

She had come to terms with her engagement almost immediately and had since felt her regard for Darcy grow steadily, to the point where she had willed him to kiss her that afternoon. Their encounter in the music room had awakened her to feelings and emotions that were new and exciting and exhilarating, and she longed to repeat them. Blushing at her own brazen thoughts, Elizabeth reminded herself that her wedding was only weeks away. And Darcy, what of him? He seemed a different man to the one that had arrogantly strode into the assembly rooms at Meryton, derisively viewing the town folk with boredom and condescension. Somehow, together, they had begun to grow into a couple. This reassured her that her future, although thrust upon her unexpectedly, was something to look forward to and embrace as a new adventure. That was until Lydia eloped with George Wickham, throwing everything up in the air.

Indeed, Lydia had done many a selfish thing in the past, but this was beyond comparison. And Mr Darcy, well hopefully he was going to be the one to restore her to her family.

Elizabeth recalled when Miss Bingley had said, 'Darcy is a man without fault.' At the time, she had scoffed at the idea of a perfect man, but with every passing day, Darcy proved Miss Bingley's words correct.

Giving herself a mental shake, she decided, she must try to get *some* sleep. These things would still be there on the morrow. Tonight, she must rest.

Knowing a book would aid her to sleep, she looked around to see if there were any in her room. There were none.

Deciding to venture downstairs to look for one, Elizabeth made her way down to the first floor, where she now knew Darcy's study was situated.

When she saw the faint glimmer of light creeping out from under the door frame, she hesitated. Was there someone in there? Was it Darcy or her father? Should she go in?

"Oh, for goodness sake girl," she muttered to herself. She had never been an indecisive person before, and she was not going to start now.

Turning the handle, she slid the door back.

There, standing before her, was Darcy, but he was not alone. A tall, rather handsome looking gentleman in uniform stood beside him.

Realising she had interrupted something, Elizabeth turned to leave.

"No need to make a retreat on my behalf, Miss Bennet, I was just leaving."

Elizabeth turned back to face the gentlemen, and as she did so, she felt her colour rise.

Darcy stepped forward and made the introduction.

"Elizabeth, may I present my cousin, Colonel Richard Fitzwilliam. Richard, this is my betrothed, Miss Elizabeth Bennet."

Richard took her hand and bowed low over it, saying,

"Charmed, madam."

Elizabeth smiled and returned the Colonel's salute.

Then turning back to Darcy, Richard said,

"I will put things in place, and you will call me when I may take charge of the goods?" he asked cryptically.

"Yes, tomorrow, the next day at the latest," Darcy confirmed.

Again, Richard bowed over Elizabeth's hand and then left the couple alone.

Standing awkwardly, it was Elizabeth who broke the silence.

"Mr Darcy, I did not mean to interrupt… that is… I came to choose a book."

The pink hue that brushed her cheeks, combined with the candle light, gave Elizabeth's skin a golden glow.

Darcy smiled. He did not know why he smiled, other than because Elizabeth was here.

It was in this very room, three weeks past, that he had finally given in to his love for this woman. And now, here she was. In his house, with him.

A surge of love and longing coursed through his body.

Instead of sweeping her into his arms and acting on these feelings, he was the perfect host.

"You did not disturb us, Elizabeth, we had concluded our business," Darcy said. "May I offer you a glass of wine?" and he turned to the bottles of on the sideboard.

Elizabeth shook her head. "No…thank you."

"Elizabeth, may I speak to you for a moment?" Darcy asked.

Elizabeth smiled and, glancing around for a seat.

Darcy quickly pulled up a chair and waited for her to be comfortable.

"Do you remember that first day, when we walked up the hill, and I cautioned you about befriending Mr Wickham?"

Elizabeth remembered only too clearly and had the good grace to colour further.

"Do not remind me. I thought you were jealous of Mr Wickahm, of his easy manner and flowing charm."

"And if he was a better person, I might well be, but that is not why I bring the subject up now. I told you about a young woman I knew, who, like Miss Lydia had fallen under Wickham's spell and was almost ruined by him?"

Elizabeth nodded.

Darcy took a deep breath, hoping to calm the quiver in his voice that was always present when he spoke of Georgiana's near ruin.

"It was Georgiana," he eventually managed to say.

The difficulty which Darcy had had to overcome to reveal this to her was evident on his face, in his expression, in his voice.

Georgiana had been the victim of a vile deception, perpetrated by George Wickham? Such a betrayal of a devoted and loving brother must have torn at his heart. Yet he had forgiven her for the part she played in it and loved her still. Was there no end to this man's goodness?

The words she spoke next were guarded and cautious.

"Your sister is fortunate, sir, to have a brother as devoted and forgiving as you, to be her champion."

A rueful smile twisted on Darcy's lips.

"Fortunate, you say? No, Elizabeth..." Darcy shook his head in a pique of self-loathing. "If I had been more thorough when checking Mrs Younge's credential, I would never have employed her, never put Georgiana in her care, and never exposed my sister to the underbelly of Wickham's character. It is something which I will have to live with for the rest of my life. That my neglect almost cost my sister everything. And now, Miss Lydia. If I had acted differently..."

Elizabeth's heart lurched as she witnessed Darcy's pain. She stood up and went to his side.

Cautiously, hesitantly, she placed her hand on his arm.

"To have a brother who loves her so deeply, who protects her so prodigiously, and bears that burden gladly. Yes, I say fortunate, sir." Elizabeth replied softly.

Darcy placed his hand over Elizabeth's and looked deep into her eyes. He needed her comfort, her understanding, her...forgiveness. If he could be sure that she was sincere in her words, it would ease the guilt he now felt over *her* sister's predicament.

As if reading his mind, Elizabeth said,

"Lydia would never have been content until she had exposed herself in society in one way or another. Mr Wickham was in the right place at the right time as far as Lydia is concerned."

"If only I could believe that, Elizabeth,"

Elizabeth could not let Darcy take all the blame for Lydia's folly.

"Believe me, Lydia has always been a disaster waiting to happen. If not Mr Wickham, then it would have been someone else."

Then, her voice soft and cajoling, Elizabeth tried to coax him out of his sombre reverie.

"Come, help me choose a book. I am in the mood for something light and entertaining."

Elizabeth turned her attention to the row of books nearest to her.

Spying a novel she had previously enjoyed reading, Elizabeth reached up to retrieve it.

Noticing where her gaze fell, Darcy too reached up for the book, saying,

"Allow me."

In the instant that followed, when their hands brushed together, an actual spark crackled in the air, breaking the silence with a burst of blue light.

"Ouch," Elizabeth exclaimed, rubbing where the jolt of electricity had pricked her hand.

"I am sorry, Elizabeth, I only meant to save you the trouble of stretching." Now it was Darcy's turn to flush crimson.

Seeing the sombre expression on Darcy's face and the redness of his cheeks, Elizabeth could not contain her mirth.

"I suspect even the ancient gods of Greece would have been envious of such a bolt of lightning, sir."

Darcy's mood lightened, relieved that Elizabeth had neither berated him for using her given name; nor reproached him for keeping Wickham's past a secret.

Returning her smile, he said,

"If you will *allow me*, Miss Elizabeth," Darcy emphasised as he reached up and retrieved the book in question.

"Tales of Fashionable Life, Volume III, Vivian. You will enjoy this more than the one I might have recommended, Marmion, by Sir Walter Scott." Darcy said as he turned the leather-bound novel over in his hands.

"I hope so," Elizabeth said retrieving the book from Darcy's hand. "Maria Edgeworth is a particular favourite of mine."

Reluctantly, Darcy let her take the book, but not before he added,

"Elizabeth…I am glad you are here."

Chapter Twenty-Two

The next morning, Mr Bennet and Elizabeth rose at their regular time and went down to breakfast. Although Elizabeth expected it was a little early for either Mr Bingley or Miss Darcy to join them, she had expected to see Mr Darcy.

As usual, Mr Bennet was engrossed in the morning paper, which had thoughtfully been placed at the side of his plate. He failed to notice that Elizabeth was perplexed about something.

Eventually, she could bear the suspense no more.

Turning to one of the footmen, she asked,

"Will Mr Darcy be joining us?"

The footman, immaculately dressed in the Darcy livery, leant closer to Elizabeth and in a hushed tone said,

"No, Miss. The master and Miss Darcy left some time ago."

"Left?" Elizabeth echoed quietly.

"Yes, Miss."

"Do you know where they went?"

Generally, James the footman, would not entertain revealing anything about the master to a stranger. However, as Mr Miller had informed the household two days ago that Miss Bennet was to be the new mistress, he felt at liberty to divulge the information.

"I believe the master had escorted Miss Georgiana to Lady Matlock's town residence, Miss."

"Oh, I see. Thank you." Elizabeth said, and then turned back to contemplate the pattern on her breakfast plate.

Just as they were finishing their repast, in bounced Mr Bingley.

"Good morning, Miss Bennet, Mr Bennet."

Mr Bennet finally came out of hiding from behind his paper.

"Bingley," he said, acknowledging of the young man's greeting.

Taking a plate from the sideboard, Charles began to pile food onto his plate. Sausage, bacon, kidneys, egg, fried potatoes and a hot muffin. Taking the seat between father and daughter, he began to attack his food with relish.

Elizabeth and Mr Bennet watched as he devoured half of his meal with alacrity before the older man could not help but comment.

"Slow down, lad. You'll give yourself indigestion wolfing it down like that, upon my word."

Bingley emptied his mouth and took a swig of the hot coffee in his cup, before saying,

"Sorry, sir, but Darcy instructed me to make haste over to Louisa's this morning. I am to pack Caroline and all her belongings back off to Scarborough. Darcy feels a period away from polite society will give her time to reflect on her disgraceful behaviour."

"Does he now?" said Mr Bennet, who then looked at Elizabeth with a cynically raised eyebrow.

"I fear it will take more than a spell at the coast to soften and mend your sister's heart and ways, Bingley. A lifetime of indulgence cannot be reversed in a few weeks by the seaside, lad. But, go if you must, and I suppose you must go. Mr Darcy has recommended it, and so it will be done." He sighed.

Bingley was puzzled by Mr Bennet's words. Mr Darcy was always most solicitous of his friend's needs, and he had often turned to him for advice and instruction.

"Sir?" Bingley asked Mr Bennet.

"I do not slander Mr Darcy, not by any means. I only meant that he possesses a forceful and demanding personality. I find he is a man one would not dare say no too."

Bingley looked down at his half empty plate, and, decided not to eat anymore, pushed it away from him. Already Mr Bennet's observation was proving correct. Charles Bingley was even now beginning to feel an uncomfortable pain in the region of his stomach.

Taking one last gulp of his coffee, Mr Bingley bid them a good day and then left, rubbing his stomach as he did so.

Elizabeth felt alone and isolated. Even though her father sat only yards from where she was sitting, he might as well have been back at Longbourn. With Miss Darcy gone and now Mr Bingley, it left only Mr Darcy, her father and her. How she missed Jane. Dear Jane, whom, she could talk freely to and discuss openly with any thoughts or notions that invaded her mind.

Kind Jane, who acted as her voice of sense and reason, subduing her impulsive and rashness that sometimes bubbled up and spilt over, causing her embarrassment and shame. Now, she felt the need to unburden herself, to hear the sound advice and reasoning that only Jane could offer her. Especially around her thoughts and dreams of Mr Darcy. Dear, sweet, sensible Jane, how she missed her.

The first thing either Mr Bennet or Elizabeth knew of Mr Darcy's return, was when they heard his raised voice call for Miller.

"Miller, in my study now if you please," Darcy shouted.

Miller, who had been a butler at Mr Darcy's London residence for the past five years, was rarely surprised by his master. That was until two weeks ago. It had been the first time young Mr Darcy had ever raised his voice to him, and today was the second.

Hurrying to the study, Miller was still buttoning his jacket as he entered the room.

"Sir?" he asked breathlessly.

"Ah, Miller, will you ask Mr Bennet and Miss Elizabeth if they would join me without delay. Then, you are to go to Coutts & Company and pick up a sum of money I ordered this morning."

"Yes, sir," said Miller, with no thought of questioning his master.

"Mind, you are to go in person, Miller. They are expecting you."

Millers' chest puffed up with pride. It was a great responsibility being Butler to a man such as Fitzwilliam Darcy, but it was also a great honour. With a reputation for treating his employees fairly and generously, Darcy had the undying loyalty of all his servants.

Miller nodded and then went to convey Mr Darcy's request to the Bennets'.

Elizabeth took a chair near the fire, while Mr Bennet elected to remain standing, as did Darcy.

"So, what news is there?" Mr Bennet asked.

Before he answered, Darcy's eyes lingered on Mr Bennet's face. Was it his imagination, or had Elizabeth's father aged since they arrived in town? No matter, if things went well tomorrow, he could return to Longbourn in a day or so.

The news he bore for them was mixed in nature. The brunt of the expense he alone would shoulder, but the emotional damage; that would be down to the Bennet family to try to repair.

Turning, so he was facing them both, Darcy got straight to the point.

"I have been to speak to Wickham this morning. His terms are harsh, but I have agreed to meet them."

Darcy recalled his meeting, omitting the less savoury remarks and insults Wickham had unleashed on Darcy and Lydia

Having arrived at the Inn a little after eight in the morning, Darcy had expected to find Wickham and Lydia still asleep. But when Wickham opened the door, not only was he dressed, but he appeared was alone.

Wickham stepped aside, allowing Darcy to enter the room.

There was no sign of Lydia.

"You took your time; I expected you to return yesterday. Why have you kept me waiting until now?"

Darcy looked around the room. The impression he got was that it was only one step above squalor, and certainly not a place to bring a young lady of breeding.

The covers on the bed were grey and rumpled, and there were several empty wine bottles scattered around the room and on the floor.

A tray with two metal plates on it rested precariously on the window sill, but only one dish of food had been eaten.

At the window, curtains that had once been bright and colourful were now held together with only dirt and spider webs, while the windows behind them were opaque with grime.

Darcy gave an inward shudder.

Wickham sat at the table and folded his arms across his chest and began to tap his foot impatiently as he waited for Darcy to answer him.

"Where is Miss Lydia, Wickham?"

"Safe enough," Wickham replied.

"I have nothing to say…or to offer until I have seen Miss Lydia with my own eyes," Darcy replied, the coldness of his voice conveying his resolve.

"Very well, see for yourself," Wickham jeered and tossed his head towards a door next to the bed.

With purposeful strides, Darcy walked to the door and pulled it open.

It was not, as he expected, another room, it was a closet. Just thick enough and broad enough to fit a single chair in. On that chair, with her hands tied to the back rails, and a cloth tied over her mouth, sat Lydia Bennet. Her dirty and tear-stained face barely visible in the darkness of the confined space, and her hair tangles and scruffy.

It took every ounce of Fitzwilliam Darcy's willpower to remain calm and project a cool exterior as he turned back to face Wickham.

From their previous encounters, Darcy knew that Wickham intended to goad and bait him until he would offer him anything to be rid of him. Though this time, Darcy had not only expected such a ploy, he had prepared for it.

"Well?"

A single look told Darcy all that he needed to know. Gone was the handsome gentleman who had smiled and charmed all the ladies of Meryton. In his place stood a man barely identifiable as George Wickham. The uniform that Lydia had been so fond of, which had drawn her to Wickham in the first place, was almost unrecognisable as it hung off his hungry frame. Where the liquor stained jacket fell open, it revealed a shirt marked with several patches of what Darcy could only assume were dried food and spilt wine. His hair was unkempt, and he was sporting at least three days of stubble. Wickham was desperate.

"I take it you have no intention of marrying Miss Bennet?" Darcy asked.

"Heavens no! Tie myself to that penniless nobody for the rest of my life? Certainly not, Darcy. There are far richer pickings for me to choose from..." Wickham paused to sneer at Darcy, before saying,

"Once you have paid me what's owing to me."

Darcy said nothing; he did nothing, only returned Wickham's stare with a steadfast gaze of his own.

Wickham became worried. Perhaps this was a trap, and the magistrates' men were waiting for him outside? He leant forward and pulled the pistol from the back of his waistband, then placed it on the table with the muzzle pointing towards Darcy.

"That is what you came for, isn't Darcy? You're not just wasting my time, are you?" Wickham asked menacingly.

"Have you touched the girl, Wickham?" Darcy asked.

It did not escape Darcy notice that no sooner had he asked this of Wickham, that the other man rubbed at what appeared to be a bite mark on his hand.

Wickham, in a show of bravado, cocked his head to one side, and said,

"Not my type, Darcy. You should know I like my women thinner and fairer... much like your sister."

For the second time that day, Darcy had to call on his willpower to stop himself from striking Wickham a blow.

Turning back to the restrained girl, Darcy gently removed the gag covering her mouth, and spoke soft words of comfort and reassurance before he asked,

"Take heart, Lydia, it will be over soon enough, I promise you." Darcy felt uncomfortable and unclean as he put the question that must be asked, to the fifteen-year-old Lydia Bennet.

"Miss Bennet...your virtue...are you...?"

Between gasping for air and her quiet sobbing, Lydia managed to say,

"I am not injured, sir."

Straightening, Darcy turned back to Wickham and asked the question he thought never to ask again.

"How much, Wickham?"

Full of cockiness and triumphant swagger, Wickham said a figure that shocked even Darcy.

"Ten thousand pounds."

"Two, and I tear up all the promissory notes I have purchased," Darcy counter-offered.

Wickham tried to tot up the amount of notes Darcy might hold of his, but the number of towns, the shops, the brothels...it was too many for him to recall. Guessing it must be close to fifteen hundred pounds, Wickham pitched.

"Five."

"Three thousand five hundred pounds, Wickham and all the promissory notes I hold. That adds up to five. It's a final and definitive offer. One that expires when I leave this room."

George Wickham knew when Darcy had been pushed far enough. If he tried to push him any further, there was every chance he would withdraw his offer and have him arrested. To part with such a sum of money, confirmed Wickham's belief of how much Darcy loved Elizabeth Bennet. Ah, yes, the lovely Miss Eliza...

"I will accept your offer, Darcy, but I have a condition."

"What is it?"

"I want you to invite me to your wedding to Miss Elizabeth?"

"You what!" exclaimed Darcy.

Wickham knew he had hit a nerve, but it was too late to back down now.

Darcy stepped forward, raising himself up to his full height, he looked down at the visibly shaken face of his nemesis, and hissed,

"If you come within a hundred miles of Elizabeth, I will personally slit your throat and throw you in the Thames."

Wickham stood and backed away a few steps, stumbling over an empty bottle as he did so. Safety seemed to lie in returning to the subject of money.

With his words tumbling out, Wickham tried to distract Darcy. "Do...do we have a deal?"

His breathing was ragged with the effort of suppressing his instinct to beat the man before him to a pulp, but through gritted teeth, Darcy replied.

"We do."

"Such a sum of money, how am I ever to repay you, sir?" asked Mr Bennet

Perplexed that the financial arrangement was Mr Bennet's first concern, Darcy's reply to him was somewhat curt.

"Repay me, sir? I need no repayment. Miss Lydia's safety is my chief concern."

Elizabeth stepped in at this point.

"And we are grateful for all you have done, sir. When may we see Lydia? We need to make arrangements to take her home."

Biting back a curse on Wickham, Darcy went on to reveal the terms Wickham had insisted on before he would release Lydia.

"I want Miss Elizabeth to be the one to give me the money in exchange for her sister," he had demanded.

"No!" Darcy replied flatly.

"No deal then, Darcy."

"Do not test me, Wickham!"

For some minutes they argued the toss, but Darcy had no intention of capitulating. Then he heard the gentle sobs of Lydia, still locked in the closet, filter out through the cracks in the wood and into the ether of the room.

Seeing him weaken, Wickham pushed his point.

"If I am to never see Miss Elizabeth again, Darcy, at least let me say goodbye. I promise I will never seek either of you out again."

As if to push his point home, Wickham picked up the pistol and rested it over his forearm.

The threat, though not spoken, was clear. Realising the status quo had changed, Darcy knew it was a small price to pay for the release of Lydia Bennet. He agreed. Elizabeth could be present, but only to aid the rescue of her sister.

It was enough to satisfy Wickham, and they agreed the handover time of 4 o'clock the next afternoon.

Mr Bennet made some minor form of protest at his favourite daughter being involved, citing the unsavoury location of the docks as his main bugbear, but all to no avail.

"I will do it father, for Lydia's sake."

Elizabeth was determined to go. Darcy and Lydia needed her to go. The safe return of Lydia depended on it. She was going.

Chapter Twenty-Three

Darcy sat at his desk, the only light was the glow from the fire. He had dashed off a brief note to his cousin, detailing the time and place of the handover of Lydia, but it did not sit well with him.

Richard was the brother he had never had, and they were close, but first and foremost, Richard was a soldier. Could he, in all good conscience, hand Wickham over to Richard and live with that knowledge? On the other hand, could he continue to go through life constantly fearing where, and whom Wickham might target next? For both financial gain and his own sadistic pleasure of persecuting him for a slight, he had not committed?

The answer was simple. No. He had already endured many situations in life instigated by Wickham's hatred and greed.

It had all started when they were children of about nine or ten. Darcy's father owned a superb gold hunter pocket watch, which Darcy was to inherit. When Wickham discovered how much his young playmate admired the watch, he started a full-out campaign to flatter and cajole Darcy's father into parting with it. Until finally, to please the boy, he had relented and given him his watch. Darcy was devastated and told his father so, only to be reprimanded for being selfish.

Wickham's relentless charm offensive had won him the prize and taught him a valuable lesson, one he would use throughout his life. And so, Wickham's turn from the path of truth and right had begun.

Elizabeth had stood silently watching Darcy for some minutes. So, deep in his own thoughts, that he had neither seen nor heard her enter his study.

It was the flickering light of her candle which disturbed the shadows on his desktop, that finally alerted him that he was no longer alone.

Surprised to see his intended at this late hour, Darcy stood and made to retrieve his jacket from the back of his chair.

"Please, do not be concerned on my behalf. The room is warm enough, and the sight of you in your shirt-sleeved does not offend me," Elizabeth told him.

Darcy replaced the jacket on the back of the chair and then turned to face Elizabeth.

"You should be resting, Elizabeth. It is past midnight."

"I could not sleep. I must do what my father has failed to do. That is to thank you, sir, for all you are doing for Lydia, for us."

Darcy's eyes wandered over the features of Elizabeth's face. Taking in the brightness of her eyes as they reflected the flame of the candle, to the soft, red bow of her lips. He missed nothing. And not for the first time, he wondered, *how could he ever have thought her plain?*

Coming from behind his desk to stand before her, he took the candle from her hand and placed it on the desktop.

Being thanked for his actions was all very right and proper, but what he wanted more than anything, was for her to love him, to show him some sign that she cared for him. To take his hand, or touch his arm or face in some small gesture of affection. To bridge that small space between them, which he felt kept them emotionally, miles apart...

Resisting the urge to reach out and pull her into his embrace, Darcy said,

"I do not want your father's thanks, Elizabeth. I think only of you... of your happiness..." he paused, then quietly added, "of our happiness."

How materially her thoughts and feelings had changed since first being proposed to by the Master of Pemberley. Her initial surprise and horror had quickly been reasoned away, to be replaced with practical acceptance. But now...having been made aware of the depths of depravity her once favourite admirer could, and had, stooped to, she was sickened when she remembered her past infatuation with Wickham. So, how could she blame or sanction Lydia, when she too had almost succumbed to his charms. But she was not the only one to have changed.

The lengths Darcy was prepared to go to, solely to retrieve her sister, was extraordinary. Besides the financial cost, there was no doubt the reminder of his own sisters' recent escape. And now, every time he looked at Elizabeth, his future wife, would he be reminded of the events of this week? Had Lydia's foolishness forever tarnished Darcy's opinion of her? Though it mattered to her more than she could put into words, that he thought kindly of her, still loved her, still...wanted her, Lydia's elopement had sullied all that might have been.

Before her courage failed her, Elizabeth took a small step forward and placed her hand on Darcy's arm.

Looking up into his dark eyes, her resolve almost faltered, but she looked away from his piercing gaze, and said,

"Mr Darcy; so much has changed since you asked me to be your wife, and very little for the better. I now understand how difficult my former friendship with Mr Wickham must have been for you, and..." she continued, giving Darcy no chance to say whatever he was about to say. "My only defence is that I was ignorant of the facts. However, considering recent events, I think it only right that I now release you from that promise you made to me at Longbourn."

Elizabeth knew Darcy was itching to interrupt, but his manners and the rapidity of her speech, would not let him.

"I cannot expect you to look on a wife who is a constant reminder of the past. The past should only be remembered with fondness and affection, not pain and disgust." Elizabeth paused just long enough to catch her breath, then continued.

"Now, tomorrow, once Lydia is safely in our care again, we will all remove to my Uncle Gardiner's house in Cheapside. From there, my father will make arrangements for us to return home, to Longbourn. I am sure this will be acceptable to all concerned, even you, Mr Darcy when you think about it." Elizabeth, her speech finished and her engagement dissolved, could not meet Darcy's stare. She feared he would see the tears she was fighting to restrain and know her heart was breaking.

Darcy looked down at Elizabeth and smiled. She did not know it, but she had just filled him with a mixture of emotions, all but one of them pleasant.

Her offer to release him had been an unpleasant shock, but her reasons were not strong enough to convince him it was what she truly desired. Coupled with her gentle touch, Darcy knew Elizabeth was only doing what she assumed, incorrectly, it was what he wanted.

Darcy raised his arms and ran his hands slowly up Elizabeth's bare arms, welcoming the tremble his warm touch produced in her. Then, with one finger, he tilted her chin and waited until she lifted her eyes and met his.

"I do not release you, Elizabeth. You are mine, we belong together. If you do not love me now, I have enough love for both of us. And not just for this lifetime, but for eternity. I love you, Elizabeth,

I loved you yesterday, I love you today, and I will love you tomorrow. I always will." His voice was like a caress, warm and soft and reassuring, though his words were masterfully delivered.

The movement of Elizabeth's head was almost undetectable, but it was enough to confirm her understanding and grateful acceptance of his speech.

Her eyes sparkled with the unshed tears, and her lips were slightly parted in an inviting pose. Darcy, overwhelmed with his love and longing for Elizabeth, could resist no longer.

Moving her into the full circle of his embrace, Darcy lowering his head, and took possession of Elizabeth's lips.

He had meant it to be a gentle kiss, a kiss borne from his love for her, but as Elizabeth had curled her arms around his neck, returning his kiss with her newly awakened passion, he found himself deepening their embrace until they were both breathless.

His hands caressed her everywhere, across her back, over her shoulders, up her neck, until finally, they cupped her face.

Now, his kisses became more urgent, more ardent, more probing. Driving and demanding and determined, and even a little desperate. Seeking from Elizabeth a satisfaction that only she could supply.

Elizabeth felt a surging tide of warmth and helplessness rush over her as Darcy took her in his arms. The graduation and intensity of his kisses made her cling to him as if her life depended on it. A swimming giddiness engulfed her, and she returned his caress with equal enthusiasm.

Her whole body shivered and tingled and pulsed with the pleasure of his kiss, and she knew she was kissing him back, participating, enjoying and prolonging it. But deep inside her, there was a yearning for more, growing stronger with every embrace, every caress that Darcy bestowed upon her.

Reluctantly, Darcy broke their kiss, knowing he was almost at the point of no return.

"Elizabeth," he whispered softly against her temple, "Tell me to stop. If you *want* me to stop, tell me now?"

When Elizabeth said nothing, he kissed her cheek, her eyelids, her brow.

"Or now?" he said before brushing her nose, her chin, her lips with his mouth.

"Or now?" he slipped his tongue into her mouth, gently probing between her parted lips, soft, yet demanding.

Elizabeth's silence spoke volumes. She pulled him tighter into her embrace, pressing her body against his, longing for him to satisfy this hunger that had set the very blood in her veins on fire.

Without releasing her mouth, Darcy swept Elizabeth up into his arms and carried her swiftly to her room.

Gently, he laid her on the bed and then covered her body with his own. Lifting his face, he looked down at her, her face glowing with adoration and longing.

He brushed a stray tendril of hair from her cheek.

"Are you sure, my love?" he asked one last time, his voice rasping with desire.

The time for hesitation was over. Elizabeth had made up her mind. Her senses had been thrown into confusion, and she felt as if she was intoxicated, drunk on love. Yes, love. She loved Fitzwilliam Darcy, and she yearned to consummate their love with every fibre of her being.

Letting her lips curl into a provocative smile, she reached up and pulled on his shirt, bringing him back down to cover her mouth with his own.

Darcy might still have been able to pull himself back from the brink, but the three words Elizabeth whispered against his lips, would either condemn him to damnation, of give him the gift of ecstasy.

"Fitzwilliam, my love…"

Chapter Twenty-Four

Darcy waited until Elizabeth fell asleep in his arms, before returning to his own room.

Their lovemaking had been urgent and thrilling the first time, with Darcy taking care to ensure Elizabeth's readiness before piercing her maidenhead, but the second time they made love, it was meaningful and tender and fulfilling for them both.

He had cradled Elizabeth in his arms and stroked her hair until she had fallen into an exhausted, but content sleep. Gazing down at her, he marvelled that a woman as wonderful as Elizabeth, now his Elizabeth, should find it in her heart to return his sentiment. He had doubted he could win her heart after Wickham had planted the seeds of lies in her mind. But Elizabeth had proved to be a mindful and determined woman, capable of making her own decisions and judgements.

As she stirred in his embrace, and then cuddled in closer to him, he felt his chest tighten and swell with love and pride all at the same time.

He had no regrets for coupling with Elizabeth before they were officially wed. Although no preacher had said the proper words required nor given them the Lords blessing, Darcy felt more bound to Elizabeth than any mortal oaths could bind him.

They were fated to be together; destiny had their future marked out long before they had even met.

No, he had no regrets. He only hoped Elizabeth didn't either.

Like a lovesick school boy, Darcy waited outside Elizabeth's bedroom door, hoping to speak to her before her father joined them. Every time a maid walked by, Darcy had darted into the empty room next to Elizabeth's apartments, desperate to protect her reputation until after the ceremony.

Though Elizabeth could not hide her surprise at seeing Darcy pacing up and down the corridor as she emerged from her room, she did try to hide her blushes.

Looking her square in the face, Darcy checked for signs of regret. Instead, he was rewarded with a brilliant smile and a slight rosy hue that crept up to colour her cheeks.

Scanning the corridor to check no servants were dawdling about their duties, Darcy pulled Elizabeth into his arms and proceeded to kiss her soundly.

"My darling, you are well this morning?" he asked with concern.

Elizabeth had the good grace to blush an even deeper crimson at his enquiry, knowing full well to what he alluded.

Smiling coyly, she said,

"I am a little tired, and a little...bruised, but nothing more."

Linking arms, like a displaying peacock, Darcy escorted Elizabeth to the breakfast room, where they were joined by her father only a few minutes later.

Elizabeth could not help herself. She could not stop smiling, and she knew Darcy knew why. They shared the odd glance over the breakfast table, but other than that, they both spoke solely to Mr Bennet.

Their attempts to act as though nothing had altered in their relationship, although admirable, were lacking. Mr Bennet, for the first time in his life, felt like he was playing gooseberry. Deciding ignorance was bliss, he did as he always did when he did not want to be involved. He hid behind the newspaper.

Last night, she had gone to release Darcy from his promise, to free him from the disgrace that was about to befall her family and relations. Instead of taking her up on her offer, Darcy had made her his own. Taking her heart, her love, and then her body.

Lydia aside, Elizabeth had never been happier.

The remainder of the day was spent preparing for the afternoon's exchange. Darcy recounted the money Miller had collected for him. Half was in gold coin, and the other half was in notes. Then he re-read the letter that had arrived for him early this morning.

It was brief and to the point.

I have arranged for the goods
to go on a long journey
RF

Darcy did not want to know the details, as long as Richard kept his promise.

Next, Darcy asked Elizabeth and her father to join him in his study, and they began to go over the plans.

Having acquired a map of the docks, Darcy worked out their route to, and from the exchange point. Then, for his own peace of mind, he memorised several alternative escape routes, should the need for one arise.

Elizabeth had brought a large blanket to wrap her sister in, while Mr Bennet had slipped a small hip flask of brandy into his pocket, just in case Lydia needed to be revived.

All was ready; all was prepared.

As the hand on his pocket watch struck half past the hour of three, Mr Bennet, Elizabeth and Darcy climbed into his carriage and began the journey to the docks. Only the burly looking coachman accompanied them.

Arriving early, Darcy had the carriage positioned to face the return route, in case they needed to make a hasty retreat.

Now, there was nothing more to do but wait.

Darcy pulled out his watched and checked it for the umpteenth time. Wickham was late. Already the sun was going down, and the mist was forming. The nightlife of the docks was changing from sailors, naval officers, and port officials, to drunks, thieves and prostitutes, and he wanted Elizabeth exposed to such people as little as possible.

Darcy was more concerned that he let on. Knowing Wickham of old, he suspected a double cross.

Mr Bennet, who had declined a hot bottle for his feet, was regretting his decision, and wondering if anyone would notice if he took a sip from the hip flask.

Elizabeth was oblivious to her father's hand occasionally dipping into his pocket, but she was very aware of Darcy checking his watch. Something was wrong. As the minutes ticked by, Elizabeth became more and more concerned for her sister's safety.

Agitated, and in need of a release for his pent-up anger, Darcy got out of the carriage and prowled up and down the path. Several minutes of pacing later, and still, Darcy felt like a wound coil ready to spring. His head snapped at every sound, every movement. Occasionally, he swung his cane at an invisible object, until finally, he heard a man's voice coming from in mist.

"Steady on, old man, you nearly hit me with that!"

Instantly, Darcy recognised it as Wickham.

He peered harder into the mist, and slowly, the form of two people emerged from the direction of the Inn where Wickham had lodged.

"Am I late? Oh, well, no matter. I knew you would wait." Cocked Wickham as he goaded Darcy to reply.

"Late? No, I do not think you are late, George. Maybe we were a trifle early. You have tidied yourself up since we last met, George. One might even say, you were…presentable?" Darcy said, playing along with Wickham.

Mr Bennet and Elizabeth had been told to stay in the carriage and say nothing until Darcy told them it was safe to do so. However, Elizabeth was finding this harder as every second passed.

Just behind Mr Wickham, masked by the mist and standing in the shadows, was Lydia. Even from several feet away, Elizabeth could see her sister trembling. Was it due to the cold, or worse, fear of Wickham? Elizabeth suspected it was the latter, but for now, all she could do was to will her to be brave and to be strong.

"Mmm," said Wickham with a false smile. "I thought I should make an effort; now I am to be a man of means. Do you like it, Darcy?" asked Wickham as he turned from side to side, parading his new suit of clothes off.

"I do hope so, I charged it to your tailor."

Darcy curse, making a mental note to write to all his suppliers telling them to deny Wickham credit.

"Now, do you have my money?"

"I do," Darcy said, "Just as you asked. Half in coinage and half in notes."

Darcy waited, hoping Wickham would just ask for the money forget about Elizabeth.

A tense few seconds of silence had passed before Wickham said,

"And where is Miss Elizabeth? I will only hand over the girl to her."

Darcy cursed under his breath, and through gritted teeth, said,
"In the carriage, waiting for her sister."

"Does she have the money?" Wickham asked, full of conceit.

"Yes," Darcy managed to say.

"Then step aside, my good man, Miss Elizabeth and I have business to conduct."

Against every fibre of his being, Darcy did step aside, giving Wickham a clear path to the carriage where Elizabeth sat waiting for him.

Wickham stopped at the carriage door and waited for the coachman to open it. If he heard the gruff mumbling of the coachman as he held open the carriage door, Wickham ignore it. Climbing in, he took the seat opposite Elizabeth, and next to her father.

Turning to Mr Bennet, he barked,

"You, old man, out!" Wickham ordered.

As protesting seemed futile, Mr Bennet climbed out onto the road and walked around to the back of the carriage, where he indulged in another hearty nip from the hip flask.

With Wickham's attention now firmly fixed on Elizabeth, and Darcy's attention fixed on Wickham and Elizabeth, no-one seemed to notice what Mr Bennet did.

With as much stealth as his old bones and liquor bolster body would allow him, Mr Bennet crept over to Lydia, linked her arm through his, and then quietly led her through the shadows and back to the main road. Once there, he quickly flagged down a hackney carriage and return them both to Darcy House.

Neither did anyone involved in tonight shenanigans noticed the two burly men that skirted around the light and shadows to follow Mr Bennet and his daughter, ensuring their safe return to Grosvenor Square.

"Elizabeth, I hope you will not think too unkindly of me in the future." Wickham began.

Elizabeth's back stiffened at the use of her given name. Too often, she realised, he had been overly familiar with her.

"A man with my background and lack of fortune must make a living as best he can. Though, if old man Darcy had not shown me there were finer things in life to be had, I might have been very content to follow in my own father's footsteps. And, if Fitz here had not shown a partiality for you, my dear Elizabeth, I would never have picked Lydia and my next...meal ticket, shall we say?"

Elizabeth remained silent, only raising a cynical eyebrow at his bold words.

Wickham tried to capture Elizabeth's hand, but unfortunately, he was too slow, and she had anticipated his move. Just in time, she pulled her hands beneath her cloak.

"Of course, my feelings were never engaged where Lydia was concerned. You, on the other hand, my feisty Elizabeth, well, I found myself becoming emotionally attached to you. The thought of becoming a farmer seemed more appealing every time I saw you. I engineered all our accidental meetings, you know? I badgered your friends to invite me to their soirees and parties. I found out which shops you like to visit and when. I even ingratiated myself with your mother, a tedious woman at the best of times. Only Charles Bingley could not be swayed, which was most annoying. He has been friends with Darcy too long. Still, I like to imagine that if I had made you an offer of marriage, you would have accepted it."

Sensing Wickham expected her to participate in the conversation, and wanting to end this interview, Elizabeth said,

"Then what turned you from your path, Mr Wickham? What made you switch your attention to my naïve, fifteen-year-old sister?"

The bitterness was only thinly disguised in Elizabeth's voice, but if Wickham noticed it, he chose to ignore it.

"Two things, Elizabeth. Mr Collins, and Darcy. Had your father's estate not been entailed to the Parson, I would have made you an offer. Not that I envisaged sticking around after the money had run out, but, it would have been a pleasurable few months, I'm sure. Yet, the entail is there, and so I saw no future for me as squire of Longbourn."

"You mean no money there for you?" Elizabeth said sharply.

"Yes, I suppose you are right. The other thing was Darcy. I could not bear the thought of him being happy. In fact, I decided long ago to make Darcy's existence as miserable as I possibly could. I only tell you this now, Elizabeth to forewarn you. Better the life of an old spinster than the one I intend for Darcy."

Sick of listening to Wickham's bragging and derogatory remarks,
Elizabeth brought the bag from under her cloak and thrust it towards him.

"I believe this is what you came for, don't let me detain you any longer. Goodbye Mr Wickham. I doubt we will meet again."

This was the signal for the coachman to open the carriage door, prompting Wickham to alight.

Wickham took the bag and climbed out of the carriage, then turned to say,

"You think we shall never meet again? How little you know men, Elizabeth. Let's not say goodbye, my dear, sweet, tempting, Eliza, instead let us just say, Au Revoir." And he took her hand up to his lips and pressed a lingering kiss on her fingers.

Elizabeth was thankful for the fashion of wearing gloves. Pulling her hand out of his grasp, she said,

"How very little *you* know women, Mr Wickham. *Goodbye*," Elizabeth emphasised her last word, which she delivered in a final and resolute tone.

"It's Miss Bennet, to you," said a deep male voice said from behind Wickham.

Wickham never saw the rifle butt that came crashing down on his skull, but he felt its effect instantly, rendering him unconscious.

"Get into the carriage quickly, Darcy, and don't look back. Wickham is no longer your problem." Colonel Fitzwilliam said in an authoritative voice.

"You will remember your promise, Richard?" Darcy reminded him.

"Yes, yes, I have not forgotten. Now make haste before someone sees us."

"My father and Lydia?" questioned Elizabeth.

"Already safely on their way to Darcy House," Richard said as he tried to hurry them on their way. "Leave now, before Wickham rouses."

Both Darcy and Elizabeth followed the colonel's advice. Neither of them looked back to see what became of Wickham.

If they had, they would have seen four of Richards most trusted men, pick him up by his limbs, and throw him onto the back of a cart.

"Mind his head, boys; I have a promise to keep," Richard instructed them.

Chapter Twenty-Five

On their return to Darcy House, Elizabeth and Darcy lost no time in tracking down Mr Bennet. However, there was no sign of Lydia.

"Papa, where is Lydia? Colonel Fitzwilliam said she was with you?"

A weary Mr Bennet rubbed his brow and gave Elizabeth the reassurance she sought.

"And so she is, my dear. Lydia was in desperate need of a bath, and a good meal. I suggested she try and rest for a while, but no doubt she will be pleased to see you, Lizzy."

Elizabeth rushed upstairs to join her sister, leaving her father and Mr Darcy alone.

Darcy went to the sideboard and poured two generous shots of brandy into lead crystal glasses, and then joined his future father-in-law by the fire. Before relaxing back into the plush folds of the fabric, Darcy handed Mr Bennet one of the glasses. Then, he let his body enjoy the comfort of his furniture, resting his head on the back as he did so.

Mr Bennet studied the man opposite him, watching as the tension visibly left his body, reducing the hunch of his shoulders and the lines on his face. Darcy was a gentleman, an honourable man, a man worthy of Elizabeth's love. Yes, she loved him…now. He had noticed the subtle changes that had occurred in Elizabeth over the past few days. The adoring looks that had once been his alone, she now bestowed freely on her future husband. Stolen glances brought a soft blush to her cheeks, and whenever Darcy spoke to her, she visibly glowed. He did not know what had brought about this transformation in his favourite daughter, but for both their sakes, Darcy as well as Elizabeth, he was happy and relieved to see that their love was now mutual.

Mr Bennet raised his glass in salute to Darcy and said, "Well done, Darcy, on all counts."

"And to you sir. You spirited Miss Lydia away with the stealth of a true soldier. Thank you, sir," Darcy replied, ignorant of Mr Bennet's double meaning.

There was nothing left to say.

Both men settled back into the welcoming embrace of their comfortable chairs, silently sipping their drinks, content with their night's work.

Elizabeth tapped gently on the door to Lydia's room, not wishing to wake her if she was already asleep. But when her sister's unusually soft voice bid her enter, Elizabeth opened the door and peeped inside.

Lydia sat on the edge of her bed, washed and in a clean nightgown. Thrown on the floor in a heap, was the blue travelling dress Lydia had supposedly loaned to Maria Lucas. It was impossible to miss the filthy state it was in. Apparently, Wickham had not allowed Lydia to changed her clothes for the duration of their time together, although Elizabeth recalled he no longer wore his uniform.

"Oh, Lizzy, how stupid I have been."

Lydia began to sob.

Rushing to her side, Elizabeth wrapped her arms around Lydia's shoulders and spoke words of comfort to her sister. As she pulled her close, Elizabeth could not fail to notice her sister had lost weight.

Some minutes passed before Lydia's crying subsided, but eventually, she wiped her nose and looked up at her sister.

Elizabeth brushed a few errant strands of hair from Lydia's face, where they had mingled with her tears and stuck to her cheek.

Quietly, she asked,

"Do you want to talk about it, Lydia?"

Lydia nodded.

Elizabeth perched on the edge of the bed, giving Lydia her undivided attention.

"He lied to me, Lizzy. Everything he said was a lie." Lydia said, pausing to dash away a fresh tear.

"I thought he loved me. George said he loved me and wanted to marry me, but the minute Miss Bingley let us out of her carriage, he changed. I have never seen a man so altered. He was vile, shouting and cursing and threatening me from the moment we were alone."

Still, the tears would not stop, though Lydia did try to calm herself so Elizabeth could understand her.

"He was wearing his uniform when we picked him up and had no other clothes with him. Wickham said it would have looked suspicious if he had started packing a bag just to go to the tavern in Meryton. Once in London, we were to stop just long enough for Wickham to get a change of clothes, and then we would travel to Gretna Green and be married."

Breaking off her narration to blow her nose again, Lydia then took hold of Elizabeth's hand.

"When I overheard George book a room, just one room, Lizzy, I knew something was wrong. I could not share a room with him; it would not be proper. So, I asked Wickham where *he* intended to sleep? Oh, Lizzy, he laughed in my face. He told me to do as he said or he would take me to the nearest house of ill repute and leave me there. He meant it too, Lizzy, I know he did." Lydia broke down again, sobbing uncontrollably onto her sister's shoulder.

Elizabeth waited until Lydia had calmed herself again, before saying,

"Go on, dearest."

In a scared voice, Lydia recalled,

"After that, he tied my hands and locked me in the closet. It was so dark and so small, I could not breathe. I was scared for my life, Lizzy, truly! I am sure he meant to kill me!"

Elizabeth rose, walked to the dresser and poured Lydia a glass of water. With her back still to her sister, Elizabeth asked,

"Did he…touch you Lydia, force you to do anything?"

"No, but he tried. I suppose because I had let him kiss me before he thought he could take liberties, but I bit him, Lizzy, and hard too."

Lydia took the glass and drank thirstily from it.

"I prayed for someone to rescue me, Lizzy. For Papa or Uncle Gardiner to come and take me home. *I* never imagined it would be Mr Darcy who would come for me, but George did. He only wanted money, I meant nothing to him, Lizzy, nothing." she said bitterly.

"Did you hear the bargain they struck?" Elizabeth asked, concerned with how indebted they were to Mr Darcy.

"Wickham wanted ten thousand pounds, but Mr Darcy said he would only pay a third of that, plus all Wickham's debts. I think the sum agreed was close to five thousand pounds, Lizzy," Lydia began to sob again. "I should have listened to you, Lizzy. You tried to warn me."

So that was the value Wickham put on Lydia. Her life, her virtue, her future, so easily bought for five thousand pounds.

How was their father ever to repay him?

Taking Elizabeth's hands once more, Lydia begged,

"Please forgive me, Lizzy, for all the horrible things I said? You know I did not mean them, don't you?"

Elizabeth smiled and squeezed Lydia's hand.

"I know dearest. We all say, and do foolish things at one time or another." Then, in a serious tone, Elizabeth said,

"Not all men are like Mr Wickham, Lydia, in fact very few people are as duplicitous as George Wickham."

Noticing the red rim of Lydia's eyes and the dark circle beneath them, Elizabeth guessed Lydia had managed to get little sleep during her ordeal.

Pulling back the bed covers, she said,

"Now, try and get some rest, and I will see you in the morning. I expect we will be going home tomorrow."

Before Elizabeth closed the door, she looked over her shoulder and smiled again.

"You will need all your strength to cope with mamma."

Darcy House was silent.

Mr Bennet and Elizabeth had retired for the evening. The servants had completed their duties and turned in for the night. Only Darcy was still awake.

Sitting in his favourite armchair, brandy in hand, Darcy stared into the flames of the fire. The recovery of Lydia Bennet had gone even better than he had hoped. It had only cost him five thousand pounds and the girl's virtue was intact. He should be happy, but he was not. His conscience would not allow him to rejoice in his success, knowing he had conspired with his cousin to alter Wickham future.

"Mind if I help myself?"

Startled, Darcy peered in the direction of the study door.

"Richard? Is that you?" He asked.

Colonel Fitzwilliam moved out of the shadows and joined Darcy by the fire. Dropping down into the other comfortable chair, he rested his head on the back cushion and closed his eyes.

"How, might I ask, did you get in? And do not tell me Miller let you in, he retired hours ago?"

"I am a soldier, Darcy, how do you think I got in? Besides, you really must have new locks fitted on the rear door. Anyone might break in."

"Evidently" Darcy replied, raising a quizzical brow.

Richard threw a bag on the table beside Darcy. It was the one Elizabeth had given to George Wickham.

"I came to bring this back to you. It's all these except for thirty pounds I gave my men as a reward."

Darcy glanced at the bag.

"It seems somewhat apt, thirty pieces of silver for my betrayal," Darcy said morosely.

Richard turned his head and studied Darcy's profile. Something was troubling him. Darcy rarely drank late at night and never alone.

"You're no Judas Iscariot, Darcy. You did what had to be done." Richard said, astonished that Darcy was taking his part in Wickham's fate so hard.

Richard watched and waited for a reply.

Draining his glass, Darcy reached for the decanter and poured himself another generous portion. His brow was furrowed and his jaw firmly clenched. Typical signs that all was not well in Darcy's world.

Leaning forward and pouring himself a brandy, Richard asked,

"Is it Miss Elizabeth, or the younger Miss Bennet?"

Darcy took another swing from his glass before answering.

"It's Wickham."

Putting his drink back on the table, Richard touched Darcy's arm.

"Have no fear, cousin, Wickham will not trouble you again. I have seen to that."

"But it does trouble me, Richard. What right do I have to decide the fate of another man? Wickham might have been redeemable if only I had given him my time, my friendship, or tried harder."

"Wickham deserved everything he got, Darcy. Have you forgotten the young housemaid he took advantage of? Or the farmer's cattle and fowl he killed, just for sport? And what about the money he stole from the universities poor box? Then there were the debts Wickham run up all over town."

Leaning forward, Richard rested his arms on his knees and continued to point out how Darcy had cleaned up after Wickham, beginning when they were only boys.

"To this day you still pay for the mother and child, keeping them on at Pemberley because you know they would not find work elsewhere. You gave the farmer funds to purchase top quality animals to restock his farm. You reimbursed the university and built them a new library, and there is not one merchant, tailor, tavern or brothel in the city that you have not reimbursed after Wickham defrauded them. There are dozens of more instances I could mention, Darcy, but you know them better than anyone."

When Richard saw his words had no effect, he reminded Darcy of his sister's encounter with Wickham.

"And Georgiana, who looked on George Wickham as a brother. Where would your sister be now if you had not come to her aid, tell me that, Darcy? No, Wickham's comeuppance was a long time coming, but well deserved."

Darcy raised his head. He had forgotten half of the incidents Richard had mentioned.

Seeing Darcy's spirits rise slightly, Richard reached into his pocket, pulled something out and placed it in Darcy's palm, with his own hand still covering it.

"Wickham is not dead, Darcy. I volunteered him for duties aboard one of his Majesties Royal Navy ships, bound for the Americas. And, I did not harm a hair on his head, as promised, although I cannot vouch for my men. But before we said our farewells, I took this from him." Richard slowly pulled his hand away, revealing something wrapped up in a scrap of cloth.

Darcy's curiosity was piqued.

Realisation of the object identity became clearer with every corner of cloth that he lifted, until finally, the object was revealed in its entirety.

Darcy felt an unfamiliar sting at the back of his eyes and fought to stop the tears from falling.

His father's gold hunter pocket watch.

"Richard, I am lost for words."

Taking his handkerchief from his pocket, Darcy buffed the gold, first on one side, and then on the other. With a touch of the button, the case sprang open to reveal the watch dial. A white enamel background with black Roman numerals, the hands indicating it was one-quarter past midnight.

"I know the men of the navy are beyond reproach, but I decide it would be prudent not to leave Wickham with anything he could use as a bribe."

"I have no words to express my thanks, Richard. I thought never to see this again, yet alone possess it."

Darcy pulled out his own very fine watch and clipped his father's excellent one in its place.

"There, it is back where it belongs, on a Darcy."

"Thank you, my friend."

Chapter Twenty-Six

The next day, two carriages set out for Longbourn.

The first had Mr Bennet, Elizabeth, and Lydia in, while the servants and luggage occupied the second.

Not wishing to intrude, and braving the December cold, Darcy had elected to ride his horse, thus giving the occupants privacy, should they want to discuss recent events.

However, inside, there was very little conversation to be had.

Lydia rested her head on her sisters should, and slept, and while Elizabeth closed her eyes, she did not sleep. Instead, she wrapped a protective arm around her sibling and listened for the reassuring sound of Mr Darcy's horse.

Mr Bennet gazed at his two children. Could there ever be two sisters less alike than these? Elizabeth was witty and charming and kind, universally liked by all. While Lydia was impulsive, selfish and argumentative, with few qualities to be proud of. But he loved them both.

It shamed him that he had not listened to Lizzy when she had warned him about George Wickham. The truth of the matter was he did not want to be bothered with it all. Why break the habit of a lifetime? Yet, because of his indolence, it was not he that had suffered, but his youngest child.

Things must change at Longbourn, he must change! He declared to himself. Although he was probably living his last decade, he hoped to implement several changed in his life, starting with his own behaviour. He would strive to be a better father, to be a better husband, and hopefully, in doing so, become a better man. They had much to thank young Darcy for, and trying to emulate him was not a bad place to start.

Darcy was cold. His great coat had felt warm and protective when first they began their journey. But once the fibres had been exposed to the cold air, they had lost that feeling of snugness. Trying to focus his thoughts, Darcy could not stop his mind from remembering several things he wished he had done differently. His dealings with Wickham, his unguarded behaviour towards Caroline Bingley, the night he spent with Elizabeth...

"Oh Lydia, my poor sweet girl, you are home at last!" Exclaimed Mrs Bennet, before turning to her husband and saying, "What took you so long, you have been gone ages, and with no word of how my poor Lydia was, whether she was married or even alive," wailed Mrs Bennet.

Pulling Lydia from Elizabeth's arms, Mrs Bennet, folded her in an oppressive bear hug, which saw the young girl's face thrust against her mother's bosom.

Struggling to break free, Lydia tugged at her mamma's arms, until finally, she could breathe freely again.

"Mamma, do not fuss so. Lizzy had looked after me, and now, I just want to go to my room, and rest in my bed, is that too much to ask for?" she huffed.

Elizabeth smiled. Lydia was back.

Sadly, Mrs Bennet would not hear of Lydia skulking off to her room the moment she returned home. Her sisters were eagerly waiting to see her and cook to make all Lydia's favourite sweet treats.

By this time, they had all alighted from their mode of transport and were filing into the sitting room.

One by one, Lydia's sisters came forward to welcome her home. Jane first, and then Mary and Kitty, who were not so enthusiastic to welcome their sister back.

Kitty had borne the brunt of her mother's distress, constantly at her beck and call, while repeatedly being questioned about her involvement in Lydia's flight.

Mary had remained as invisible, as always.

"Are you two not pleased to see me? If you come to my room, and I will tell you all about my adventure."

A hush descended over the room.

Mr Bennet was about to speak, but to everyone's surprise, it was Kitty who stood and let loose with a volley of reproach and criticism.

"Your foolish elopement could have cost this family dearly, Lydia. It was not some wild adventure you went on, but a disastrous and selfish elopement that could have seen you dead, or worse. Mamma has been at her wit's end with worry. You have put your own father's life in peril, and jeopardised the engagements of both Jane and Lizzy. You are selfish, thoughtless and thoroughly spoilt, Lydia Bennet, and you don't deserve all the attention you are getting."

Several pairs of eyes swung between Lydia and Kitty before finally, Mr Bennet said,

"Well said, Kitty. I could not have put it better myself. Though I expect this will not be the last misdeed, Lydia will involve us all in. Now, I for one could do with a large slice of cook's excellent apple sponge."

Lydia was ashamed. As she had sat crying, tied to that chair in the darkness, cold, hungry and afraid, she had sworn an oath to God. If He spared her life and restored her to the bosom of her family, she would strive to be a better sister and a better daughter. She would do as her mamma asked, and would share her things with Kitty. And finally, she would never let another man kiss her unless he was her husband. Kitty was right. Mr Darcy had been right, and though it pained her at the time, she now knew, Lizzy had been right. It was time to grow up and be a woman.

Walking over to her Mamma, Lydia gently put her arms around her neck and kissed her cheek.

"I will never give you cause for concern again, Mamma, I promise."

Mrs Bennet began to cry all over again, wiping her tear away with a soggy, and well-used handkerchief.

Stifling a tear of her own, Mrs Hill stepped forward and began to slice up the cake, while Mrs Bennet rallied and poured everyone a cup of tea.

Elizabeth turned to speak to Mr Darcy, only to find the space empty. She looked out into the hallway, but there was no sign of him there either. Somehow, she knew in which room to find him.

For some inexplicable reason, he always seemed to gravitate to this room, the music room. Perhaps it was because it was the furthest and most remote room in the house. Somewhere Mary could play and practise on the pianoforte for as long as she liked without disturbing everyone. So, there was little chance of them being overheard in here.

Darcy stood with one hand resting on the piano and the other behind his back. Turning only slightly, he acknowledged Elizabeth's arrival with a curt nod.

Leaving the door ajar, she moved to stand by his side.

As Darcy turned to face her, Elizabeth expected him to take her in his arms and kiss her.

Instead, he folded his arms behind his back and stood stiff, drawing himself up to his full height.

Elizabeth noticed his jaw was clenched and a muscle in his cheek ticked under the strain.

"Mr Darcy?" she questioned, instinctively knowing there was something on his mind.

Darcy came to the point with little fanfare or warning.

"Elizabeth, two evenings ago my behaviour was reprehensible. It does not sit well with my beliefs of how a gentleman should conduct himself. It has played on my conscience, and I can no longer remain silent on the matter." Darcy paused to pull in a ragged breath as he fought his emotions.

"As a man of the world, I knew what I was asking of you...what I was taking from you. Until the preacher has joined us together, as man and wife in the eyes of the law, and of God, I had no right to do what I did, to take what I took. I can only ask that you will forgive me for my momentary lack of self-control and error of judgement." The anguish and contrition in his voice were profound.

Elizabeth thought for a few seconds. She wanted to ask, why now. Why not the next morning, or sometime during the day? Why now? But it was impossible at that moment, to trivialise his heartfelt apology. Instead, Elizabeth resolved to admit her part in her own seduction, and in doing so, hopefully, ease his burden of guilt.

"Mr Darcy, as it appears to be the time for confessions and making apologise, you must allow me to make mine...to you."

Darcy interpreted her to say,

"I wish you wouldn't, Elizabeth. You can have nothing to confess and certainly no apology to make to me! Besides, one is rash and the other superfluous. I would far rather hear neither."

"I am afraid, sir, like you, I must make a clean breast of things. Apparently, neither of us are willing to enter into this marriage with a lie standing between us." With natural assurance, she continued. "I have entirely misjudged you, even as recent as two days ago. My opinion of you was so full of errors and misjudgements. I have thought you proud and arrogant and full of prejudice, against me, my family, and indeed, the entire populace in general. But you have proved me wrong again and again. Yes, the pride was yours, instilled in you by your history, your pedigree, your parents, but the prejudice was mine. I thought your attitude and motives were driven purely for selfish reasons. I gave you no information as to where my dislike came from and no chance for you to defend yourself against it. I let the opinion of others influence me and feed my prejudice. But now, I have come to know the man behind the mask. The kind, honourable, responsible and respectable man called Fitzwilliam Darcy, and I no longer feel that way."

Darcy blushed, accepting compliments never sat well with him.

"I have acted poorly, childishly, and naively. I am a grown woman and should have known better…did know better. Therefore, I can only tell you how sincerely sorry I am, and humbly ask for your forgiveness."

Elizabeth lingered for a moment, then quietly asked,

"Does that make us even, sir?" She asked coyly.

"This is no time for flippancy, Elizabeth."

Darcy broke his stance and took hold of Elizabeth by the shoulders.

"I am an adult, Elizabeth, a gentleman, not some callow youth who is unable to control his basic urges. I took from you something which is not yet mine to take."

Elizabeth raised her hands and placed them on his chest. Even through his several layers of clothes, she could feel his heart beating. Strong, regular, reassuring beats, just like Darcy himself.

She had come to know the man behind the façade, and he was as good as everyone had said. His sister, Mr Bingley, even Miss Bingley had reassured her he was an honourable man. A good, kind, respectful and loving gentleman. And now, without a shadow of a doubt, she knew this for herself.

He had not taken advantage of her that night. There had been several opportunities when Elizabeth could have told him to stop, but…she had not wanted him to stop.

Looking up at Darcy, meeting his gaze, Elizabeth leant in closer, lowered her voice, and whispered,

"No, Fitzwilliam, but it was mine to give…"

Under her palms, Elizabeth felt the rhythmic beat of his heart change. It grew stronger and faster and bolder…

There were no more thoughts to think, only feelings and sensations.

Darcy felt the weight of the sky lift from his shoulders as Elizabeth uttered those words. There was no reproach, no anger, no regret… just love…Elizabeth's love.

Mr Bennet watched as the young lovers became entwined in one other's arms, their passion, mutual and matched. If someone had told him that Lizzy, his favourite daughter, would willingly go into the arms of Fitzwilliam Darcy, he would have told them it would be a strain on credulity to think such a thing. Yet, if ever there was a man that was labelled 'misunderstood', it was Fitzwilliam Darcy.

Closing the door shut, he left the lovers in peace, satisfied that Elizabeth's future, and happiness, was safe in Darcy's care.

Chapter Twenty-Seven

Elizabeth slipped out of the back door, along the lane and was soon skirting around the edge of Longbourn's boundary, as she made her way to Oakham Mount.

The last few days had seemed like a dream, and she felt the need to escape and spend some time alone to reflect on events.

The duplicity of Mr Wickham had come as a complete surprise to all her family. Mr Darcy had forewarned only she, and even then, she doubted his word. Sadly, everything he had said and alluded to about Mr Wickham's character had been true. Wickham had lied, cheated, used and abused the vast majority of Meryton's townsfolk. But he had singled out her family to bear the brunt of his vitriol.

Once his true character had been revealed, she wondered how she had ever been so blind...so gullible? To seek out his company and listen enrapt by his every word. On at least two occasions she recalled ignoring the rules of propriety to walk alone with him in the garden. Thankfully, there had been no improper contact, only his lips on her hand as he bid her farewell. If only Lydia had been as circumspect.

But Elizabeth could not blame her sister for all her actions, no matter how irresponsible, untimely or dangerous they had been. Lydia had thought herself in love. And why not, Wickham encouraged her in that belief, even propagated it. Lydia had been his pawn, a means to an end.

She could see now that Wickham was driven by an unjustifiable jealousy and hatred of Mr Darcy, coupled with an overwhelming desire to hurt *and* extort money from him. And he had almost succeeded.

Then there were Wickham's victims. The people he had stolen from, whether it be blackmail, unpaid bills or emotional theft. He had left a trail of devastated people wherever he went. And he appeared to have no boundaries. Georgiana had known him as a brother, but even that did not protect her from his bile.

Throughout all this, spanning several years, it appeared Darcy had remained, as ever, a gentleman.

There was no doubt she had misunderstood him from that very first night at the assembly rooms. Such a trivial slight has set her on a path that she was heartily ashamed of now. Without his intervention, where would all these people be now? Where would Lydia be?

A shiver ran down Elizabeth's spine as she thought of what might have happened to Lydia, to her family had Mr Darcy not intervened.

With the peak in sight, she decided she would no longer dwell on Mr Wickham. Thankfully, he was no longer part of their life, nor would be ever again.

Having reached the top of Oakham Mount, Elizabeth sought out her favourite rock, wrapped her cloak around her legs and sat down.

Turned her mind to more pleasant things, she conjured up an image of Mr Darcy

Her intended had proven to be quite a man. In fact, unlike any man she had ever encountered before. He was kind and conscientious and charitable, he was honest and decent and fair. He was warm and handsome and loving. The perfect gentleman, husband and...lover.

Such a man deserved to be loved. To be loved by the woman who was to be his wife. And she did. Her foolish and shallow notion of being swept off her feet now seemed like both a childish fantasy and a reality. Though it had not been love at first sight, she had come to love Fitzwilliam so very dearly. The mere thought of him set her pulse racing and made her cheeks flush.

The night she had abandoned her maidenhood and willingly gone into Fitzwilliam's arms and his bed, she had already surrendered herself to the reality that she loved him. Loved him passionately, ardently and unreservedly. And more than anything else in the world, she wanted to become Mrs Fitzwilliam Darcy. And in just a few days' time, she would be.

Darcy watched as a myriad of emotions changed Elizabeth's features. One minute she was frowning, the next shaking her head and looking to the heavens.

He could not help but wonder what she was thinking. Was she worried about her family, her sister Lydia? Or was she thinking about him, regretting their night together or concerned about their future together?

Desperately, Darcy wanted to go to her side, to take her in his arms and reaffirm his undying love for her, but, how could he?

Locked in a battle with his own conscience and emotions, Darcy still could not believe that Elizabeth loved him, had come to him willingly, ergo, he must have taken advantage of her. Henceforth, he decided, it must be Elizabeth to first instigate any sort of closeness or physical contact.

Darcy lingered in the clump of trees on the edge of the clearing, frantically wanting to join Elizabeth, yet fearful of being discovered, of being rejected.

Turning to leave, hoping to creep away unnoticed, he stepped on a twig. Too late, he realised he had been discovered.

Elizabeth turned.

"Mr Darcy!"

"I am sorry, I wanted to join you, but you seemed so lost in thought, and I did not want to intrude," Darcy said.

Inside, Elizabeth beamed. The very man that was filling her mind and warming her cheeks was standing before her.

"If you prefer, I can leave?"

Elizabeth realised her inward happiness had not transferred to her face.

Smiling, she offered him to join her on her seat.

"You seemed distracted, Elizabeth?"

"Oh, I was just thinking, about Miss Bingley and you," she admitted with her usual candour.

"You must know that I did not encourage her in any way, Elizabeth. Any affection Miss Bingley felt towards me was totally unreciprocated."

"I suspected as much, although it was quite evident to me that she had set her sights on you from the first moment I met her. Or rather, on what being Mrs Darcy could offer her," Elizabeth said honestly.

"I am sorry she was hurt by my rejection, but what else could I do? I only ever looked at her as the sister of my friend, nothing more."

After a brief pause, Darcy asked,

"Is that all you were thinking about?"

"No. I was also thinking of how your selfless actions have saved my family from total mortification, and the price it has cost you."

Darcy thought for a moment. He had done what he hoped any decent gentleman in his position would do. Wickham had only been at liberty to act as he had, because of Darcy's silence. Besides, Mr Bennet did not have the large funds at his disposal as Darcy did. In truth, he was only thirty pounds out of pocket, a trifling sum in the larger scheme of his wealth.

"I am not out of pocket, Elizabeth, Richard returned the money I paid to Wickham."

Seeing the startled look on her face, he went on to reassure her.

"Oh, fear not, he has not harmed Wickham. Richard merely persuaded Wickham of the advantages and benefits of joining His Majesty's Navy."

Elizabeth understood his meaning perfectly, and although being press-ganged was illegal, she suspected the fate the colonel initially had in store for Mr Wickham had a more final outcome. Elizabeth also suspected that the only reason the Colonel had not ended Wickham's life, was at the express request of Mr Darcy. Considering the alternative, life at sea seemed a preferable option.

With the silence between them stretching into minutes, Darcy asked the question he had sworn not to ask.

"Do you regret us, Elizabeth?"

The human and vulnerable side of Darcy was finally shining through the chinks in his gentlemanly armour. For her eyes only she suspected, but Darcy was finally sharing his insecurities, his concerns, his worried. And it made her love him even more.

"Do I regret meeting you and being slighted? No, not any longer, I understand why you said what you said…now. Do I regret your interference between Jane and Mr Bingley? I did at first, but how could I hold a grudge when it was you that reunited them. Do I regret your… original proposal? Initially, but no more. I think I was more surprised than anything. Do I regret your involvement with the rescue of my sister, Lydia? How could I, you saved us all from a life of ruin and invisibility."

Pausing to take his hand in hers, Elizabeth continued,

"Do I regret consummating our love before we were married? No" she stated firmly, and then raised his hand to her lips and placed a soft kiss on his fingers.

The pounding in his chest felt as if his heart was about to burst free from its confines. His emotions had soared, and his head spun with the things he wanted to say and to ask.

"So, you truly have no misgivings about…that night, or marrying me?"

"No, my love. Did you know that I have Scottish ancestors? Well, in Scotland, they have a tradition called Handfasting? It is similar to being engaged, but if they choose to anticipate their wedding vows, it instantly becomes a marriage. I considered myself married to you from that moment, Fitzwilliam. In fact, I would marry you here, right now, if I could." Elizabeth murmured with feeling.

"You would?" Darcy asked.

Elizabeth nodded.

"Then why do we not do it, here, now. I will go and get the Preacher, and we can be married within the hour."

Elizabeth freed her hand and cupped his cheek tenderly.

"Without your sister, without your groomsman, without the Colonel?"

Darcy visibly slumped as Elizabeth pointed out the impracticality of his suggestion. He so very much wanted to be married to Elizabeth. His heart longed for her, his soul needed her, and his body ached for her.

Never one to sway from a challenge, Elizabeth said,

"Though I suppose if you send an express, and they do not mind travelling at night, we *could* be married tomorrow. Of course, the food will not be as fancy or as plentiful but…"

Whatever Elizabeth was going to say was lost in Darcy's mouth as he covered her lips with his own.

Never had a kiss felt so sweet, so full of promise, so full of tomorrows. Neither of them wanted it to end, as they savoured the love and essence of each other.

No-one missed Elizabeth at breakfast, and the staff at Netherfield were accustomed to Mr Darcy's long absences. Not even Odin questioned the length of time he was left to tarry alone, as he searched out the odd green blade of grass to nibble on.

Seated on several benched carried, up by the farm workers from Longbourn Farm and Netherfield Park, were approximately two dozen wedding guests. All but five were related to the bride. Colonel Fitzwilliam, Georgiana Darcy, Mr Bingley and Mr and Mrs Hurst were the few people the bridegroom had deemed to invite. While the brides' side boasted the Lucas's, the Gardiners from London, Mr and Mrs

Philips, Mr Collins and of course the brides' immediate family. Total guests, twenty-four.

Reverend Muir had at first been opposed to conducting a wedding ceremony outside and so far away from the sanctified ground of the church. However, a sizable donation from the bridegroom, enough to repair the church roof, purchase and install a new church organ, and money in the bank to refurbish the rectory, soon had the rector extolling the virtues of an outdoor wedding.

Noticeable by their absence, was Lady Catherine De Bourgh and her daughter Anne. Mr Collins, however, had managed to smuggle out of Rosings, a brief note passed to him by Miss Anne De Bourgh.

It read;

My Dear Mrs Darcy,

Please accept my best wishes for both
you and my cousin on this most joyous
of days. Feel assured that I bear you,
nor Fitzwilliam, any animosity.
Our match was never to be.
It was never his intention,
nor my desire, to marry each other.
I hope, sometime in the future,
you will invite me to visit you
both at Pemberley.
Until such a time is possible,

Your new cousin,
Anne De Bourgh

These few lines, penned by Miss De Bourgh, touched Elizabeth deeply. With her marriage to Darcy, she had likely condemned Anne to the life of a spinster. It was a sobering thought.

Standing before Reverend Muir, Fitzwilliam Darcy and Elizabeth Bennet made their vows.

"...for better, for worse, for richer, for poorer, in sickness and in health, to love and to cherish, till death do you part, for so long as you both shall live; according to Gods Holy law?"

"I do" they both said.

"…therefore, I pronounce them husband and wife."

Taking Elizabeth's' hand, he placed it in Darcy's' and closed the ceremony.

"Those whom God has joined together, let no man put asunder. Amen."

Self-consciousness of the number of people watching them, Darcy placed a light, chaste kiss on Elizabeth's' lips.

"Is that the best you can do, Darcy? Kiss her man!"

Darcy knew it was Richard calling out.

Smiling down at his new bride, with her face aglow with love and her lips curved into an enchanting smile, Darcy was unable to resist the magnetic pull of her eyes, those beautiful, mysterious eyes. It was an invitation he no longer needed to resist.

Darcy slowly, he slipped his arms around Elizabeth's waist, and then in one deliberate move, he pulled her close.

Then, oblivious to their surroundings, and with eyes, thoughts and love only for each other, Elizabeth and Fitzwilliam Darcy sealed their marriage with a deep and passion fuelled kiss.

Epilogue

Wickham had a new focus for his wrath, Captain Wilberforce. Compared to Wilberforce, Darcy, and his vile cousin, Colonel Fitzwilliam, were harmless simpletons.

Wilberforce was cruel, just for the pleasure of it. Once he knew Wickham had a fear of heights, he took great pleasure in sending him up to the crow's nest at every opportunity. Although scrubbing the decks was just as bad. His hands were chapped, and his knuckles were split from the cold and constant exposure to saltwater and soap.

For the third time that day, Wickham hung his head over the starboard side of the ship and lost the contents of his stomach. Not that it mattered much, the food was appalling, and the rum was no better. Wickham was a wine and brandy man and had no taste for beer and rum.

His fine suit of clothes has soon been confiscated and a rough clothed uniform issued to him. It chaffed his skin, and his feet ached from wearing the flat canvas deck shoes, also issued to him. He suspected his clothes and boots had been sold and the money pocketed by the boson, but he had learned quickly to keep his opinion to himself.

Though sleeping below deck in a hammock was surprisingly comfortable, all things considered. Even though it was December, the overcrowded sleeping quarters meant that at least it was warm, unlike on deck, where the biting cold wind seeped through the fibres of his clothes and attacked his skin with relish. He was cold, he was hungry, and he was exhausted.

Wickham's only consolation was that the voyage should only last twenty-five days. The ship was heading to Boston, and once there, he intended to jump ship and make his way inland. If he never saw the ocean again, it wouldn't bother him. Besides, he was confident the ladies there would be most receptive to a gentleman from the homeland. And, if things went his way, he could be married to some rich American before the winter was over.

Charles Bingley had managed to return to Longbourn just in time to see his friend Darcy marry Miss Elizabeth. Though it had been a close call.

Once he and Caroline had arrived in Scarborough, Charles had wasted no time in calling in a physician to assess Caroline's physical and mental condition.

Being a no-nonsense northern gentleman, he came straight to the point, telling Charles that, *A period away from society, with complete quiet, and maybe a little bit of hard work, will do her a power of good.*

"In my opinion, Miss Bingley has a surplus of yellow bile. Her humour's need to be restored, and quickly, or it could be the mental institution for her," the doctor had said in his practical way.

Nevertheless, it still came as a shock to Charles, when his sister had suggested she spend a few months with the nuns at the convent of St Agnes. The order observed strict silence, daily prayers and encourages visitors to participate in serving the community.

Caroline Bingley had decided she couldn't stand to be in the company of men for a moment longer than she had to be. But the only place she knew she could truly be isolated from them was in a convent. It would do. Besides, as she was just visiting, and not taking holy orders, she only had to commit to being there for six months at a time. One flunky bringing her tea in the morning was much the same as another. How hard could it be?

Once Mr & Mrs Darcy had left on their honeymoon, Charles and Jane had wasted no time in planning their wedding. They had decided on a spring wedding. It meant Elizabeth and Fitzwilliam would be back, and able to attend, plus, all the time, money and effort Mrs Bennet had expended in arranging Elizabeth's wedding, would not be wasted.

So, Jane was happy, Mrs Bennet was happy, and Mr Bingley was deliriously happy.

Only Mr Bennet felt any displeasure at the thought of Jane's marriage. He had already lost his Lizzy, and once Jane had gone too, who would keep him company then? There was, he decided, very little prospect of any intelligent conversation once Jane had moved away.

Mind you, he thought, Kitty had been following Jane around more than Lydia since the event that no-one mentioned. Perhaps there was hope for him, and her, yet.

On the Pemberley estate, two of the unused cottages had been converted into one large dwelling, in preparation for the arrival of its new tenant.

Furnished and equipped for direct use, there was nothing for the tenant to do but move in and make it their own.

An elderly lady greeted Sarah and the children.

"I am Mrs Reynolds, Sarah. Mr Darcy has told me all about you and the young ones."

Mrs Reynolds took them into the house. The children, all seven of them, sat on the floor, frightened to move or speak.

Mrs Reynolds addressed Sarah.

"Now, I have arranged for cooked meals to be sent up three times a day for the first week, just while you find your feet and get settled. Jessie will come and help you clean and change the beds once a week. As there are so many of you, Mr Darcy has said all the laundry can go to the wash house next to the buttery. There is plenty of linen in the cupboard, so you won't have to wait for its return. Is that clear?"

"Yes Ma'am," replied Sarah as she bobbed a curtsy.

"Tomorrow, I will take you into town and have you all measured for one set of Sunday best clothes, and two sets of work clothes each. From Monday, the children are to attend the Pemberley Tennant's School. Can you read and write, Sarah?"

"No, Ma'am," she said meekly.

"Well, I'll speak to the master about that. You will all attend church on the Lords day and bible classes once a week. Now, is there anything you want to ask me?"

"I…what will Mr Darcy want from me in return? No-one does nice things for nothing."

Mrs Reynolds looked at the young woman. Only eighteen years of age and already so cynical.

"Your loyalty, Sarah, nothing else."

With the door closed, and the children off exploring, Sarah pinched herself, and then again. Only a month ago she had no dreams, no prospects and no hope. Her only thoughts were how to feed the children and how to avoid Mrs Younge's wrath. Now, everything had changed. They were on the cusp of starting a new life, in a beautiful place with food and clothes and no stick on their backs.

Not knowing where the church was, Sarah fell to her knees and thanked God for their good fortune.

Lydia Bennet physically shuddered every time she let her mind wander in the direction of George Wickham. Since returning to Longbourn, she had often thought of what might have befallen her had Mr Darcy and his cousin, Colonel Fitzwilliam not rescued her from what she now realised would have been a fate worse than death. Previously, her mamma had encouraged her to enjoy herself in the company of the officers, but there was no denying that her elopement has shocked even Mrs Bennet.

Once things had returned to normal after Lizzy's wedding, Lydia had tried to follow in Jane's and Lizzy's footsteps, but it was a struggle. Reading books, sewing samplers and practising on the pianoforte was very boring, but with Mary's help, she had progressed in all areas.

However, since the Reverend Muir had become a frequent visitor to Longbourn on the pretext of discussing church matters with Mr Bennet, Mary had not been as ready to spend time with her as she did discussing sermons with the preacher.

So, Lydia now spent at least some of each day with either Maria Lucas or her Aunt Philips, who was very much like her own Mamma.

Indeed, her Uncle Philips had a very nice clerk working in his solicitor's office...

The spot Darcy had chosen for them to honeymoon, was idyllic. Having discovered that Elizabeth desired to visit the lake district someday, he immediately arranged for them to hire a small cottage overlooking Lake Windermere.

It was located high enough to be isolated and off the usual tourist route, yet not so high or remote as to suffer from severe weather conditions or curtail their love of walking.

With the town of Ambleside only a mile away, he had also lodged a few of his trusted servants in the local tavern. In their usual fashion, these faithful retainers were discreet and invisible, while looking after their master, and his new wife.

To all intents and purposes, the young couple were honeymooning alone.

Peering around the sitting room door, Darcy was not surprised to find his new bride, sat in front of the glowing fire.

"Come, Fitzwilliam," Elizabeth said, and patted the space next to her.

Joining Elizabeth on the floor now seemed as natural to Darcy as breathing. With no business to tend to, no events to attend and no people to talk to, they had spent the last weeks becoming more familiar with each other, and not just in the biblical sense.

They had spent time discussing literature and their favourite authors. What foods they each liked...and disliked. They discussed plays and operas, and music and composers, ballets and recitals, anything and everything. Next, they discussed their childhood, their parents their siblings, and even Wickham. Where fate would take him and whether he could overcome his hatred of Darcy.

It was a time to expand their bonds of humble and mutual affection, with no distraction but their love. And that love had indeed, distract them.

Twisting to lay his head in Elizabeth's lap, Darcy closed his eyes and enjoyed Elizabeth's ministrations as she gently stroked his hair.

At length, Darcy said,

"I never knew such happiness existed, until I met you, Elizabeth."

Elizabeth bent down and placed a soft kiss on his brow.

"Even though you thought I was not handsome enough to tempt you," she teased.

Darcy opened one eye and looked up at her.

The curve of her lips told him she was teasing, and he replied in kind.

"Mrs Darcy, will you never cease reminding me of my one, inappropriate remark? You know very well I only said it to shut Bingley up. It was a hot night, the room was crowded, and I knew no-one."

"Oh, so it was nothing personal?"

For the umpteenth time, Darcy patiently explained.

"I was instantly drawn to you Elizabeth, but I was not wife hunting. I had only agreed to join Bingley at Netherfield so I could be free from the Mamma in town, who were constantly trying to marry me off to one of their simpering and insipid daughters. Besides, the attraction I felt for you was a new sensation for me. It scared me. To know someone could make my heart race, with just one glance."

Elizabeth bent and kissed him again.

"I made your heart race, Fitzwilliam?"

"You did, you know you did," Darcy said, looking up at her lovingly.

"One glance of those beautiful eyes, and I was lost, Elizabeth. I fought it at first. Men like me do not believe in love at first sight. But that was what it was; only I was too blind or too stubborn to recognise it. I was back in London by then, but once I acknowledged the depth of my feelings for you, everything fell into place. I couldn't wait to see you again. So, I rushed back to Hertfordshire, anxious for your feelings…and that I might be near you. I dreamed, no I hoped, that I might have a chance to win your love."

Elizabeth let a ripple of laughter escape her as she recalled their first meeting on his return to Hertfordshire.

"Yes, I remember. You threw yourself at my feet."

Darcy loved to hear her laugh. It was sweet and genuine and melodic.

He smiled up at her, watching as she allowed her happiness and mirth to shine, enjoying her relaxed and easy demeanour. How far they had come in just a few weeks. How much they had both grown, and shared, in that time. If Darcy had believed in soul mates, then Elizabeth was his.

Looking up into her face, the light from the flames reflecting in her eyes, he asked,

"And you, Elizabeth? When did you begin to love me?"

Elizabeth stopped laughing. The time for pretence and subterfuge was long gone for this couple. Now, they were totally free of all misunderstanding, lies, and secrets.

"When I stayed at Netherfield with my sister, I still had not fathomed you out. A rich, desirable and eligible man who surrounded himself with the likes of Caroline Bingley and the Hursts. One minute you were vocal and affable, the next you were withdrawn and sullen. Slowly, I began to warm to you. Then my mother happened. I watched as she exposed herself to the room that day. Her condescension and rudeness, tumbling from her mouth. I was ashamed. I expected you could cut her with just a few words, but you did not. Rather than engage her or belittle her, you walked away. I watched as you shut yourself off, retreating behind the façade I came to know so well. Finally, much later, I understood. Your silence was your protection."

"But you did not love me until much later?"

"No…like you, my guard was up. Mine because of Wickham and yours…well, I expect we all seemed very provincial and dull to you. But gradually, your kindness, your patience and your devotion chipped away at…my shield, I suppose. You had been honest with me about Wickham, even though I questioned your integrity…your very honour, at the Netherfield ball. And at first, when you proposed, I did not want it to be true. My opinion of you was still so full of errors and flaws. Yet, you came to me and wooed me. Gradually, my head allowed my heart to open up and let my feelings grow and blossom into the love and admiration I feel for you now."

"Many things conspired against us from our first meeting. Wickham, Miss Bingley, Lydia, your family, my aunt." Darcy said, acknowledging the many obstacles they had overcome to be together.

"Yes, your pride," replied Elizabeth in a tease.

"And your prejudice," retorted Darcy with a smile.

"But now, Fitzwilliam, I love you with all my heart. I could not imagine myself being married to any other man, then you."

Her new husband's face glowed as she openly declared the depth of her feelings for him.

"And now you have me forever, to love and to cherish, until death do us part." she said brightly.

Darcy smiled. Her love had grown gradually, steadily increasing as he revealed more of his character to her, emotionally, mentally, and now physically. Such a love he was sure could only continue to grow. As for him? His love for Elizabeth was bound into the very fabric of his heart. Every bone, muscle, sinew, and tendon in his body throbbed with love and admiration for the woman he now called wife. Fate had brought them together, and he was confident that destiny would keep them together. He would never, could never, love anyone other than Elizabeth.

Looking up at her soft, red, cupid bow lips, slightly parted and inviting, Darcy said.

"Yes, till death do us part, Elizabeth, but for now, I prefer to concentrate on the, to love and to cherish."

Darcy gently pulled her next to him the floor, and Elizabeth went willingly into his arms, eager to ignite and share in the passion they sparked in one another.

Making love, loving each other, living together, loving together, exploiting their mutual adoration and relishing in their freedom to express that love in both an emotional and physical way.

Their love, Elizabeth and Fitzwilliam's love, would last not only for a lifetime, but for eternity and beyond.

The End

Mr Darcy's Struggle

Elizabeth felt tense as they approached Lucas Lodge. Darcy had insisted that she rode with him and Georgiana. She was pleased with not having to endure the overcrowding of the Bennet carriage, and she must get used to travelling with Darcy, but still, the closeness of him tonight made her uneasy. His dark, penetrating eyes rarely left her face. She had tried to make polite conversation with them both, but Georgiana was too excited at the prospect of attending a real ball, and Darcy was unwavering in his attention and replied only curtly. As they pulled up to the entrance, the footman jumped down to help the ladies out of the carriage, but Darcy brushed him aside and completed the task himself.

Once inside and relieved of their cloaks, Darcy admired Elizabeth's gown. The under layer was pure white and reached the floor, where her matching slippers peeped out. The sheer over layer was decorated with small silver flowers and leaves, intricately woven into the fabric. Her dark locks were in the Grecian style with silver-headed pins holding it in place. She was stunning; he was under no illusion that he would be the envy of every man here tonight. He glanced around the room, and then frowned; there were too many people, too many men. The prospect of other men coveting his fiancée was extremely distasteful to him.

He must also be circumspect over Georgiana. As she was not yet 'out,' Darcy should have refused her plea to accompany them, but he saw no harm in her attending a small family gathering. Of course, she would not be able to dance with anyone other than Richard and himself, but she was content with this arrangement. Her delicate features glowed with excitement, and it made her look younger than her sixteen years. The delicate gown of lemon, with small green vines growing up from the hem, suited her perfectly. He would have his work cut out this evening, ensuring the well-being of both his ladies. As usual, Darcy was dressed impeccably, with his waistcoat complimenting Elizabeth's dress perfectly, embroidered with a pattern of silver knots.

Sir William and Lady Lucas greeted them, offering felicitations on their upcoming nuptials. Then Sir William bade them enjoy their last night as single people, and he winked at Darcy. It was kindly meant, but inappropriate with two unwed females at his side. Sir William had a tendency to put into words, sentiments that should remain thoughts, but his jolly demeanour showed it was said in jest, and not with malice. Charlotte and Mr Collins welcomed them next, and Darcy's brow furrowed again. He offered the clergyman the curtest of nods in acknowledgement of his greeting, then swept the women into the ballroom. Elizabeth was mortified that Darcy had let Mr Collins's presence affect him so. She alone understood the reason behind his action, yet to others, it would appear as though he had been excessively rude. She would have to remind him that his actions now reflected on her, too.

It turned out to be more than the intimate gathering she had been led to believe, but at least most of the guests were friends or family. Spying Colonel Fitzwilliam, she hoped he would ask her to dance; they had enjoyed a warm friendship when both in Kent.

Elizabeth watched as Georgiana gently disengaged herself from her brother's arm and went to talk to Elizabeth's younger sisters, who were now standing with Maria Lucas. She felt a pang of envy at how carefree and happy they seemed and longed to join them as they laughed and chatted together. Six short weeks ago, she could have done just that, Elizabeth thought ruefully.

Elizabeth and Darcy would be expected to open the dancing, but she knew he did not care for such frivolities. Charles had once told her, 'Darcy never lifts a hoof, even though he is most proficient in all aspects of the dance.' A sigh escaped her as she realised if Darcy did not take her to the floor, she could accept no other man's offer. It would be an unpardonable breach of protocol. No, she must resign herself to enjoying it vicariously. Slyly glancing over at her escort, she noted that yes, he was *still* watching her, only now his piercing stare was accompanied by a smile. As the musicians struck the chords for the minuet, he bowed and asked,

"Miss Bennet, may I have the honour of the first dance?"

Elizabeth was taken aback by his offer, and for a moment, words failed her. Her surprise must have registered on her face, and she stumbled over her reply.

"I did not, that is, I did not think that.... yes, I thank you."

Darcy raised both brows in a questioning pose and then held out his hand. She placed her hand in his, and mutely they walked to the dance floor. Uncomfortably conscious that all eyes were upon them, Elizabeth realised every step, every expression would be scrutinised by the people assembled. With Darcy's intense dislike for large gatherings, or being the centre of attention, she felt more than a little nervous. The music started, and they performed the customary salute before meeting, circling, and returning several times as the dance dictated. Fellow revellers slowly joined them, and Elizabeth observed Darcy's shoulders relax, happier to now be one of many. As the dance continued, she realised Charles was right, Darcy was indeed an excellent dancer and conducted the steps with an easy air.

"Sir, you dance with an abundance of style and grace; why do you dislike it so?" she asked playfully.

"You are mistaken, Madam. I do not dislike dancing; I enjoy it a great deal. It is that I find it difficult to secure a partner who meets my standard," Darcy said honestly. "I recall the first time I saw you dance; it was with the imbecile Collins. He was out of time, and trod on your slipper, dislodging a flower."

Elizabeth remembered how mortified she had been at Mr Collins's ineptitude, and that she had to correct him constantly.

"I did not realise you had observed us, sir, or that you had noticed the state of my slippers. I am surprised you would concern yourself with such trifling matters. Do *I* meet your exacting standards, Mr Darcy?"

As the dance drew them together, Elizabeth caught her breath. Darcy's gaze seemed more intense than ever, and she felt as though his penetrating stare had somehow pierced her very soul. Taking both her hands, Darcy held them over his heart and replied with quiet, yet devastating passion.

"From our very first meeting, Elizabeth, my eyes have followed only you. There is not one moment when in each other's company, which I cannot recall the gown you wore, the style of your hair or who your partner was. For every smile, I remember the time and the place. Every word, every glance you have ever bestowed on me, kind or otherwise, they are all indelibly committed to my memory. Not one heartbeat have I forgotten."

Elizabeth felt spellbound; his words exposed the depth of his love, and they washed over her like an embrace. She had longed for such love, a passion that even after possession, it was not sated. They stood motionless while all around them danced.

"Come, Darcy, you must not monopolise Miss Elizabeth in this fashion. I believe she is promised to me for this dance."

As the fog of emotion cleared, and reality returned, Darcy became aware that the dance had ended, and the musicians were still. They stood alone on the dance floor, being silently observed by the rest of the guests. Realising it was Bingley who had come to their rescue, Darcy turned and muttered,

"Thank you, Charles, maybe the next one."

Without words, but still, in possession of her hand, Darcy led Elizabeth from the ballroom and out onto the deserted terrace. The biting December air enveloped them, but neither felt it. Stopping at the veranda's edge, Elizabeth took hold of the stone balustrade. The impact of his words still reverberated around her mind. She had read about such powerful loves, in the books of poets and Master Shakespeare, never dreaming she could be the recipient of such herself. She had always professed this would be the only thing that could induce her to marry, but now that she had found it, she could not, in all honesty, say she returned the sentiment. Oh, she wanted to, so very much she wanted to, but her feelings were unclear even to herself. If she professed to love him and it was false, it would mean heartbreak for them both. No, it was better to stay silent until she was sure. Again, the immenseness of Darcy's declaration washed over her, the power of his all-consuming love saturating every fibre of her being, and she began to tremble. She tightened her grip on the rail lest Darcy mistook her shaking for shivering, but too late. He slipped off his coat and draped it over her, his warm hands lingering on her shoulders. Hesitantly, she covered them with her own, and then leant back on him for support.

"I did not know," she murmured.

His warm baritone voice whispered close to her ear,

"You did not know what, Elizabeth? How those months apart were torture for me? How I risked my friendship with Charles in order to reunite him with Jane? Or maybe you are referring to Lydia, and the sacrifice I was willing to make to restore her to her family. That I have openly disregarded my family *and* society, by choosing to marry for love? Tell me that you know how my heart burns with a passion so violent, that you are the very air that I breathe. Surely you must know, Elizabeth; all I have done, I have done for you, only you."

The anguish in his voice deafened her to propriety, and she turned and sought his lips with her own. She wanted to kiss away all the pain her family had caused him, to thank him for helping Lydia and Jane, and to fill the void of his absent family. And as their lips met, she felt his arms slide around her waist, drawing her still nearer. His acceptance of her imperfect family brought tears to her eyes, and unable to restrain them, they silently slid down her cheeks.

Her kiss was bittersweet in so many ways, Darcy thought, as the salt mingled on their lips. This was not the response he had hoped to provoke with his declaration. The uncertainty of what lies behind her actions was nothing short of agony. He longed for her caresses to be given with love, but suspected they were in gratitude. But for now, he would take whatever she offered. Hopefully, she would come to love him in time, for he could not, would not, live without her by his side.

Elizabeth, unable to hold back the sobs any longer, tore her mouth from his and buried her face in his coat. Darcy comforted her with soft words of reassurance until finally, Elizabeth managed to regain control of her emotions. Then Darcy lifted her chin to look deep into her eyes. Beautiful limpet pools of the darkest brown, still glistening with tears. He un-tucked his neckcloth and used the end to dry her eyes, knowing Fletcher would admonish him for it later. Concerned they had been gone too long already, Darcy tenderly stroked her hair, and then her cheek, before offering his verbal reassurance.

"My love is constant, Elizabeth. I will wait a lifetime if that is what it takes, but for now, I fear we must return. You are promised to Charles for the next dance, are you not?"

Retrieving his coat from her shoulders, he quickly shrugged himself back into it. He had not meant to cause her such distress and was heartily ashamed of himself for revealing the extent of his love in such a way. Sighing, he knew there was little hope their actions had gone unnoticed, but they must return.

Elizabeth was also disinclined to return to the frivolity of the dance. Instead, her mind was focused on easing Darcy's pain, while trying to sort out her own feelings. The last thing she wanted to do was make merry and engage in meaningless chatter. Darcy's tender embrace was far more alluring at this moment. Instead, she gave him a weak smile and placed her hand on his arm. Together, they silently turned and walked back inside.

Darcy to the Rescue

Darcy was waiting on the steps of Netherfield as the carriage rolled to a halt and Charles Bingley jumped out. Having left town before the clock struck eight, Bingley was pleased to finally stretch his legs. They briefly exchanged pleasantries about the weather and Bingley's journey and then adjourned to the library for a hot toddy. Stevens had left the coffee pot and whisky decanter on the table for the gentlemen to help themselves as instructed. Darcy half filled their cups with coffee and then topped them up with a generous glug of the whisky. Passing one to Bingley he said,

"It's good to see you, Charles."

Bingley took a decent swallow of the potent brew before replying,

"Thank you, Darcy. I very nearly didn't come. My sisters had arranged several outings for us. But your letter was so cryptic, curiosity got the better of me." He reminded Darcy of the brief contents of the missive.

Charles
Return to Netherfield,
I implore you not to delay.
Come alone.
Darcy

"Yes, I'm sorry about that, Charles, but I know your sister Caroline has a habit of *accidentally* opening letters that are not addressed to her," Darcy explained.

"Well, what was so urgent that it demanded my immediate return?"

Darcy knew he must make a clean breast of things regarding his interference between Miss Jane Bennet and Charles, but how? He did not want to upset or alienate his closest friend, but he could hardly stand by his opinion that Jane was unfit to be Charles's wife when he intended to make Elizabeth his own. Feeling suddenly unprepared to make his confession, Darcy merely leant forward and refilled his glass saying,

"Nothing that won't keep," he lied. "I was lonely, that's all. Perhaps we can talk after lunch?"

Bingley agreed to this plan and then went to wash before the noonday repast was served.

Usually, Elizabeth would have walked to Netherfield, but seeing the state of the paths, she was glad that her mother had insisted she take the carriage. Mrs Bennet had intended to send the footman over with an invitation for Darcy to dine with them, but Elizabeth knew he would most certainly be expected to deliver it on foot. So she was happy to deliver it personally and save the poor man a wretched walk.

She set off straight after luncheon and arrived at Netherfield a little after two. The footman showed her into the day room and then withdrew. She expected her host to arrive momentarily, but after several minutes had elapsed and she was still alone, she decided to look for him herself. The entrance hall was deserted, but she could hear voices coming from the upstairs drawing room. Determined to deliver the invitation in person, she began to climb the stairs. As she neared the top level, the voices seem to get much louder, too loud in fact. Taking care to make no noise herself, she crept closer until she could hear each word that was spoken. The occupants appeared to be in the middle of a heated discussion. Although manners dictated she either retreat or make her presence known, Elizabeth did neither.

"You, engaged to Miss Elizabeth? You can't be. I won't believe it, Darcy."

"It's true, Elizabeth and I are engaged to be married," Darcy confirmed.

"How can you be when you steered me away from such a union with her sister Jane?" Bingley scoffed. "They have very little money and no worthy connections, you said. Her heart appears untouched where you are concerned Charles, that's what you said. Do you deny it, Darcy?"

"No, I do not deny it, Charles, but if you pause for just one minute, I will explain," Darcy said as he tried to reason with his friend.

"Explain? What is there to explain?" Bingley asked raising his voice to an even greater level. "You can marry Miss Elizabeth because that is your desire, yet Jane and I are to remain estranged. You are a two-faced hypocrite, Darcy, and I never thought I would see the day you put your own self-interests above all others. In light of your declaration, I no longer feel bound by your council," Bingley bellowed and then opened the door to leave.

Unfortunately, Elizabeth was blocking his exit. Unperturbed, he stepped around her with only a slight incline of his head in acknowledgement of her presence.

"Charles, come back and let me explain. There is much more to…" Darcy fell silent the minute he saw Elizabeth. His first thought being, how much did she hear? Her next words told him, everything.

"How could you? Oh, I suspected you did not approve the night of the ball. The look of disdain on your face gave you away. But to stoop so low as to try and separate two people, who are clearly very much in love, well, it confirms all the defects of your character I previously thought you possessed," she spluttered, then turned on her heels and sped down the stairs.

Darcy followed her down the stairs pleading,

"Elizabeth, let me explain. It's not as bad as it sounds. Elizabeth, please, won't you, at least, hear me out?" he beseeched.

Elizabeth spun around and faced her intended. In her eyes, there was no explanation he could give that would redeem him. She threw her mother's invitation at him and spat,

"If you have any semblance of a gentleman about you, you will make your excuses." She hurried through the front door and into her carriage before he could stop her.

Darcy stood open mouthed. How could so much have gone awry in just a few minutes? Unaccustomed to having people leave when he was mid-way through a sentence, he briefly thought them in the wrong, but only briefly. He realised his actions had been the cause of both Charles's and Elizabeth's outrage, and rightly so, from their perspective. But in his heart of hearts, he had only tried to protect his friend from what he thought, at the time, was another fortune-hunting mamma forcing her daughter into a loveless match. These past few days he had seen first hand how Jane pined for Charles, and he now knew he had been mistaken in his opinion of her. He must make amends and today. Yet Darcy doubted he would be welcome at the Bennet's now.

Then he saw the crumpled piece of paper Elizabeth had hurled at him and stooped to pick it up.

It read,

Dear Mr Darcy,
Mr Bennet and I would be honoured
if you and Mr Bingley would accept our
heartfelt invitation to come and dine
with us tonight.
Yours,
Fanny Bennet.

Darcy knew instantly that he still intended to go, and if he could talk Bingley 'round to attending with him, so much the better. Whether he wanted to listen or not, Charles would hear his explanation and then his apology. After that, it was up to him to decide his own future.

Available worldwide as an eBook (Kindle) or Paperback at
Amazon, iBook's, Kobo, Nook, Barnes & Noble
And Createspace

To Love Mr Darcy

Elizabeth flung open the door, and before the poor footman could lower the steps, she had jumped down onto the forest floor.

Having won his point, Darcy followed her from the carriage and then ordered the driver to return to Longbourn and wait for him there.

Elizabeth, who knew the road intimately, set a swift pace. Darcy increased his stride to keep up with her.

"Elizabeth, will you not wait and let me explain…" he began, but Elizabeth was in no mood to listen.

She turned and let loose with a scathing reply.

"I have not given you permission to use my given name, sir. You will address me as Miss Bennet. You dare to call yourself a gentleman. What I see standing before me is a bully and an oaf. And after that disgusting display of barbarism, I cannot imagine you have any excuse to offer."

Elizabeth continued along the path.

This was a step too far for Darcy. Coming to terms with his offer of marriage was one thing, but insulting his integrity was quite another. Taking hold of her hand, he pulled her to a halt.

Elizabeth twisted her hand this way and that as she tried to break free, but his grip was too firm. She was only succeeding in making her wrist hurt. Reluctantly, and with a petulant stamp of her foot, Elizabeth stopped struggling and stood still.

"That's better," Darcy said while maintaining his grip.

"Firstly, I was not about to offer an excuse, I do not need, nor do I intend, to make excuses for my behaviour. It was unfortunate that you witnessed my lapse in self-control, but one day you will understand why Wickham's actions received such a response. I was merely going to explain that the bad blood between George Wickham and myself is deep-seated and personal, and not the result of a jealous tantrum on my part. He is not the gentleman he professes to be, Elizabeth. Secondly, I was disappointed that the prospect of spending time with me this morning caused you to flee your home."

With no acknowledgement from Elizabeth, Darcy spoke sharper than he intended. "Very well, if you prefer that we spend no time together until we meet before the Parson, so be it. However, I had hoped that we could use these weeks to get to know one another better."

"So, you are still determined to marry me, even after this morning's fiasco?" Elizabeth demanded.

"Nothing could induce me to break our engagement, Elizabeth, and I suggest you resign yourself to becoming my wife," he told her soberly.

Elizabeth's shoulder slumped in resignation. Seeing this, Darcy gauging she was no longer a flight risk and released her hand. Testing his theory, he walked over to a fallen tree trunk and sat down. When she did not immediately follow him, Darcy beckoned for her to come hither and sit with him.

With leaden steps, she obliged.

Darcy could not bear to see how sad and dejected her demeanour had become. Was the prospect of becoming his wife really, so abhorrent to her?

"Elizabeth, I fear we have got off to a poor start. I thought, after our time together at Netherfield, that you held me in some regard and would welcome my proposal. I did not realise you despised me so vehemently," Darcy said sadly.

"Then you release me?" Elizabeth asked hopefully.

"No," he said resolutely. "We will be married as planned, but I would like us to try to become better acquainted before we marry. I would ask that you at least, give me a chance, Elizabeth."

With Darcy being so honest with her in regards to his intentions, Elizabeth also spoke her mind.

"Forgive me, but I too must be candid. I do not despise you, Mr Darcy, but neither do I love you. When I nursed Jane at Netherfield, I thought we dealt very well together. I judged us as more than acquaintances, friends perhaps. And though you may believe that it is a childish fantasy, I had hoped to marry for love," Elizabeth informed him bluntly.

"A marriage such as your parent's perhaps?" Darcy retorted, then instantly regretted it.

"Their marriage is of a peculiar kind, I admit, but it has been a long and happy one," Elizabeth said in defence of her parents. "Can you guarantee ours would be filled with such affection and of such a duration?"

Darcy knew, in all honesty, he could not.

Available worldwide as an eBook (Kindle) or Paperback at

Amazon, iBook's, Kobo, Nook, Barnes & Noble
And Createspace

About the Author

I was born in a small rural town in Hertfordshire, England. My ancestry has been traced back to the 3rd century AD in Nottingham, England. Prior to this, we were Danish Vikings. (I guess we were part of an invasion party).

Until the early 20th century, we were landowners and farmers in Kent & Essex. With the modernisation of farming techniques, we sold up and moved nearer to the capital, finally settling in Tring.

My paternal grandparents, who inspired my love of the past, were both teachers, specialising in English and History.
My paternal grandmother was also a descendant of the Scottish Clan of Galbraith. We have our own clan tartan in the colours of black, green, blue and white squares.

My mother is descended from the single family of Standingford, (often spelt the Anglo-Saxon way of Stanton). There is only one family with this name and all, no matter how distantly, are related. We have our own heraldic shield and family motto. *Dum Spiro*, While I Breathe.

I am the middle of five children, with an older sister, a twin brother and a younger sister and brother.

My hobbies include reading, writing, listening to classical music, swimming, walking the dog and jet skiing.

I enjoy a variety of authors, including Oscar Wilde, Shakespeare, Noel Coward, and of course, Jane Austen, while my favourite composer is Bach.

I am a full-time writer, but I also contribute articles to various magazines, charities, and private publications.

Before I decided to become a full-time writer, I worked for the British Government.

My husband and I have been married forty years, and we have two daughters, four grandchildren and one dog.

Phew!

Printed in Poland
by Amazon Fulfillment
Poland Sp. z o.o., Wrocław